Breaking Beautiful

Breaking Beautiful

JENNIFER SHAW WOLF

Walker & Company
New York

Published in the United States of America in April 2012
by Walker Publishing Company, Inc., a division of Bloomsbury Publishing, Inc.
www.bloomsburyteens.com

For information about permission to reproduce selections from this book, write to Permissions, Bloomsbury BFYR, 175 Fifth Avenue, New York, New York 10010

Library of Congress Cataloging-in-Publication Data
Wolf, Jennifer Shaw.
Breaking beautiful / Jennifer Shaw Wolf.
p. cm.
Summary: Allie is overwhelmed when her boyfriend, Trip, dies in a car accident, leaving her scarred and unable to recall what happened that night, but she feels she must uncover the truth, even if it could hurt the people who tried to save her from Trip's abuse.
ISBN 978-0-8027-2352-9 (hardcover)
[1. Accidents—Fiction. 2. Memory—Fiction. 3. Dating violence—Fiction. 4. Brothers and sisters—Fiction. 5. Twins—Fiction. 6. Dating (Social customs)—Fiction. 7. Mystery and detective stories.] I. Title.
PZ7.W81855213Bre 2012 [Fic]—dc22 2011010944

Book design by Regina Roff
Typeset by Westchester Book Composition
Printed in the U.S.A. by Quad/Graphics, Fairfield, Pennsylvania
2 4 6 8 10 9 7 5 3 1

All papers used by Bloomsbury Publishing, Inc., are natural, recyclable products made from wood grown in well-managed forests. The manufacturing processes conform to the environmental regulations of the country of origin.

For David, for showing me the power of true love

For Jason, who taught me that the strength of your spirit cannot be bound by the limitations of your body

Breaking Beautiful

Chapter 1

The clock says 6:45, even though it's really 6:25. If everything were normal, the alarm would ring in five minutes. I'd hit the snooze button, wrap Grandma's quilt around me, and go back to sleep until Mom came in and forced me to get up. I used to stay in bed until the last possible minute and then dash around getting ready for school—looking for my shoes or a clean T-shirt, and finally running out the door to the sound of my boyfriend, Trip, laying on the horn of his black 1967 Chevy pickup.

Nothing is normal, and no one makes me go to school.

Mom comes in and stands at the door to see if I'm awake.

I'm always awake.

"You think you can handle school today, Allie?" Mom's quiet, so if I am asleep I can stay asleep. I shake my head without rolling over. She hovers for a minute or two, so I can see her concern before she leaves to get ready for her orderly world.

Andrew is next, twin telepathy guiding him to my door. He knows or at least senses more than anyone how much I'm hurting. I know he does, because until now it's been me on the other side, watching him hurt. You can't share a womb with someone for nearly seven months without creating an unbreakable bond.

His wheelchair hums and bumps against the wall. Our house is small, one level, and old. Perfect for Andrew. The hallways and doors are wide enough for him to maneuver his chair.

A tap at my door, barely audible. A thump against the wall. He grasps and then loses his grip on my door handle. When we moved in, Dad changed all of the doorknobs to long handles so Andrew can open the doors, but it's still hard for him. I should get up and help him, but my body feels like lead.

The latch clicks, and his chair pushes against the door. He moves forward until the door opens enough for him to see my bed. I roll over so I can see him, but he stays in the doorway. That's new, the invisible wall between us, a barrier at the threshold of my room that he never crosses anymore. He breathes hard and speaks in his halting voice that almost no one outside our family can understand. "Okay, today, Al? School?" Andrew is smart—brilliant—but most people think he's mentally retarded because of his body and the way he talks.

Andrew has cerebral palsy, brought on by a lack of oxygen when we were born—eight and a half weeks early. I came out screaming like a full-term baby. He was cold and blue. His body is twisted and barely in control, but his mind is sharp. His injuries from our birth are easy to see. Mine are less obvious.

I shake my head and avoid Andrew's eyes, but I'm drawn

there. His eyes are soft, brown, and deep. The pain I see there, pain for me, makes me look away.

"You . . . should." He licks his lips and his bad hand shakes. He forces a smile. "I could . . ." He's trying so hard to talk, so hard to convince me to get out of bed. For his sake, I wish I could get up.

I burrow deeper into the quilt, worn flannel patches my only protection from everything I'm not willing to face. "I just"—don't look him in the eye—"I can't." The waver in my voice matches his. "Not yet."

He lingers. I close my eyes so I don't have to see his face.

"Andrew, breakfast." Mom's voice floats from the kitchen. Andrew's chair whirs down the hall. The red numbers slide by on my clock. Morning sounds float muffled through the walls and into my room. Dishes clink, the sink turns on and off. Dad tromps across the kitchen floor. Mom helps Andrew with breakfast. His bus pulls up out front.

Our house is so small you can hear everything that everyone does or says. Not a good place for keeping secrets. Even the outside walls are thin. The parade of life going by sounds so close it could be marching through my bedroom. Grade-school kids laugh. Another bus hisses to a stop. A motorcycle roars by; Trip's friend Randall, probably with Angie Simmons glued to his back. If I sat up and opened the blinds, I could watch the whole thing from my bed like some reality TV show—a reality I've never belonged to.

How can they keep going like everything is normal?

The days have started to run together, but I think it's the fifth day of school, the second week of what would be my senior year. Over a month since the accident and three weeks since I came home from the hospital. There's an untouched pile of schoolbooks and papers in the corner by my desk. Blake brings my homework by every day—at 3:08—part of my new routine.

I slide out of bed because Andrew didn't close the door all the way. The outside air coming in around the edge makes me feel exposed. I catch a glimpse of myself in the mirror over my dresser when I stand up. Wounded, scarred. Ugly. I can't even look at myself. I'm glad Trip can't see me like this.

He would hate my hair.

Trip never wanted me to cut it, not even just a trim. Before the accident it hung—long and thick and gold—to the middle of my back. I run my hand through what's left. It still surprises me how soon I reach emptiness. They shaved a swatch a couple of inches wide and almost six inches long across the back of my head, but someone in the hospital took pity on my blond locks. They left enough length to cover the gash. For a while I had a morbid, half-bald, punk ponytail to go with the Frankenstein stitches across the back of my head and over my right eye. When I came home, Mom's friend layered it into a sort of bob that brushes against my neck and sort of covers the bald spot. It looks horrible.

I touch the wound that's morphing into a scar on the back of my head. Coarse new hair pokes through where the stitches used to be. It itches. I guess that means it's healing.

Trip's eyes follow me to the door. Bits of our relationship are mounted on every wall and rest on every flat surface of my room. Pictures of us together are lined up on shelves and stuck in the corner of my mirror—prom, homecoming, us just goofing off.

Only the last one, the one from the cotillion, the last picture ever taken of Trip, is missing. I put it on the top shelf of my hutch—the shelf I need a chair to reach. I shoved it there without even looking at it. Trip's parents gave it to Mom after the memorial service because I was still in the hospital. Memorial service—I guess you can't have a real funeral without a body.

I reach to shut the door but hesitate when I hear Mom and Dad talking in the kitchen. I'm still not used to hearing Dad's voice. He was deployed for almost eighteen months and then back and forth between here and Fort Lewis for the last six. Now that he's retired from the Army, he's been trying to get his auto shop going. His being home this late is a bad sign—no appointments and no cars to work on in the shop. He's a really good mechanic, but business hasn't picked up yet because everyone in town is loyal to Barney's Auto Shop. Dad says that Barney's is a rip-off, but they've been the only shop in town for like forty years.

"The guys at the café were talking yesterday," Dad says. A chair scrapes against the wood floor. "I guess there's a new cop at the police station." At least they're talking about something other than me. Dad isn't a coddler. Twenty years in the Army made him tough. He harps on Mom to make me get up, go to school—get on with my life.

"Oh?" Mom sounds amused. "How long do you suppose this one will last?" Pacific Cliffs is a small town, one of those places where everyone knows everyone and no one locks their doors at night. The long arm of the law is Police Chief Jerry

Milton—Mom's date to junior prom. Chief Milton by himself has always been sufficient police for Pacific Cliffs, until now.

Dad's heavy footsteps cross the floor. "This guy was brought in from Seattle, some kind of special investigator or detective or something."

"A detective? Here?" Mom laughs, but it's a nervous laugh.

"My guess is Mr. Phillips has been putting pressure on Chief Milton to reopen the investigation." Dad sounds casual, but the weight of what he's saying presses against the scar on the back of my head. I open the door an inch more and take a half step into the hall.

"Why would he . . . ?" But Mom works for Mr. Phillips. She knows that answer almost as well as I do.

Dad sets his coffee mug down on the countertop. "My guess is he thinks Chief Milton didn't take the accident investigation seriously. That maybe there was something he missed."

I grip the door handle. I want to shut the door and shut out what he's saying. Instead I slide between the door and the frame and listen closely.

"He wouldn't want to talk to Allie, would he?" Mom's trying to match his casual tone, not quite pulling it off.

"If he's reopening the investigation, she's the first person he'll talk to."

More questions? Things I can't answer. Things I don't remember. Things I don't want to remember. I was too sick, too hurt before. Everyone felt sorry for me. But now . . .

"Hasn't she been through enough?" Mom sounds sincere. I wish I could believe that she could protect me, but I know better.

"Honestly, Lu." Dad sets the coffee mug down again. "I think he might be right. If I were Roger Phillips, if it were my kid who got killed, I'd want it all looked into, too."

"I don't know what good a 'special investigator' will do." Mom says the title with disdain. The sink turns on and Mom raises her voice. Does she know I'm listening? "Everyone knows Trip was reckless in that truck, and that there was probably alcohol involved—"

"No way to prove that one way or another. Not with the little bit they got from the accident scene. Seems like they should have spent more time looking for—"

"—small town, remember?" Mom sounds offended, like Dad made a personal attack on Pacific Cliffs. "We don't have the resources—"

"—exactly why Mr. Phillips brought in this guy. It will help everyone if—"

I take another step forward and my foot comes down on something soft and fuzzy. My scream mingles with the cat's yowl as she streaks away toward Andrew's room. I stumble forward and reach for the door handle, but my hand slips and I end up on the floor.

"Allie." Mom's voice wavers. "Is that you?"

I want to crawl back to my room, but Dad's already coming down the hall. Caught by my clumsiness. Again.

He reaches a hand to help me up. "Are you okay?"

I don't answer. It's too hard to lie to Dad.

"Hungry?"

"No, sir." That's the truth. There's no room for food around the hole in my stomach.

"No school today?" His voice is gentle, but I can feel his eyes boring into my forehead.

"No, sir." I roll a piece of lint caught in the pocket of my sweats between my fingers. Mom stays hidden in the kitchen. I can hear the dishes clink as she loads the dishwasher.

Dad puts a hand on my shoulder. I flinch, but control it enough that I don't think he notices. "You need to get back into life. This staying in your room all the time—"

"Is someone else going to come talk to me?" The question slips between my cracked lips before I can stop it.

"Were you . . . did you hear?" Dad's voice is sharp. I lower my head. He's been gone long enough that I'm not sure what the penalty is for eavesdropping.

"The door was open." My voice comes out hoarse from lack of use.

He nods. "I guess it's better if you know. Yes, somebody will probably want to talk to you."

"About the accident?" Stupid question.

"About the accident."

"But I can't . . . I don't remember anything." I plead with my eyes. Maybe he can protect me.

"Are you sure, Allie? It might give the Phillipses some peace if they knew exactly what happened that night." He squeezes my shoulder. I think he means it to be gentle, but it makes me feel trapped. "I think it would give you some peace, too."

"I don't remember anything." I pull away and back toward my bedroom. "I'm sorry. I'm going back to bed. I . . . I . . . don't feel good."

He half reaches for me again, but I keep moving.

"My head hurts." That's the truth, too. I close the door tight behind me while he watches from the other side.

Instead of going back to bed I'm drawn to the closet. The doors are closed so I can't see it, but in the back there's a black garment bag, so long and full that it could be a body bag with an actual body stuffed inside. Sometimes I imagine that it is a body bag and if I open it up I'll see Trip. It really holds the dress—long and bloodred, strapless, with little pearls and white lace across the front. It isn't really a color I would have chosen, but I didn't pick the dress out for myself.

The scar on the back of my head throbs.

"Do you like it? It's to wear to cotillion."

Cotillion is a big deal in Pacific Cliffs. It goes along with the Beachcomber's Festival, the biggest event in town. There's a fair with vendors and tourists, a pageant, and then the dance. Last summer, the last summer I had planned to *ever* spend in Pacific Cliffs, the cotillion fell on my eighteenth birthday.

"But it's not a birthday present."

Trip was such a little boy whenever he had something to give me. His crystal-blue eyes would sparkle and his expression would vary from excitement to fear and doubt, and back to excitement. I can still see his face, the way he tilted his head. How excited he was for me to see the dress. The pain spreads from the back of my head, cuts across my right temple, and curls around the smaller scar above my eye.

"I'm saving something special to give you on your birthday."

My whole head throbs.

It hurts too much to remember.

Chapter 2

Blake shifts his weight from one foot to the other. He's standing at the door to my bedroom like he's held back by the same invisible wall that keeps Andrew out. "I brought your homework." He holds the paper out for me to take but doesn't move to come inside. All of my schoolbooks are already in the corner so we're down to assignment sheets.

I cross the room to him and run my hand through what's left of my hair, knowing how bad I must look.

He won't look me in the eye. Funny how we've gotten to this point again—him at my door, coming to see me every day. Like we've erased two years of hurt feelings and not speaking to each other. But not entirely erased. There's still a barrier between us, like scar tissue left behind from a wound that's been forgiven but will never be forgotten.

Pre-Trip, Blake was my best—make that my *only*—friend in

Pacific Cliffs. Our grandmas were next-door neighbors and best friends. Since he lives with his grandma and I visited mine for a couple of weeks every summer, we saw each other a lot. During our summer visits he was my coconspirator in adventure, my partner in crime, and the only kid who wasn't weirded out by Andrew's wheelchair.

Blake was also my first kiss.

Trip was jealous of my friendship with Blake. For those two years, it was better for Blake and me to pretend that we didn't know each other. I guess I don't have to worry about that anymore.

"Do you have anything for me to take back?" Blake shifts his weight again as I take the paper from him. "Anything you've finished?"

I shake my head no and step back into my room.

This is the point when he should leave, when he always leaves, but today he leans against the door frame. "The assignment for art is kind of weird. I could explain it to you. What's written on the paper probably won't make much sense."

"I'll figure it out." Not that I have any intention of actually doing the assignment. Last year I killed myself to get good grades. Studied until my eyes crossed and my brain hurt. It went along with my plan for getting out of Pacific Cliffs permanently. But it doesn't matter anymore.

Blake rubs the front of his neck, clears his throat, and then rubs it again—a nervous tick he's had as long as I can remember. Even Trip noticed. He used to do that when he made fun of Blake. He clears his throat one more time before he finally speaks. "When are you coming back, Allie?"

I touch the back of my head. "I don't know." The truth is, I'd be happy to never leave this room. No, happy isn't the right word, maybe comfortable. Except comfortable doesn't fit my self-imposed prison either. The only word that fits is terrified. Terrified to leave this room and face . . .

What? I'm not sure. It's not like anyone is going to be mean to me. They'll all be nice. Dripping with niceness. And that will be worse.

Even Hannah George will be nice to me now, keeping up her "Beachcomber's Queen" appearance. Hannah was never nice to me before. Not that I could blame her. She was Trip's girlfriend before me. They'd been together since seventh grade. But the summer I turned fifteen she spent a couple of weeks at a basketball camp in California—the same couple of weeks I was in Pacific Cliffs. The summer Blake was gone.

I had watched Trip skim boarding along the edge of the surf for a long time before he acknowledged me. It was July, but the beach here is pretty much always cold. I was wearing a bikini top and board shorts—hoping he would notice.

"Hey. Cat girl, right?" Trip had called. The summer before he had helped me rescue Sasha, a little tiger-striped kitten, from a crab cage, a cage Blake was convinced Trip had put her in.

"Allie," I yelled back.

"Right, Allie. You still got that cat?" He tucked his skim board under his arm and started walking toward me.

"Yeah." I shrugged, but my heart was pounding under the narrow string that held the two halves of my swimsuit top together. "She lives with my grandma."

In his wet suit, the blue one that brought out his eyes, Trip looked like a surfer Ken doll. The suit hugged his chest, and his hair fell in wet waves over his ears. He stepped closer. "So, you around for a while?"

I tried to stay casual and barely glanced up from my magazine. "A little while."

He stopped so his shadow fell on the page I pretended to read. A drop of water slid off his hair and onto my arm. "Long enough for me to teach you how to skim?" He nodded to the board under his arm.

I remember looking up, seeing his grin, and wondering how anyone could get tan on this beach and how anyone could have teeth that white.

I never figured out how to skim, another in a long line of coordination-required, failed sporting attempts. It was really just an excuse to hang out with Trip. I didn't know about Hannah then, or if I did, I'd forgotten. It didn't make much difference. When Trip kissed me good-bye at the end of my visit, I didn't expect to see him for at least a year. I didn't know I would be back six months later, this time as a resident of Pacific Cliffs. Dad was being deployed again—the last time before he retired from the Army. Grandma's health wasn't good so we moved here before he left. Pacific Cliffs was my mom's hometown and where Dad promised her we would live once he was out of the Army, so we stayed even after Grandma died.

Trip dumped Hannah for me as soon as I moved in. That was enough to make every girl at Pacific Cliffs High School despise me. They were all loyal to Hannah because they'd known each other since they were in diapers. I was the outsider who stole the hottest guy at school. They've all hated me since

I moved in, one of about a million reasons for me to avoid going back there.

Blake is still at the door—waiting for something. Sasha, the kitten Trip rescued—now a fat cat—weaves herself between his feet. He bends down to pet her and she raises her head and rubs against his hand. She used to arch her back and hiss at Trip whenever he tried to touch her. "A lot of thanks I get for rescuing that beast," he would say, and laugh. It made me wonder if Blake was right about Trip locking her in the cage.

"Why don't we go for a walk? We could go to the beach. It's actually a nice day, and you need to get out of the house." He nods toward my window.

"I can't." It hurts when I shake my head. Even if I wanted to go, there are two major problems with me and Blake going for a walk. One, the cliff road that Trip drove off that night is visible from any point on the beach, and I don't know if I can stand to see that place again. And two, the second I go anywhere with Blake the rumor mill will be unleashed. Some girls have to worry about a story getting around school. In a place the size of Pacific Cliffs, the whole town knows your business almost before you do. Like my house, Pacific Cliffs isn't a good place for keeping secrets.

"Oh, yeah, well." He looks down at the floor and digs into his pocket. One lock of sandy hair slips over his eyes when he looks up at me. I resist the urge to brush it back. He clears his throat—"Um"—and brushes his hand across his neck. "I have something for"—he clears his throat again—"something that's yours." He holds out his hand.

I gasp and take a step back.

He's holding a palm-sized stone, round and polished smooth, dark brown with gold stripes that dance in the light like they were alive.

Guilt flashes across his face. "It's yours, isn't it?"

"Where did you find it?" I barely breathe. My heart thumps, and my scar pricks for attention, but my fingers ache for the familiar smoothness of the stone's surface, for the bumps along one side, and for the rough spot in the middle.

He swallows. "Up the cliff. By the road." He breathes in. "Where they found you that night."

The side of the road by the cliff is covered in loose rocks, sand, and scrubby beach grass. Blake finding the tigereye by accident is improbable. Finding it even if he searched for a long time would probably be impossible. But I don't question him. I reach for his hand, dig the rock out of his palm, and slide my thumb across it.

It feels warm from Blake's touch.

"Tigereye stone," the old woman at the fair had said, "beautiful and rare, like your eye."

"The freaky one," Trip said, and James and Randall laughed. My left eye is normal—dark brown, but the right one has a streak of gold in it. A little bit of extra pigment. Something that made me feel special when I was a kid. Now it just makes me feel like a freak. And now that my "freaky" eye is framed by a lumpy scar it looks freakier than ever.

Trip didn't buy the tigereye the woman was trying to sell him. That one was bigger and strung on a silver chain. He told her it was cheap junk. The woman gave me this smaller stone when I came back to her table looking for my lost purse.

"Tigereye is powerful," she said. "It gives the bearer the attributes of a tiger—empowerment, strength, courage."

I press the stone into my palm until it hurts. I look up at Blake. "Thank you."

He backs away. "I'd better go."

I nod and push the door closed. Before it clicks shut he adds, "I'll see you tomorrow."

Chapter 3

I can get away with staying in my room for most of the day, but I'm still required to eat dinner with the family. As soon as I get to the table, I know something's up. It's the way my parents are sitting—their chairs a little closer together, a little farther from me. Mom twists her napkin. Dad has his hand on her back.

I've seen this too many times before not to know what's going on. They're presenting a "united front."

Mom and Dad and their united front always meant something in our lives was about to change or that I was in trouble—another move, Dad being deployed, problems with my grades.

Usually when they do this, Andrew and I sit opposite them, close together, my hand touching his under the table—our own united front. In seven moves, six different schools, four states, and two foreign countries, our only constant was each other. Dad got deployed, Mom cleaned and purged and organized. Andrew and I stuck together.

Only this time there's a subtle difference. Andrew's chair is parked closer to them than to me—too far away for me to reach his hand. And he won't look at me.

Dad clears his throat. "Allie, we need to talk." Mom nods to show their unity. "We know the accident was hard on you. And losing Trip, but you have to get on with things. You need to go back to school. You can't stop living because—"

I look up at him. Meet his gaze hard. Dare him to finish that sentence. *Because Trip is dead.*

He looks away—a first. I've never been able to stare down the sergeant major before. He stands up, breaks ranks, and walks all the way around the table. He looks down at me. This time I look away. I'm used to Dad being strict and unfeeling, but the tenderness in his eyes I can't take. "Trip is gone, honey." He touches my arm. I study the brown-gold patterns in the scarred wood floor. They remind me of my tigereye. "He isn't coming back. And it's time for you to start living again."

They keep saying that. "Trip is gone." Like I'm holding out some hope that he'll come back, pull up to the driveway, bound up the front steps with flowers or a present for me, to apologize for being gone so long.

"We think maybe you need to see someone." Mom's voice cracks. "Ms. Holt from the school said she knows a woman down in Aberdeen. A grief counselor—"

"No." The sharpness of my voice surprises me. I tear away from Dad's hand and face them from the other side of the room. "No!"

"Allie, you need to—" Mom starts.

"—calm down," Dad finishes. He moves toward me.

I glare at him again. "No shrink. No counselor. No way."

"Hon, it will make it easier, if . . ." Mom slides her knife closer to her plate. "If"—she adjusts her spoon—"if . . ."

"If the new investigator wants to question you," Dad finishes for her.

I stop and blink once, and then again as that thought settles on me. That's what this is all about. Everyone wants to get into my head and find out what's buried there. What I don't remember. What I do.

Andrew is watching me—concern and fear in his eyes. His body shakes. It's harder for him to control his movements when he's upset. "A-A-l—"

His tremor snaps me back to the table. I glare at him, too. I can't believe he's on their side. "No." I turn on my heels and flee. Run to my room and slam the door.

I expect someone to come after me. I've only slammed the door a few times before when Dad was around. It was always followed by him stomping down the hall, flinging open the door, and yelling, "That kind of behavior isn't tolerated in this house!"

But no one comes. Not Dad with his heavy footsteps, not Mom with her clicking heels, not Andrew in his chair.

I stride to my dresser. The sudden urge to throw something, break something, is overwhelming. I clench my fists to keep from sweeping the dresser and knocking everything on it into a broken heap on the floor.

I won't go to a counselor.

I'm not crazy.

I throw myself on the bed and stuff my pillow into my mouth so I can scream without them hearing.

No.

I can't have anyone prying into my head, pulling out the secrets I don't want to share. Things I can't remember. Things I have to keep hidden. Since the accident my mind is so full of fuzz that I can't trust the lock on my brain.

I press the pillow against my eyes and try to shut everything out, take in a few breaths, to get control. Blood pounds in my ears. My head throbs between the scar on the back of my head and the one over my eye. My hands are shaking with anger that I don't understand.

What gives them the right to care now?

Now that it's too late?

The stone that Blake brought me is still on my nightstand. I set it there before I left my room for dinner. I didn't know I would need it.

My hands shake as I reach for it now. My brain wants to explode. I could throw it hard enough to break the mirror. Hard enough that the pictures of me and Trip would shatter into a million pieces. I slide my fingers over the smooth surface and take in another breath.

Courage.

I wonder what the woman knew about courage. About the kind of courage I would need. Or about the courage I lack.

I hold the stone to the light. The stripes dance. I find the rough spot in the middle and rub it, concentrating on making it smooth.

I'm eighteen. An adult. Short of having me committed, putting me in a straitjacket, and hauling me off in a little white ambulance, they can't make me go anywhere. They can't make me talk to anyone.

I breathe in and try to count the stripes on the stone, but they swirl and move too fast. Breathe again. Count. Breathe. Close my eyes to shut out the dancing stripes and my throbbing head.

The hall floor clicks with Mom's footsteps. I should have known it would be her. Dad doesn't deal with emotions and Andrew won't even come all the way into my room anymore.

She knocks, but I don't answer. I slide the stone into the pocket of my sweatpants and sit up on the bed. I don't look at her when she comes in. She sits beside me, sighs, and glances around my room—taking it all in. Clothes on the floor, the pile of schoolbooks in the corner, and my "clutter"—posters, stuffed animals, shells, snow globes, knickknacks. Stuff I've collected from all of our moves. I'm the family pack rat. Mom is a neat freak and ultraorganized. My room is a constant irritation to her. I wonder what she'd have done if I had swept everything off my dresser and onto the floor. Everything is such a mess she might not have even noticed.

She reaches over to run her fingers through my hair, forgets and brushes against the scar, then recoils before she can stop herself. She touches my back lightly, but settles for her hands in her lap. "I don't know why you're so angry with us. We're only trying to do what's best for you." She sighs. "I'm not equipped to deal with this. I need some help. You need some help."

"No." I study the handmade rag rug on the floor, something I saved from Grandma's house.

"You can't live in this room forever."

I touch the stone in my pocket. "No."

Mom starts picking at her perfect nails. "I know you're hurting, but you have your whole life in front of you. It's your senior year. You have to move on. Having someone to talk to about things, someone trained in this sort of thing, might be the best thing."

I run my fingernail along the bumpy side of the stone, three "things" in a row. And not one mention of the word "death."

"You can't go on like this."

I press the stone hard into my palm.

She breathes in and then speaks deliberately. "I want you to be able to move past this."

I grit my teeth and close my eyes. What she wants is to have her orderly life back. To pretend nothing happened. To pretend there's nothing wrong with me. Just like before. I open my eyes and look into hers. Now that my whole family is after me about the counselor thing I won't have any peace.

What are my options? Let some grief counselor sift through the pieces of my mind that are left, or go back to school and pretend everything is normal? Not like I haven't done that before. "I'll go back to school tomorrow." The words come out so quiet that for a minute I hope she didn't hear them.

But she grabs on to them immediately. "If that's what you want." She adjusts the band on her watch. "And only if you're ready." She looks at the piles of clothes on the floor. "I could throw something in the wash so you would have something clean to wear. And I have some cute scarves, or maybe a hat, you could use to cover your hair." Her eyes trace the wound on the side of my face. I lean forward and cup my hand over my eye scar.

Unbelievable. She made the leap from "Are you sure you're up to going?" to "What will you wear?" and "How will we cover your scar?" in less than a heartbeat.

She pats my knee. "I'm sure it will start to fade soon anyway." She stands up. "It might be hard for you at first, but I know this is the right decision. It'll be good for you to be back at school, back with your friends. I'm sure they're worried about you."

Friends? I press the stone hard against my thigh. After eighteen years it still amazes me how little Mom knows about my life. She sees what she wants to, even now.

She stands up. "I'll bring you in some food, okay? And I'll get these"—she scoots my dirty clothes into a pile with her foot—"into the wash for you." She tucks the pile of T-shirts, sweats, and underwear under her arm. She pauses at the door. "I think going back to school is probably the best thing. It will give you a chance to share your feelings with other people who loved Trip. People who understand what you're going through." She walks out and closes the door with her foot.

Share your feelings? Did she get that out of some "Helping Your Child Deal with Grief" pamphlet?

People who understand?

I cross the room to the shelf above my desk. I set down the stone and pick up one of about a hundred pictures of me and Trip. My long blond hair, his clear blue eyes and dark good looks, set against the background of a mountain stream and pine trees—we look like an ad for Abercrombie & Fitch—the perfect couple.

"Watch your head." He reaches up and holds the branches away from my face. I stumble over a vine and slip in the mud, but he catches me. "Careful. Maybe I'm going to have to carry you."

I laugh. "No, just don't let go of my hand."

"Don't worry." He presses my fingers to his lips. "I won't."

No one understands.

"Here it is. My special place. I found it when I was four-wheeling. No one in Pacific Cliffs knows about it but me."

"It's beautiful." I turn a full circle and look up; a canopy of green-filtered sunlight falls over a meadow of wildflowers, moss-covered boulders, and a bubbling stream.

He steps forward and cups the side of my face. "Not as beautiful as you." I blush and look away. He slips his hand in mine. "And now for my surprise." He leads me around the back of the tree. Carved in the trunk are the words TRIP LOVES ALLIE.

"Oh." I cover my mouth, barely able to believe that he wrote that for me.

He wraps his arms around me. "Now it's our special place."

I trace the letters on the tree behind us in the picture.

No one knows what's churning inside of me.

Crushing guilt.

"We have to hurry. Dad wants us at his dinner meeting tonight." He opens the door for me and then stops, staring at my boots and the bottom of my jeans. "What the hell did you step in? Mud? It's all over your pants."

I look down. "I guess that happened when I slipped. It'll wash out." I start to get in the truck, but stop when I see the expression on his face.

"I plan this great surprise and you have to screw it up." His eyes blaze fire. He slams the passenger door shut, almost catching me in it. "Now we're going to be late."

Pain.

"It's just a little mud. Maybe we can go by my house and I can change. Your dad won't mind if we're a little late—"

His fist crashes into my stomach. I gasp as all the air leaves my chest. Stars fly in front of my eyes as I fall backward into the mud. I can't breathe. I can't move. I'm not even sure what just happened.

"I guess I'll have to go by myself." He walks around to the front of his truck and opens the door. "If you're going to get muddy, at least you should do it right." He climbs in, slams the door, and peels out. His tires spray me with mud, bits of pine needles, and little rocks as he drives away.

Relief.

All mixed with knowledge that Trip is never coming back.

Chapter 4

The doors to the Pacific Cliffs combined middle and high school look ominous. My head is throbbing and all morning I fought the urge to throw up.

I ignored the pile of clean clothes Mom left outside my door—my button-down red shirt and white tank sitting on the top, ready for me to put on. Instead I grabbed a ratty pair of jeans and a wrinkled T-shirt that was scrunched in the corner of my drawer. The T-shirt says "The Fighting Falcons"—from the high school I went to in Texas. I needed something that didn't remind me of last year. Just before I left I pulled on the knit cap that Mom had set with my clothes. Something to cover the mess that used to be my hair.

The jeans are too big, the gap at the waist a testament to the weight I've lost since Trip died. The T-shirt is too small. I guess my chest has grown since I was fourteen. The falcon stretched across the front is probably too sexy for a girl who's supposed to be in mourning, but I know it will annoy Mom and Dad.

I ended up throwing my gray sweatshirt on over the T-shirt on my way out the door, anyway. The sweatshirt was my constant companion and hiding place last year. I always wore it, even on the rare occasions when it was actually warm—another thing that annoyed my fashionista mother.

Sitting in Dad's truck in front of the school, all of my rebellion melts away and the terror is back. I can't shrink far enough into my gray sweatshirt today. I would do anything to avoid going through those doors. Anything but go to the grief counselor in Aberdeen.

"You'll be okay." Dad follows my gaze down the long sidewalk to the double door. "I'm not going to tell you it will be easy, but you can do it."

Not much of a pep talk. You'd think with Dad's experience sending troops into battle he would have some canned speech about being brave. I touch the stone in the bottom of my pocket, but I don't feel an influx of courage.

He puts his truck in gear, a subtle hint that it's time for me to get out. "Hang in there." I open the door, slide out slowly, and reach for my backpack. He gives me what is supposed to be an encouraging smile. "Have a good day." I can only nod, sling my backpack over my shoulder, and face the firing squad.

Dad is habitually early, so there aren't very many students here yet—thank God. The few who are turn and whisper to each other when I walk by. I keep my eyes on the ground all the way to the door and head for the office. I have no idea what my class schedule is or where my new locker is. I don't even know if they're expecting me. The hard marble eyes of the school mascot—a stuffed bobcat trapped in a glass case—accuse me as I pass by.

The secretary, Mrs. Byron, and Ms. Holt, the school nurse/guidance counselor/girls' sports assistant coach, are chatting with their backs to me. The only one who sees me walk in is Clair, the part-time office assistant who was a student here less than three years ago. She gasps when she looks up. "Allie." She puts her hand over her mouth. "Your hair." I touch the hat and feel little spikes of hair sticking through the back. The other two turn, but they have time to check their expressions before they see me. I put my hand over the side of my face to cover the scar there.

"Hello, Allie." Mrs. Byron gives Clair a stern sideways glance. "Your mom called this morning and said you would be here today. It's good to see you."

Clair nods, but her hand hasn't left her mouth and her eyes are glistening.

"I have your schedule and locker assignment," Mrs. Byron says. She starts shuffling through some papers on the desk.

Ms. Holt gives me a weak smile that I try to return. I've made it a point to avoid her since my visit to her office last year. I slipped on the sidewalk at lunch and scraped up my elbow. My stats teacher sent me to the nurse's office when he saw the blood dripping through the paper towel I was holding over my arm. All Ms. Holt had to do was give me a Band-Aid. Instead, she made me sit on her little paper-covered bed and take off my sweatshirt so she could clean out the wound. When she saw my arms, she asked a lot of questions. I gave her my canned "clinical clumsiness" excuse. I think she bought it, but after that she was always watching me, the way she's examining the scar above my eye now. At least I have a viable story for that one.

"How are you doing?" Clair's eyes are nearly brimming over, but she's forcing a smile.

"Okay," I mutter. My fingers find the rough spot on the stone in my pocket.

"You poor thing, you've really been through it." Clair sniffs and pulls a tissue from the box on her desk. "We all miss Trip around here. He was so alive, you know, always—" Another firm look and head shake from Mrs. Byron shuts her up.

Mrs. Byron shuffles through the papers on the desk and produces a little blue card, just like the one I got when I enrolled in school two years ago. She leans over the desk and points to my locker number. "Your locker is down the new hall, on the right." By "new hall" she means the hall that was added on to the school in 1979.

"Do you want us to have someone take you there?" Clair asks.

"No, thanks." I ignore the obvious stupidity of that question. Pacific Cliffs' combined school is about one-quarter the size of my grade school in Maryland, and I navigated that when I was five.

"Your advisor is Mr. Hamilton," Mrs. Byron continues. "He's out in the portable this year."

I nod and reach for the paper. Before I can grasp it, I hear a familiar fake-sweet, singsong voice behind me. "Mrs. Byron, where can I copy the flyers for the bonfire?"

I don't turn to face Hannah—willing her to leave without seeing me—but in another second she's beside me.

"Allie," she gasps. Then she does the last thing I expect her to do. She wraps her arms around me and pulls me against her ample chest. I'm stuck with a face full of her blue silk blouse and musky perfume. I can't lift my arms to hug her back. All I can think is how different this greeting is from the one I got from her when I moved to Pacific Cliffs.

Hannah was waiting for me in front of the school after Mom dropped me off that first day. She knew exactly who I was and what had happened between me and Trip the summer before. Mom hadn't even driven away when Hannah fell into step beside me. We walked together the last three steps into the building, just long enough for her to spit one word in my direction: "Bitch."

I'm sure she was responsible for that same word painted across my locker in red fingernail polish a week later. The janitor used acetone to remove it, which made the old paint bubble underneath. Even after the locker had been repainted the same sickening orange brown, you could see what had been written there. If I went to locker 18-B now I'm positive I would still be able to read that label across the front—my greeting every day when I came to school.

"Oh, Allie." Hannah releases me and wipes her eyes. "It's so good to see you. I'm so glad you're okay."

Clair is full-fledged crying, and even Ms. Holt is dabbing at her eyes. Only Mrs. Byron seems unaffected. She reaches for the flyer in Hannah's hand. "I'll make the copies."

Hannah takes my blue card from between my fingers. "We

have our first three classes together. Come with me. I'll walk you there."

I have no choice but to let her put her arm around me and guide me down the hall, past the whispers and stares, toward my new, unmarked locker.

Hannah and I walking down the hall together causes more of a stir than I could have made on my own. I reach to brush my hair against my face, to cover the scar, but there isn't enough left. Instead, I tug the hat down farther. I'm sure everyone is asking themselves the question I've thought of a million times. How could Trip ever choose me over Hannah?

Hannah is beautiful—long black hair that hangs satiny and straight down her back, green eyes, and an olive complexion that makes her look perpetually tan. She's taller than me, and athletic—star of track and basketball.

The difference between us is glaringly obvious as we walk together. Not only do I look like a freak now, but I stumble along with my eyes on the floor. Hannah smiles and floats down the hall like the pageant queen she is—poised and confident. She won the Beachcomber's Queen contest without blinking.

I know who Trip would choose now.

My whole life people have told me I'm beautiful. Way back when I was in fourth grade I remember my mom talking about me over the phone. She said, "Allie has a hard time in school. She'll never be smart like her brother." Then she laughed and said, "Yeah, at least she's pretty."

Maybe before I *was* pretty. I had my hair—long and thick, and a honey-gold color that guys go for. I've always been decently thin with an okay chest—not eye-poppingly huge like Hannah's, but okay. Some people even thought my freaky eye was cool. Because we moved around so much, I was always the new kid. Maybe that's what Trip saw in me—something new.

I go through the first half of the day without seeing Andrew. I've made it past the opening round of whispers, stares, and the sympathy that drips off everyone. The only bright spot today is that so far the teachers have excused the work I missed. So much for Blake's valiant efforts. I haven't seen him either, something that's hard to do in a school the size of Pacific Cliffs, even if he's a junior and I'm a senior.

By the time I put my books in my locker to go to lunch, I'm exhausted. I wonder if Dad or Mom would come rescue me if I called. Doubt it. I'm tired of being the center of attention so I go to the special ed room to eat lunch with Andrew.

He's already at the table when I come in. He could eat in the commons with the other kids, but it embarrasses him to eat in front of people. He has one hand that works okay as long as he's not excited or upset, but eating takes a lot of coordination between his hand, his head, and his mouth. The food doesn't always reach its intended destination.

The aide is busy on the other side of the room with another student, so I help Andrew pull on the vest that protects his clothes. I get his cup out of his backpack and pour "Thick-It"—a powder that thickens liquid so he doesn't choke—into his apple juice.

He picks up his spoon, weighted so he can get it to his mouth with less shaking, and smiles at me. Maybe he's wondering if I'm still mad. "Th-th-thanks, Al."

I look away, almost dissolving into the tears I've fought all day, and slide a chair next to him.

"No food?" he asks.

I shake my head. "I'm not hungry."

He pushes his tray toward me, ground turkey, mashed potatoes, green beans, and applesauce. I make a face and he makes one back. "You . . . can . . . live on it—"

"—but death might be better." I finish the joke we've shared forever.

I need to feel Andrew next to me, so I put my hand on his knee under the table. He pushes his feet against the footrest of his chair and his hands against the seat. He half stands with his shoulders pressing against the restraint holding him in and adjusts his position. His body is always in motion like that, even when he sleeps. Mom says it's nerves and habit. Andrew says he does it to build up strength. On good days he can support his own weight long enough to get from his chair to the bed. When he was a little kid he got around by rolling and army crawling, but he's gotten too tall and too old for that.

I wonder what it would be like if things were different—if I had been the one born second and blue from lack of oxygen. Even with his twisted body, Andrew is gorgeous. His hair is the same color as mine, but curly, falling in soft waves over his ears. His brown eyes are framed by long eyelashes and he's tall, with Dad's broad shoulders. He would have filled out like Dad, played football and basketball, and every girl at school would've been after him. I could have been strapped in that chair instead of him. Dad talks about people coming back from the war with survivor's guilt. I've had survivor's guilt since birth.

"There you are, Allie." Hannah sweeps into the special ed room. "Hi, Andrew." She puts a hand on his shoulder. He drops the spoonful of potatoes he was working into his mouth and turns red. She smiles at him. “Did you actually grasp what Mr. King was trying to tell us in physics yesterday?” Andrew bobs his head up and down. “I might have to pick your brain later,” she says. Andrew beams, and Hannah turns back to me. “I saved you a place at lunch.” She hesitates. “Unless you want to eat in here. I could bring you a tray.”

I can’t believe Hannah is being nice to me. I would rather stay with Andrew, but he waves me off so I follow Hannah to the commons. Her friends Angie and Megan are already there. James and Randall, Trip’s friends, aren’t around. Last year Angie and Randall were joined at the hip and usually the lips. I must have missed a break-up somewhere. That doesn’t surprise me. They fought all the time when they were dating.

When I saw James and Randall in the hall, they wouldn’t look at me. I couldn’t look at them either. It must be weird for them to see me without Trip. Truthfully, it feels weird for me to be walking around school without him.

Lunch is strained conversation and awkward silence. I pick at my food and wish I had stayed with Andrew. It’s a relief when lunch is over, and Hannah heads to the opposite end of the hall for her honors classes.

I finally see Blake when I walk into art. He’s lying with his head on his desk, the hood of his white Volcom sweatshirt pulled up over his ears and a black cord trailing from the hood.

I glance around, out of habit, to see if anyone is watching before I approach him. He startles when I tap him on the shoulder, pulls the earbuds out of his ears, and blinks up at me like he’s surprised to see me, or maybe just surprised I’m talking to him in public. “Why didn’t you tell me you were coming back to school?”

I sit in the desk next to his. "I didn't really plan on it. It just sort of happened."

He coils the cord from his earbuds around his fingers. "So you and Hannah are buddies now?"

"I don't know." I squirm. He must have seen me sometime this morning, even if I didn't see him. "She sort of accosted me when I walked in."

"She's been playing the widow since you've been gone. Playing up her relationship with Trip to get attention. Now that you're back, I guess she'll have to share that attention." There's an edge to Blake's voice that bothers me, like he's accusing me of using Trip's accident to get attention, too.

"She could be sincere."

"Doubt it."

"What if she's genuinely hurting?"

"Right." Blake kicks the leg of his desk and it pings loudly. "Hannah can't stand that your accident took all the attention away from her winning the pageant. The only loss she's mourning is the death of her spotlight."

"People can change, Blake." I'm not sure why I'm defending her, except that she was nice to Andrew. "Why don't you give her a chance?"

"Maybe because nobody in this town has ever given me a chance." To signify that our discussion is over he puts his earbuds back in his ears and lays his head back down on the desk.

I want to say more, but the teacher, Ms. Flores, walks in. She ignores Blake, but I'm not so lucky. She makes a big fuss about me being back in school and how everyone was so worried about me, and did I get the cards her seventh graders made? By the time she gets to the lesson, my head is spinning. How did everything get so mixed up? I'm back in school. Trip is gone. And I'm defending Hannah George to Blake.

He frustrates me so much sometimes—like saying no one in this town has ever given him a chance. Okay, he may be right about that. Blake has been the center of small-town scandal since before he was born, because his mom, Phoebe, ran away with the high school drama teacher the night of graduation. When she came back, nearly two years later, she was a drug addict and pregnant with Blake. She left him with his grandma, but every few years her maternal instincts kick in and she reappears in his life long enough to mess it up again.

One of her motherly episodes earned Blake a criminal record when she swept him away to live with her and her new husband in Reno. Blake was there for about eighteen months—six months longer than his mother's marriage. He got arrested for breaking and entering, and spent some time in juvie before his grandma brought him home. By the time he got back, my life had changed so much that we didn't fit together anymore.

I wish I could blame his mom for what happened between me and Blake. But it was my fault.

With his hood pulled up gangsta-style and his flagrant disregard for Ms. Flores's demonstration of pastels, Blake isn't doing much to change his reputation.

But I remember a different Blake. Expert kite flyer. Always making grand plans. Excited over caves and rocks and seashells. And the summer I turned fifteen—awkward for both of us. My family had spent a few weeks in Pacific Cliffs every summer for as long as I can remember, but when I was twelve, Dad was posted to Germany and we went with him. It was three summers before I saw Blake again. I knew how much my body had changed in that time. Worse, I knew Blake saw it, too. Andrew was sick most of that summer—getting over a scary bout with pneumonia—so it was just me and Blake.

Then there was the thing with Trip, the kitten, and the crab cage. After Trip left, Blake was fuming. He was so sure that Trip had trapped Sasha on purpose to get my attention. When I defended Trip, Blake sounded almost jealous. He stomped back to his house and left me standing in my doorway with a wet kitten wrapped in Trip's T-shirt.

I didn't see Blake again until the day we left. He showed up at my door and asked if I wanted to go to the beach.

For that afternoon, it was like no time had passed. We flew a kite and played in the waves—talked and laughed the way we had when we were little kids. Then we went to the cave that had been our hiding place for so many summers. The awkwardness crept back in when I sat on the ledge in the back and he scooted close to me. He put his arm over my shoulders. "Texas again, huh?"

"Yep." I tugged the front of my shirt up higher, but I didn't move away.

"How long?"

"I'm not sure." I could feel him watching me, but I couldn't look at him. I jerked a thread off the bottom of my cutoff shorts and rolled it between my fingers. "Dad only has a couple of years until he retires."

"And then what?"

I kept rolling the thread between my fingers. "Here, I guess.

He promised Mom we'd live here when he got out of the Army." I looked up and caught Blake staring at me, hard, intense. And I couldn't look away.

"You guys here all the time would be cool."

"Yeah. It would be."

Then he kissed me. My first. Probably his, too, but it didn't show—somewhere between a movie kiss and a quick peck. It was beautiful and amazing and perfect.

After we went to Texas, I waited for a phone call, or an e-mail, something. When I didn't hear from Blake, I thought the kiss didn't mean as much to him as it did to me. I didn't know his mom had dragged him off to Reno until we came back the next summer.

Then Trip came along and I didn't think I needed Blake anymore.

Big mistake.

If anyone at this school has a right to hate me, even more than Hannah George, it's Blake.

Chapter 5

"Allie."

I roll over, still half-asleep, and jump when I see his face.

"Open the window."

I put my finger to my lips and listen in the direction of Mom's room. Silence. I slip out of bed, make sure I miss the squeaky floorboard, and slide the window open just a crack. "Trip, you scared me to death."

He slips his hand through the crack and opens the window up farther. A breath of cold ocean air blows in my room. "I've been trying to get ahold of you all day." His face is in the shadow, so I can't read his expression.

I cross my arms over my chest, feeling exposed with no makeup, an oversized T-shirt, and no bra. "I was helping Mom clear out Grandma's house."

"You should have told me where you were going." His voice echoes through the quiet of my room, but I don't dare shush him. "What took you so long? Who else was there?"

"No one." I should be flattered by his concern, but something in his tone makes me nervous.

"I need to know where you are." He pushes the window open all the way, so hard that it bangs against the frame. I glance at my door, wondering what would happen if Mom caught Trip in my room. He doesn't climb inside. Instead he pushes something smooth and black across the windowsill. "I got you something."

I take it from him. "A phone?"

"I got it this afternoon. I added you to my plan."

"Thanks, I—"

"—my number is speed dial two. Try not to lose it."

"Allie."

I sit up in bed, not sure if the voice was part of my dream or if it was real. I try to focus in the dark, and strain my ears.

"Allie." It's a guy's voice. Not Dad. The rumble of an old truck, like Trip's, passes in front of my house.

Electric prickles run down my spine.

"Trip?" I whisper toward the window, my heart racing. Then I remember. That's not possible.

My clock says 12:38. The last thing I remember is lying on my bed after school. I'm still wearing the clothes I put on this morning. No one woke me for supper.

I've almost convinced myself that the voice was my imagination when it comes again. "Allie." But it's a different voice, a little girl, or maybe a boy. A long pause. A woman answers, but I can't make out what she's saying. My whole body is shaking. I am going crazy. For a minute I think about how old this house is, or who might have lived here before. But I don't believe in ghosts.

The kid's voice is back. I swing my legs off the bed and look out my window again, expecting or maybe hoping to see someone passing by, but all I see is misty rain under the porch light and a deserted street, no sign of the truck I heard before.

"Allie," the child says. My hair stands on end at the base of my neck and around my scar.

The stone is still in my pocket, pressing against my thigh. I touch it and stand up, following the voice past the ghostly image reflected in my mirror, down the hall. Listen again. Nothing. I creep closer to Andrew's door and lean my ear against it.

"Allie." It is Trip's voice.

I throw the door open. Andrew isn't in his bed. There's a light in the corner, on top of his desk. He's there, hunched over his computer.

"Andrew," I whisper loudly. He jumps and nearly slides out of his chair. He's in sweats, and not strapped in, which means he got himself out of bed after Dad put him there. "What are you doing?"

"Did . . . I . . . ?" he begins.

I cross the room. "Wake me up? Scare the hell out of me?" I move closer to see what he has on the desk in front of him. It's flat and black and electronic looking, about the size of a notebook or a small laptop.

He slides his hand across the screen and the voice I heard before says, "Sorry." Up close the voice sounds electronic and not as much like Trip, but it still sends a chill through my whole body.

He changes the screen a couple of times, traces down, touches the screen again, and "sorry" comes out in the little boy's voice.

The tension gets to me and I laugh. "What is that?" My voice sounds too loud in the quiet room.

He pushes the board toward me. It says DynaVox, the company that makes the augmented communications device Andrew has been wanting.

"A communicator? You got it?" I slide my finger down the smooth side. The communicator has a touch screen with a bunch of pictures and a menu of voices.

His whole face lights up with excitement. He reaches for the device and I push it back to him. "This . . . one?" He moves his finger down the screen and then touches it with his finger. "Allie," it says in the voice so close to Trip's.

Icy fingers slide down my spine. I shake my head.

His smile fades. His hand shakes as he moves his finger down the menu. The screen changes to letters. He touches T . . . R . . . I reach over and cover his hand with mine to stop him. I can't stand to hear the voice say Trip's name. Andrew sighs and bobs his head. He changes the menu so I can see a list of different voices. I touch "young woman." Andrew presses another part of the screen. "Sorry" comes out in a high-pitched woman's voice.

Andrew rolls his eyes and shakes his head. He slides his finger down the menu and chooses "elderly woman," then pushes a box that says "Allie," in a voice that reminds me of Grandma.

"Definitely you."

Andrew grins. He shakes his head and starts to giggle like a little kid. I reach for the board. He tries to keep it away from me, but he's laughing so much that he loses his balance. The screen falls onto his lap and slides down his legs and onto the floor. He reaches for it and starts slipping out of his chair. I grab his shoulder to keep him from falling out but he's too big for me. We both end up in a heap on the floor.

Andrew's laugh consumes his whole body. I laugh, too, but the sound is hollow, like an electronic laugh from the communicator. I lean my head against his chest. We used to lie on the floor all the time when we were kids. I would tickle him, and he would giggle until his whole body shook.

He reaches up and touches my hair. "Okay . . . now . . . Al?"

"Trying." I close my eyes.

"Sorry," he says in his own halting voice. His fingers brush the scar on the back of my head. His leg twitches. He pulls his hand away with a jerk, and he catches my hair between his fingers.

"Ouch," I say, but I don't move. I can feel his breath and the quick thump of his heart under my cheek. It feels so nice that even when my legs go numb, I don't want to move. Instead of going back to my room I pull a couple of blankets off Andrew's bed. I cover him with one and then curl up next to him.

"Missed ya, sis," he says softly. We've never been apart our whole lives, but I understand. With Trip around, I spent less and less time with Andrew.

"Missed ya, too," I whisper back. With his heart thumping under my ear, I fall asleep.

Chapter 6

I sit with Hannah and her crowd every day at lunch. Not really by choice. Hannah walks me from class to the lunchroom so I'm stuck. From the outside it might look like I'm part of their group now, but they don't voluntarily include me in their conversation and I don't speak up. I'm more of an extra chair at the table.

I pretty much tune out what they're saying anyway—gossip about the school and sometimes the town. The people they talk about are familiar, but they might as well be talking about aliens. I'm so disconnected, have always been so disconnected, from the normal part of the Pacific Cliffs combined school, that none of it matters to me.

I thought it would be different. I was a stranger during my summer visits, but I had hoped that once we really lived here, I would be accepted. I dreamed about being part of a crowd—

any crowd. Trying out for cheerleader, or sports, or the school play. Maybe even doing the Beachcomber's Queen contest. Mom talked about high school a lot, about what it was like to know everyone in town, to have a bunch of friends, and how cool it was when she won the pageant.

Before we moved here, Pacific Cliffs was my haven—the "home" that would always be there no matter how many times we moved. I used to calculate how old I would be when we lived in Pacific Cliffs for real. Being the "new girl" all the time made the idea of living where everyone knew you seem like a dream.

I didn't know how bad it could be.

". . . so gorgeous," Hannah says, "makes me want to speed past the billboard on Willow Street just so he'll pull me over."

"Who?" My interest is piqued, thinking about what Dad said about the special investigator. Hannah stares at me—the vacant chair speaks—maybe she forgot I was here.

Megan shakes her head. "Detective Weeks, the new cop." She looks at Hannah. "She has a 'thing' for him." Hannah blushes, something I didn't think she was capable of.

"But he's totally old," Angie throws in. "Like thirty or something."

"Twenty-seven." Hannah even has a pretty blush. "Not that old."

"He is hot." Megan points her fork at Hannah. "I'll give you that."

"But old." Angie rolls her eyes.

"Not that old," Hannah says again, and flips her hair over her shoulder.

"He probably won't be around very long anyway. He's just here because . . ." Megan looks at me and then takes a bite of her hamburger instead of finishing her sentence.

"He said he likes it here," Hannah huffs.

"You talked to him?" I shouldn't ask, but I'm curious.

Hannah shrugs casually, but smiles at the same time. "I sat by him during a town meeting. Something I had to do for Beachcomber's. He's nice."

"Oh, yes, very nice." Megan fans herself.

"She did more than talk to him." Angie leans in. "She followed him to Westport so she could watch him surf."

"Stalker." Megan grins and pops a fry into her mouth.

Hannah keeps blushing and scowls at both of them. It's weird to see them be kind of nasty to each other, but I've never had close friends. Maybe that's how friends act.

"Big deal," Angie says. "I've talked to him, too, every time he comes in for groceries." Angie's dad owns the only grocery store in town. "He's more interested in Allie than you." A familiar jealous hatred settles into Hannah's eyes. "I mean, that's what they brought him for anyway, right? To investigate the accident?"

I look down at my tray.

Angie points at me with her fork. "He asked me whether I knew you and Trip. If Trip was a big drinker—like I'm going to answer that." She sticks a forkful of salad in her mouth, chews, and then points at me again. "He wanted to know if you were back at school yet. I told him I didn't know if you'd ever be back." I'm still looking at my tray, but I can see Hannah giving Angie distinct "shut up" signals. She doesn't seem to notice, because she swallows and keeps talking. "There was a rumor that you were in some hospital in Seattle. That your brain wasn't right after the accident and you were in a wheelchair like your brother. Someone else said it was a mental hospital. That you went crazy after Trip died." She looks at me and shakes her head. "You look pretty normal. I guess it wasn't true."

Hannah and Megan look somewhere between embarrassed and irritated. Angie finally catches their expressions. "What?"

My face burns. My eyes water. I stand up so fast I knock over my chair. "I have to go. I forgot I was supposed to go in for tutoring." I spill my uneaten fries on the floor when I pick up the chair. I leave them and dump my tray on the way out. I'm moving so fast that I don't see Blake on the other side of the glass doors until I run into him.

"Hey!" He catches me in his arms. "Are you okay?"

I pull away and shake my head. I mean to say "yes," but with the tears gathering in my eyes it probably looks more like "no." I'm not sure why I am so close to crying. I don't cry anymore. Not ever. I've gone through way worse than Angie's stupidity.

"What did they say to you?" Blake looks through the doors toward the table I just left.

"Nothing." I keep my eyes down. "I just . . . I need to—"

"Allie." Angie comes through the door behind me. "Hannah told me I needed to apologize. She thinks I upset you."

"It's okay," I mutter. "No big deal."

"Hannah seems to think it was." Angie rolls her eyes. "The Queen is so PC these days." She sees Blake and wrinkles her little freckled nose. "Oh, hi, Juvie, I thought I smelled something." She turns back to me, like I didn't hear her insult Blake—like he's nothing to me. "So we're okay, right, Allie?" I can only blink in response as she reaches into her purse to pull out her cell phone. "Later." She waves and heads down the hall.

"Some friends." Blake pushes his earbuds into his ears, stuffs his hands in his pockets, and walks away.

Chapter 7

"You about ready to go? School starts in a half hour." Dad pours coffee into his silver "Go Army" thermos and checks his watch.

"Just a sec." I pull a granola bar out of the box from the cupboard, wondering if I'll actually have the stomach for this one.

He watches me, then pours the last of the milk into a cup and hands it to me. I drink it because he's watching. "Looks like we need to add milk to Mom's list." He picks up the pen next to her "Things We Need" tablet and writes "milk," then looks over the list. "This is getting pretty long and I know Mom's working late again. What are you doing after school today?"

I have to think about it before I answer. My time after school used to belong to Trip. He'd get mad if I had something to do that didn't involve him. But that's not a problem anymore. I shrug. "Nothing."

"Could you go to the store?" He rips the list off the notepad.

"I guess so." Going to the grocery store in Pacific Cliffs is the last thing I want to do, but saying no to Dad isn't usually an option.

"You can drop me off at the shop so you'll have the car to get groceries on your way home. Just make sure you come get me at five thirty sharp." He pulls a fifty-dollar bill out of his wallet, looks over the list again, and adds a twenty. "I expect change back."

"Yes, sir." I stick the money in my pocket, next to the tigereye. At the high school I went to in Texas I would have been scared to have that much money on me. In Pacific Cliffs it's no big deal.

If Dad had dropped me off at school and I'd gone to the main entrance like normal, I might have noticed the car—black, immaculate, expensive. Maybe if I had been paying attention when I came in from student parking, I'd have seen him in time to duck into a bathroom. But after a week of unwanted attention and sympathy I was trying to be invisible—head down, hands buried in the pocket of my sweatshirt, clutching the tigereye between them. That's why I don't see Mr. Phillips coming out of the office until I'm almost on top of his Italian leather shoes.

"Excuse me," he says, and steps sideways. When I look up, he gasps. "Allie." Mrs. Phillips, the green leather pumps to his right, gasps, too. I haven't seen them since cotillion, the night of the accident, before Trip died.

I'm face to chest with Mr. Phillips's dark suit and silk tie. Farther up are the same broad shoulders that Trip had, then the square chin. I don't dare look higher than that.

He puts his hands on my shoulders, heavy. I brace myself to keep from pulling away. "It's good to see you, Allie."

"What are you doing here?" I blurt out. I punish my tongue by biting down on it hard.

Mrs. Phillips sniffs. She pulls her brown fur coat around her, like she's cold. I've never seen Mrs. Phillips without a fur coat—her way of showing everyone she's above them. She's the sole heir to the oldest money in town. According to Trip, she didn't think I was good enough for him.

Mr. Phillips drops one hand from my shoulder and pulls his wife against his side. I look up. Her eyes—crystal blue, like Trip's—are swimming. She catches my gaze, then looks at the ground.

Mr. Phillips clears his throat and swallows. "We came to talk to Mr. Barnes about setting up a scholarship fund in Trip's name."

"Oh." I put my hand over the side of my face and study his shoes. They could be brand new. There isn't a scratch or a speck of dirt anywhere on them.

"We would like to help you with school, too, Allie," he says. "If you choose to go to college." He puts his hand back on my shoulder. "And I've been meaning to reinstate your phone on our plan."

I step back, still within his reach but farther away. "That's nice, but . . ." My throat closes so the words can't come out. "I couldn't . . ." I'm dying for the bell to ring, anything to save me.

His hand gets heavier on my shoulder. My heart thumps against my chest like I was a cornered rabbit. "It would be no trouble. After everything you meant to our son—" He glances at his wife. "What's the use of having all this money if we have no one to share it with?"

Mrs. Phillips twists the strap of her purse around her fingers.

Guilt and fear make the milk boil in my stomach. I could throw up, right here, on his perfect shoes. Then maybe he'd leave me alone.

The first bell rings. I almost slide to the floor in relief. But Mr. Phillips doesn't let go of me, even as the sea of gaping faces moves past us toward class. "I'll talk to your mom about it." He lowers his head so I can see perfect teeth and his smile. "You should come by the house sometime. It feels so empty without Trip." He finally takes his hand away and uses it to steer his wife toward the door. "We'll be watching for you."

I tug at the sleeves of my sweatshirt and force myself to nod, but the chill down my back comes way before the wind that blows in when Mr. Phillips opens the door for his wife.

After the Phillipses leave I just stand there, frozen in place, unable to move, like Mr. Phillips's hand on my shoulder was some kind of freeze ray that sucked all the warmth out of my body.

The second bell rings. The hall empties. I slowly thaw back to motion, but instead of going to my locker, getting my books, and heading to class, I retrace my steps back to Dad's truck in the parking lot.

The truck's engine roars so loud that it makes me jump, but no one comes running out of the building to stop me from leaving school. I crank the heat up full blast to try to relieve some of the numbness that grips my chest. I exhale as I drive past the WELCOME TO HISTORIC PACIFIC CLIFFS sign and realize I've been holding my breath.

A few miles out of town I start to feel alive again. The highway feels free; the hum of the tires, the slap of the windshield wipers, even the feeling of control I get when I step on the gas and Dad's truck responds with a roar. I can't make myself stop.

Nearly three hours later I pull into a gas station in Olympia with the gas light on Dad's truck burning bright. Only then does it hit me how far I've driven. Only then does it hit me that I did something really stupid.

I try to estimate how much gas I'll need to get back to Pacific Cliffs and how much money I'll need to buy all the groceries on the list. I even pull out the manual Dad keeps in the glove compartment to see how many miles per gallon the truck gets so I can divide it out, but math was never one of my strong subjects.

I give up and spend sixty-six fifty of Dad's seventy dollars on gas. Then I drive to a pier overlooking the Puget Sound, get out of the truck, and watch the water while I try to figure out what to do.

For a flash of a second I think about calling Trip. He would berate me for being stupid enough to drive all the way out here, but he'd come pick me up, probably even pay for the groceries.

Then I remember he's gone.

Anyway you look at it, I'm screwed. I have no money. Period. Not here. Not at home. Not even in the bank. I wanted to get a job last year, but Trip said it would cut into our time together, that anything I would get at Pacific Cliffs was beneath me, and "don't I take care of everything you need anyway?"

An ugly, scrawny seagull pulls a yellow fast-food wrapper with a little bit of cheeseburger stuck to it out of the garbage can in front of me. Before she can eat any of it, a bigger seagull swoops down and snatches it away. Then a bunch of other seagulls join him. They tear the wrapper apart and squawk and fight over the pieces.

I think about what would happen if I kept driving and didn't ever go home. I could drive until I ran out of gas again. Find a place where no one knows me.

Or I could point the truck toward the ocean and drive until I run out of land.

The truck has Davis Auto on the side and a big winch on the front—conspicuous. Besides, Dad needs it for work.

And then there's Andrew.

The drive back to Pacific Cliffs is slower. The rain is coming down in sheets so the wipers can hardly keep up. Every mile that ticks by feels like a lead weight pressing on top of me. What is Dad going to do to me when I come back without the money, and grocery-less?

When I get to Hoquiam, a lit yellow sign catches my eye. PAWN X-CHANGE: ELECTRONICS, GUNS, JEWLERY.

My stomach clenches. I reach up and finger the diamond stud earring in my left ear.

"I got you something."

I slow down as I pass the pawnshop. The neon sign blinks OPEN.

"They're the real deal. Nothing's too good for my girl."

I keep driving for three blocks.

"I got them to make up for things . . ."

Three more blocks slip past.

". . . to show you how sorry I am for what happened last night."

I turn around.

"Please look at me, Al."

I drive back and pull into the parking lot of the store next to the pawnshop. My freaky eye accuses me from the mirror, so I focus on the earrings—turn my head back and forth and watch them sparkle.

I remember his hand on my face, his fingers tracing my sore cheekbone.

"I just lost it, okay? The whole day with my dad—I can never do anything right when he's around."

I turn off the truck's engine and stare at the yellow sign until the letters are burned into my retina.

"It will never happen again. I promise."

I've worn the earrings since Trip gave them to me. The skin has grown around them so I have to twist to get them out. My right ear bleeds a little. I wipe it off with a napkin I find in the center console of the truck.

In my hand they seem so tiny. Trip said they were real. How much could they be worth? The grocery list is still sitting on the seat next to me. How much do I need? Fifty dollars? Dad thought seventy would be enough, with some change left over.

If I ask for seventy dollars, will they laugh in my face?

I hesitate, rubbing the rough spot on my stone. Then I go inside.

The man behind the counter is younger than I expected, like twenty-something. He has dark hair and a mustache and his arms are covered in tattoos. He's trying to look respectable, wearing a clean blue polo shirt tucked into jeans, but not quite pulling it off.

I'm grateful for my gray-sweatshirt shield that keeps him

from seeing whatever his eyes are perusing for as they take me in. I cover the side of my face with my hand and keep my head down. My other hand is clutching the earrings, digging them into my palm.

"Can I help you with something?" He smiles, but it's a slippery smile, like any minute it could slide into something more sinister.

I grip the earrings tighter but force myself to pull them out of my pocket. "I wanted to—" My voice squeaks, so I swallow and try again. "I was interested in what I would get for these." I open my hand. The earrings have left angry red marks on my palm. I should have thought through the presentation better.

"Let's have a look." He pulls out a piece of black velvet and motions for me to set the earrings on top of it.

"They're real." I go for confident, but it comes out more like a question.

He reaches under the counter, pulls out some kind of magnifying glass, and studies the earrings. "You have a fight with your boyfriend?"

My hand automatically goes back to the scar over my eye. "No. It was an accident. I mean, I got this in a car accident."

He looks at me strangely. "I meant why are you selling the earrings? You trying to get back at the guy who gave these to you?"

"No, he's de—" I bite off the word and say, "Gone," instead. He looks at me hard, but I acquire a sudden and deep interest in a piece of artwork on the shelf behind him—a collage of faces, different expressions and different colors flowing into each other.

He goes back to the earrings, studying each one with the

glass while the clock ticks by agonizing second after agonizing second. He finally looks back at me with no expression. "What did you want for them?"

I've seen enough bargaining on TV to know I should start higher than what I want. "One hundred fifty." I bite my lip and wait for him to laugh in my face.

"Hmmm, I don't think so." He steps back and shoves his hands in his pockets. "Try again."

"One twenty-five." All of the faces in the painting laugh at me.

He fingers the earrings. "I won't go higher than a hundred."

I look down at the studs, sparkling hopefully even in the grimy fluorescent light. I feel like they deserve better than to end up in a place like this, but I look away from them and say, "Okay."

"Done." He grins.

I only wanted to get Dad's money back so I wouldn't be in trouble, but as fast as he agreed, and as big as his smile is now, I get the idea I'm being taken.

"There are a lot of jerks out there, Al. That's why you need me around. I'll always be here to protect you."

The man scoops the earrings into a little box and a bubble of panic hits my throat. What is Trip going to say when he finds out I . . . ? I squash that thought with my hand pressed against my forehead. Trip can't find out anything ever again.

Chapter 8

On the way home, my ears—used to Trip's earrings—swell in protest. They feel bare and I keep pushing insufficient wisps of hair around them. I wonder if anyone will notice that they're gone. Mom will. Now that we're pretending everything is normal again she barely notices me, but missing earrings? That she'll notice. But maybe because everything is supposed to be normal, she'll pretend she doesn't.

Dad's truck feels huge and loud as I pull into the parking lot at Simmons' Grocery. Since it's the only store in town, Simmons' sells everything from groceries to pocketknives to souvenirs for tourists. I spent so much time getting home that I've hit the after-work crowd. Instead of the store being empty, there are five other people shopping. The aisles are too low to hide behind, so I feel everyone's eyes on me as I try to find the stuff on Mom's list as fast as possible.

The first reactions I get from the other customers are mixed—a sympathetic smile from an old man who holds the door to the fridge open so I can get the milk and an open-mouthed stare at the side of my face from a kid standing by the candy aisle.

Then I see Grandma's old friend, Sherry Clark, one of the gossip-seekers who came to see me in the hospital after the accident. She's talking on her cell phone, but stops midconversation when she sees me. In a voice loud enough for the person on the other end and the entire store to hear she says, "Allie Davis, it's good to see you out."

I mutter something like "thanks" and try to squeeze by her, but her body seems to swell enough to fill up the aisle. "I remember when I lost my Patrick, I couldn't bring myself to go anywhere for nearly six months." She looks at me over the top of her glasses. I feel like I'm being examined for acceptable signs of mourning. I automatically reach to pull my hat down over my scar and, if possible, to cover my bare earlobes.

"Dad asked me to go shopping. I have to pick him up. I need to hurry—" I try again to push my cart in the little hole between her and the canned tomatoes.

"Just seeing other people, people getting on with their normal lives, is such a hard thing after you've lost someone so close to you."

"Yes. It is." I look down at the floor and try to look appropriately shattered.

She pats my hand. "Hang in there. You're a trouper." She lets me by, but I'm not even to the next aisle when I hear her on her phone again, even though she's trying to whisper. "Huge scar on the side of her face . . . horrible, poor child. She was such a pretty thing."

I can't leave fast enough, so I get the basics, skip the rest of the list, and push my cart to the front of the store. Angie's mom is working the only open register.

I start unloading my cart. Angie's mom looks at me like she's surprised. "Oh, Allie, how are you feeling?"

I'm not sure how I'm supposed to answer that question anymore. I stick with a quiet "Okay."

"Angie told me you were back at school. That you've been eating lunch together. I think it's nice that they're reaching out to you." She's running the groceries through, superspeed. She barely misses a beat when James walks in. "You're late," she says without looking at him.

I shrink back instinctively, but there's nothing to hide behind. "Sorry," he mumbles. He throws his coat under the counter, sends a dark look in my direction, and starts bagging my groceries.

Angie's mom picks up her conversation with me without missing a beat. "Have you seen the monument they put by the cliff?"

I don't know what she's talking about, so I just shake my head. "No." James is still watching me. His dark eyes bore into the side of my face, but I can't look back at him. Why is he staring? What is he thinking? Does he notice the earrings are missing?

". . . They did a beautiful job on it, but I would imagine it would be hard for you to go up there." Angie's mom hands me my receipt and says pleasantly, "This is such a sad thing for you to have to go through." She pats my hand. "Tell your mom I said hi."

"Thanks," I mutter, and reach for my cart, but Simmons' is a full-service grocery store. James grabs the handle before I can. I walk around him and head for the doors. He follows me out, pushing the cart, his gaze on the back of my head. I want to tell him I can get it, that I don't need his help, but I don't dare say anything. We stop at Dad's truck and I fumble around the tiger-eye for the keys in my pocket. I'm probably the only person in Pacific Cliffs who locks their car door, and now I wish I hadn't. James's close proximity and silent glare make me nervous. My hand slips off the handle once, but I manage to get the door open. He reaches past me and puts the groceries behind the seat. He straightens up but doesn't leave.

"Thank you." I study the front tire of the truck.

He lets out a heavy breath and then says through his teeth, "Nobody has forgotten anything. You aren't going to get away with pretending everything is okay." He turns around, shoves the cart hard, and heads back to the store.

I'm so shocked I can't move. His words chill me as bad as Mr. Phillips's touch. I stand for a minute, letting the rain soak through my sweatshirt, before I recover enough to climb in the truck.

What is that supposed to mean? Pretending everything is okay? I've been walking around school with my head down. Talking to no one. Looking at no one. How am I supposed to be acting?

I'm so distracted that I miss the one red light in town. When I'm halfway through the intersection, a horn blares. I slam on the brakes, slide on wet pavement, and barely avoid hitting a blue clunker Ford Maverick. Every heartbeat sends sparks of adrenaline through my body. The driver, Marshall Yates, a sophomore with a garage band and a huge attitude, flips me off and keeps going.

I take half a breath before I see flashing lights in my rearview mirror and Pacific Cliffs' new, unmarked black Charger behind me.

I pull over and lean my head against the steering wheel. How could today possibly get any worse?

Then the officer gets out—tall, blond, definitely not Chief Milton. He leans in my window. "How are you doing today?" Dumb question. "Do you know why I pulled you over?"

Hannah was right about the new cop being hot, but I'm not in the mood to try to flirt my way out of a ticket, and the way I look now it wouldn't work anyway. I swallow hard. "I missed the red light."

"Kind of a hard one to miss, don't you think?" His blue eyes laugh at me. "License and registration, please."

I pull my license out of my purse and reach for the registration in Dad's glove box. The door sticks so I have to hit it and jerk on the handle a couple times before it falls open.

I glance at the clock—5:55. Between the ticket and my being late, Dad will never let me take his truck again, even if he never finds out that I ditched school.

He takes my license and registration. "Be right back." Why are cops so friendly while they ruin your day? I wonder if Dad was wrong about this guy being some kind of detective. Traffic stops seem like grunt police work. Maybe it's all a rumor and he's just a regular cop.

Through the rearview mirror I watch him walk back to his car. He stops at his door, looks at my license, then turns around and comes back. "Allison Davis?" He's still looking at my license when I roll the window down again. I keep my eyes forward, so my scar is hidden on the other side of my face.

"Yes." I lick my lips because my mouth has gone dry. "Is there a problem?"

He smiles—even friendlier. "It might take a while to run your license through the system—old computer. I don't want to stand out here in the rain. Do you mind sitting in the car with me?"

I do mind, but I don't think I'm allowed to say no to a police officer. I slide out of the truck and follow him. He opens the passenger-side door of his car for me. I climb in and bury my hands in the pockets of my sweatshirt. The damp seeps into my skin and I have to hunch my shoulders to keep from shaking. The outside of the car looks like a regular Dodge Charger—sneaky—but inside the dash is covered in blinking lights, wires, and even a laptop. I focus on the dash while he gets in his side.

"So." He reaches over to turn down the dispatch radio. The only thing coming over it is someone talking about the high school football game. "You're Allie Davis?"

I nod and continue to study the dashboard while my heart pounds. I'm not sure what he's doing. If he was going to question me, wouldn't he do it at the police station? If he was going to arrest me, wouldn't he have put me in the backseat?

"I want to talk to you about the accident last summer." So much for him being a benign cop.

My answer is quick and sounds too defensive. "I don't remember anything."

He continues like I didn't answer. "There were some inconsistencies I was hoping you could explain to me." His mock-friendliness is gone. Now he's all business. "I talked to one of the EMTs who was on the scene that night. He told me that there were some unusual things about your injuries. That your head injury wasn't consistent with the way you were lying against the rocks. And that there was a lot less blood than he would have expected, considering how much you had lost."

"I wouldn't know." I meet his eye with a look that I hope is braver than I feel. "I was unconscious. Did he mention that?"

"I also talked to a nurse at the ER in Aberdeen. She wouldn't go on record, but she mentioned bruising on your arms and legs." His gaze works to penetrate my shell. "Bruises that weren't consistent with the accident. Old bruises."

"My medical records are confidential." My voice wavers, but I try to keep it steady. We learned that in civics last year. It was something I remembered clearly.

"Smart girl. You're right. Without a warrant I can't get those records. And maybe she shouldn't have told me what she did. But it would be okay if you told me where the bruises came from." His voice is coaxing but sure—he's a guy who's used to getting what he wants because of the way he looks, like Trip.

I keep my mouth shut, exercising my right to remain silent. He waits.

"Detective Weeks, we have that license info for you." The dispatcher's voice crackles over his radio. I don't miss the word "detective" in his title. He ignores the voice and turns the radio all the way down. He crosses his arms, looks at me, and waits.

I scrape my fingernail against the rough edge of my stone

and wonder how long in a police car constitutes unlawful imprisonment. We studied that in civics, too. But the pressure of his silence and the pounding of the scar on the back of my head are killing me. "Mild cerebral palsy." The canned answer comes out easy enough.

"What?" He leans forward, eager.

"I have mild cerebral palsy. My brother and I were born eight weeks early and deprived of oxygen at birth. Me, just a minute or two, him for much longer. He's in a wheelchair. I don't read so well, and I don't have the best balance so I fall a lot. Thus the bruises." I level my eyes at him and work to keep all emotion out of my face and out of my voice. "If my license is cleared, I need to go. I'm supposed to be picking up my dad right now."

"Actually I want to—"

Something hits the window. I jump. Detective Weeks reaches for his gun. Outside the patrol car is Dad—standing in the pouring rain and pounding on the window. He's soaking wet, and he looks pissed.

Detective Weeks calmly moves his hand from his gun, opens the door, and steps out to meet Dad. He shuts the door behind him so I can't hear what they're saying, but I don't think I've ever seen Dad look this mad.

Tight-lipped all the way home, Dad doesn't mention my being late, or the ticket that Detective Weeks still dared to give me. I don't think he knows I ditched school—at least he doesn't mention it. We're sitting in the driveway before he says anything. Then he turns to me. "Is that the first time that cop has talked to you?"

"Yes, sir." I sit up straight. Dad is in full sergeant-major mode.

His hands grip the steering wheel. "If he ever does anything like that again, I want you to let me know."

"Yes, sir."

"If he wants to question you, with the proper paperwork and down at the station, then we'll cooperate. But I don't approve of his methods."

"Yes, sir." I say it again, because I don't know what else to say.

He sighs and turns off the truck. "Did you get the groceries?"

"Yes."

"Good, because you're grounded from driving for the rest of the month."

I sit in the car for a minute and watch Dad walk inside. I can't get the image of him toe-to-toe with Detective Weeks, yelling at him, defending me, out of my head. I wonder if things might have been different if Dad had been around.

Chapter 9

Something feels off when I walk into school the next day. Clair takes my forged excuse note—*Allie needed some time off yesterday. Please excuse her absence*—without her usual sad smile and without comment.

When I walk down the hall the whispers are back—not that they ever completely left. But the sympathetic looks and half smiles are gone. I feel accusations all around me. But I might be imagining it because of what James said to me at the store.

When I reach my locker, Hannah, Megan, and Angie are there, talking with their heads together. Like they can sense me coming, they all turn—a three-headed, ultrapopular monster—and glare at me. I recognize the look on Hannah's face.

I press my book against my chest for protection. "What's wrong?"

"Like you don't know." Angie's long fingernails tap out disgust on her thigh.

"I don't—" I take a step backward.

Hannah strides toward me. "You little slut!" She gets so close that I have to take a step back. "It wasn't enough that you stole Trip and got him killed. Now you have to go after Jonathon, too!"

My mind races. "Jonathon? I didn't—"

"Jonathon Weeks, the new cop. Don't even try to deny it. Half the town saw you in the front seat of his car." She sucks in an angry breath. "And because your dad caught you together, and blamed it on him, he's going to get fired and have to leave!"

I cower against the lockers as she pushes her face even closer to mine. I can't believe how ugly she is with her face twisted like that.

"You poison everyone and everything that gets near you," Hannah spits out. "I wish you had never come here." She's still screaming at me, but I shut it out. Rub the stone in my pocket and let her words wash over me—a wave crashing against the cliffs on the beach.

She finally stops to take a breath. "Aren't you going to say anything?"

I blink, wondering what I could possibly say to her. "No."

That sets her off again. From the corner of my eye, I see her hand move. My reflexes are quick, like a tiger, and I catch her before she slaps me. I twist her wrist around and dig in my fingernails. She screams and tries to pull away, but I don't let go. When she finally wrenches away, my nails leave angry streaks of red across the back of her hand.

She's bleeding, holding her hand, and still screaming. I can see her mouth moving, but all I can hear is another voice.

"Don't ever touch me again."

I back away, not sure if I said it out loud.

"Allie!" Someone puts a hand on my shoulder.

"Don't touch me!" This time I know it's my voice. I jerk my shoulder away and flee toward the door.

"Allie. Stop!" It's Ms. Holt. I ignore her, shove my way past all of the open mouths, down the hall and outside. I'm gasping for breath, but I don't stop. I run as hard as I can. My head is pounding, and my ears are ringing with the voice inside my head. Never again.

I keep waiting to hear footsteps on the sidewalk behind me—an angry mob coming to grab me and drag me back for digging my claws into the queen, or for the murder they're all sure I committed—but no one follows.

I'm not sure where I'm going until the sidewalk changes to a boardwalk and the ground starts to get sandy, past where Grandma's house used to be. Past Blake's house, gray and blue, with its sagging porch and peeling paint contrasting with the neat condos all around it. Toward the ocean, where the sound of the waves shuts out the screaming in my ears.

I head down the steep path that leads to the beach, stumble, fall, and slide for a few feet. Sea grass whips against my face and slices my cheek. I stand up and run toward the cliffs.

The tide is out and I can see the mouth of the cave—our cave. It has a wide entrance tagged with graffiti, and cans and other garbage wedged into various holes by the tide. The floor is wet and sandy with the charred remains of a bonfire in one corner. A few feet farther back, the sides of the cave close in, getting steeper and narrower, so narrow that it looks like the cave ends, but I know better. I keep climbing and slipping over the slimy-smooth rocks, clawing my way to the back, willing the cave to swallow me. It gets darker and narrower, but I keep going. When the dark is so heavy that I can feel it and my brain is screaming for me to turn back, the cave opens up and a dim light spills in from a crack in the ceiling that reaches the surface.

I scramble onto the ledge against the back wall where Blake and I used to hide from the world. Well above the watermark is another ledge where we kept our treasures—sea glass and shells, a smuggled box of cookies, the walkie-talkies we bought at the thrift store. We quit leaving things in the cave after a high tide submerged it and everything was swept away. A couple of times we carried Andrew into the back of the cave with us, but usually he stayed at the entrance and played lookout with his walkie-talkie.

The musty, salty smell is sickening, but sweet and familiar at the same time. The walls are covered with green slime and seaweed. I lean back against the wall of the cave so my scar rests on the dry rock above the waterline. I tuck my knees up under my gray sweatshirt and reach for the stone in my pocket.

I should have run when I had the chance. Not yesterday, months ago—before the accident.

When I close my eyes, I see Hannah's face contorting in pain and shock—so different from the fake-sweet Beachcomber's Queen of the last few weeks. I was stupid to think she had changed.

I'm not sorry.

Hannah deserved what she got. No one is going to see it that way, but I'm glad that I hurt her.

I wonder if that means I'm crazy.

The ocean roars in my ears. I run my fingers over the stone in my pocket and shrink farther into the darkest corner of the ledge—hidden. I wish I could stay in here forever. In the creepy blackness of this cave, more than anywhere else in Pacific Cliffs, I feel safe.

"Allie." His voice echoes from the front of the cave. "Allie. I know you're here. I saw your footprints."

Blake. His voice brings a prick of tears to my eyes. He shouldn't have followed me. He should let the tide come in and sweep me out with the rest of the garbage in the entrance. I don't answer, but he keeps coming. It's harder for him to squeeze through the crack than it used to be, and he has to stay low, even in the back. I guess we've both grown since the last time we were here.

"Hey." He says it like we were still in school, greeting each other between classes. He climbs on the ledge next to me and sits directly in the light from above. "Slimier than I remember." He wipes a film of green from his hand onto his jeans. "Smells worse, too. Nothing compares to the fertilizer plant, but still bad." Blake works at a plant up the coast that makes fertilizer out of leftover fish parts. Because of his job, most of the kids at school greet him with their noses plugged. I've never noticed any smell, but I have noticed the broad back and thick biceps Blake developed loading bags of fertilizer into the trucks all summer.

I keep my face in the shadow. "What are you doing here?" It comes out more abrupt and more accusing than I mean it to.

He rubs his throat. "You know, boring day at school. I thought I'd go for a walk, get a soda. Maybe huddle in the back of a cave for a while."

I glance at him. The light from the crack in the ceiling falls on his face. "You think I'm crazy."

"Yeah," Blake says. "I knew you were crazy the first time I saw you crawl all the way back here. I thought we were going to get stuck and die, but you kept going." He grins, but I can't return his smile. "What you did today, finally giving Hannah what she deserved, that wasn't crazy. In fact, that's about the sanest thing I've seen you do in a long time. Much saner than pretending those girls are your friends. Much saner than going out wi—" He looks down so the shadow from his bangs falls over his face. I know he wants to say, "Much saner than going out with Trip Phillips."

He's more right about that than I'll ever let him know.

He scoots closer, so his cologne masks the smell of seaweed a little bit—still not close enough to touch me. He clears his throat. "You've been through a lot. You're allowed to freak out once in a while."

I stare at my fingernails, remembering that I dug them into Hannah's hand—definitely crazy.

Blake is watching me. "What did that new cop want to talk to you about, anyway?"

I jerk my head up. "You know about that?" Dumb question; of course he knows.

"Your dad made a pretty big scene in the middle of the street. You know how it is around here. By now half the town thinks you're pregnant with Detective Weeks's love child."

I shake my head. My whole life I wanted this—to live in a place where everyone knew me. Stupid.

"By the way, remind me to never tick off your dad." Blake

lifts his head and grins so the light falls on the little gap between his front teeth. The one he tries to hide whenever he laughs. His hair is still in his eyes. If I reached over I could brush it out, but the barrier is still there, the one that keeps his left hip at least two inches from my right one. "So, what did he want?"

"Questions about the accident." I pick at a piece of seaweed stuck to the bottom of my jeans. "Things I can't remember anyway."

"What things?" His grin disappears, and there's an edge to his voice that goes beyond curiosity or concern—I'm not sure what.

"Nothing." I dislodge the seaweed and flick it onto the ground, then slide off the ledge. I can't handle questions, even from Blake. "I'd better get back so they can arrest me or something."

"Juvie's not so bad," Blake says. I stop. This is the closest we've ever come to talking about what happened in Reno. "I've been in worse places. Pacific Cliffs comes to mind." He stands up, bumping his head on the top of the cave.

"I won't go to juvie," I say. "I'm eighteen, remember?"

Blake rubs his head. "Hannah won't press charges. It would just give you the chance to spend more time with her favorite cop." He leans against the wall and crosses his arms over his chest. "So you think that guy's really here just because of the accident? That Mr. Phillips is paying him to find out what happened? Or is that another famous Pacific Cliffs legend?" The edge is still there, even if he's trying to sound like he doesn't care.

"I don't know." The silence echoes between us in the cave. I turn the tigereye over in my hand. My scar feels tight, and the knot in my stomach and the smell of the cave are making me sick. "You'd better go." I gesture toward the entrance. "You don't want to get caught with me. Who knows what kind of nasty things they'll say about you."

He stands up, but not enough to hit his head again. "Rumors don't bother me. I've lived with them my whole life." His voice is lower now—gentler. "But we do need to get out of here. The tide's starting to come in."

I stand up, follow him through the crack, and pick my way over the rocky path to the cave's entrance. I catch my foot on one of the rocks and stumble forward. Blake puts his hand on my shoulder to steady me. Then he crosses the barrier and slides his hand into mine. His touch is warm against the chill of the cave.

He faces me, still holding my hand. "The bottom of the cave is pretty wet. We need to take our shoes off." He grins. "Unless you want me to carry you."

I can't tell if he's teasing or not. I roll my eyes and shake my head. I lean over to take off my shoes. A piece of hair falls forward and sticks to my check. Blake reaches to brush it back. Instinctively, I flinch away.

"I'm sorry." He takes a step backward and worry fills his eyes.

"It's okay." I duck my head, finish taking off my shoes, and walk out of the cave without looking at him.

He doesn't try to touch me again.

Chapter 10

I get suspended for two days for tearing up Hannah's hand. Like I wanted to be at school anyway. Hannah gets detention, as if she'd actually have to serve it. I spend my suspension cleaning up Dad's shop, and I'm grounded for the next two weeks, like there was anywhere I wanted to go, anyone I wanted to be with anyway. And I'm supposed to apologize to Hannah.

Not a chance.

Oh, and the school decided that "recent events indicate we didn't plan sufficiently for the aftermath of emotions following the death of one of our students." Or so it says in the letter they sent home. They're bringing in some counselor from Aberdeen, maybe even the one Mom was going to take me to in the first place. The counselor will be "available during school hours for any student to come in for counseling."

Voluntarily.

Except for me.

My counseling is mandatory. The Monday after my suspension, I get a note that I'm supposed to go straight to Ms. Holt's office. So much for going back to school. I would have been better off staying in my room.

They put the counselor in the back of the health room, so I get to sit a few feet away from Ms. Holt while I wait my turn. She acknowledges me and then turns back to a pile of papers on her desk and focuses on them like her life depends on it.

After a few minutes, the door opens and the counselor shepherds Hannah out with an arm protectively around her shoulders. Hannah's eyes are red and she has a little smudge of mascara on her otherwise perfect face. Her right hand is covered with four neon-green Band-Aids. When she sees me, her prettiness fades, and her eyes harden into green stones.

The counselor squeezes Hannah's shoulders. In the same motion, she reaches her hand out to me. "You must be Allie. I'm Karen Vincent."

Ms. Holt turns from her paperwork and offers to check Hannah's hand while Ms. Vincent guides me through the little door.

Ms. Vincent is on the heavy side, with short brown hair and a pair of thick black-rimmed glasses. Her "office" was probably the health-room supply closet up until a few days ago. The quarters are tight, with just enough room for a little folding table, a vase of flowers so big that it looks ridiculous perched on top of it, a desk chair for her, and a hard plastic chair for me. Behind Ms. Vincent's chair there's a whiteboard and two markers.

"So, Allie," Ms. Vincent says warmly. She tries to avoid staring at my scar. "How are you today?"

I erase all emotion from my face and stare back at her. I have one defense left. Silence. They can make me sit in this chair, but no one can make me talk.

She riffles through some papers. "I've been through your file. It sounds like you've had a pretty bad few months."

I wonder what those papers say. Why should I answer if she already has all the information she needs to pass judgment on me?

"Maybe we should start with something easier and not go back so far. We could start with what happened last week." She laces her fingers together. Her fingernails are painted red, and she has little jewels on each of her thumbs. "I've heard Hannah's version of the story. Maybe you'd like me to hear yours."

I blink.

She's unfazed. She swivels her chair around in the sparse space and picks up a red marker. Fumes permeate every inch of her closet when she uncaps it. The smell brings forward the ache in the back of my head that's always waiting for an opportunity to start throbbing. "Have you ever heard of the stages of grief, Allie?" She doesn't wait for an answer: maybe she's figured out she won't get one. "The model I follow has seven stages." She says them as she writes: "Shock and denial, pain and guilt, anger and bargaining, depression, the upward turn, reconstruction, and, finally, working through." She turns back to me. "These aren't always linear. Sometimes you can stay in a stage for a long time, sometimes you can revert back to an earlier stage, rarely someone will skip a stage altogether." She caps the marker and sets it on the table. "What stage would you say you're in now?" She rolls the marker back and forth on the table with her fingers.

The fluorescent bulbs above us hum. Ms. Holt coughs in the next room. Somewhere down the hall a ball bounces. "Do you mind if I take a guess?"

I keep my eyes on the jewel on her right thumb.

She uncaps the marker again and swivels back around. She circles the "anger" part of "anger and bargaining," and then turns back to me with a smug smile. "In this stage, people do things they wouldn't normally do. Hurt or push away the people who are close to them, kind of a defense mechanism, to keep from getting hurt again. Sometimes they even revert to physical violence, like what happened with Hannah. You'll probably find yourself getting angry. Blaming what happened on your friends, your parents, God, or even"—she catches my eyes in her muddy brown ones—"yourself."

My whole face gets hot, and I drop my eyes. I reach into my pocket, pull out the stone, and rub it between my fingers.

"What happened to your boyfriend wasn't anybody's fault. It was an accident. I know it doesn't help that you were there, too. That you survived the crash, and, as I understand, due to some heroics on the part of Trip."

I jerk my head up. Ms. Vincent smiles sympathetically. "Hannah told me that Trip pushed you out of the truck to save your life when he realized he was going over the cliff. Survivor's guilt is a very common thing in this sort of situation."

I blink. Is that what everyone thinks? That Trip saved my life and that's how I ended up on the side of the road? Or is it something that Hannah made up so everyone would hate me more? Everyone thinks I have survivor's guilt. What would they say if they knew what was really inside?

"It feels like you have a lot of bottled-up anger." She glances down at my right hand, now wrapped so firmly around the tiger-eye that my knuckles are turning white. "I want you to try channeling that energy into something positive. Get involved at school. Do charity work. Do some kind of vigorous exercise. If it gets too bad, beat up your pillow." She smiles and touches my fist. "And you can always call me." She hands me a card with her picture on it, in a sharp blue business suit, without glasses and about fifteen pounds lighter. "I'm at the school the rest of this week and then available for counseling sessions at my office."

She stands up to indicate that our session is over. I stand, too. She opens the door so Ms. Holt can hear us. "It was nice to meet you, Allie. Think about the things we talked about. We'll talk again soon."

I don't wait until her back is turned to throw the card in the garbage.

When I step into the hall I almost run into James. He steps back quickly, like I was contaminated, and then glares at me. I look away from him and find that the hallway is a sea of angry faces. Amazing how quick the groupthink at a small school can change from sympathy to loathing. Your boyfriend dies and you're the center of their compassion. Fight back against the queen and you're public enemy number one.

I know what they're thinking. They wish I had died instead of Trip.

A lone friendly face meets me at my locker. "How was—" Andrew starts.

"My appointment with Dr. Freud?" I jerk open the door to my locker. "Classic." I push against the tower of books that's threatening to fall on my head. "She thinks I'm angry." I yank out my English book and shove the rest of the stack back in so hard that a pile of papers slips off the top and scatters on the floor. "Dammit!"

"Angry?" Andrew is smart enough not to laugh, but there's a smile threatening to bubble over.

"Shut up, okay?" I kneel down to retrieve the papers. "I don't need it from—" The writing on one of the papers stops me. I pick it up and look at it closer—three words written in red marker.

We're not through.

Fierce, slanty handwriting I've seen too many times not to recognize.

I lean against the wheel of Andrew's chair for support. Andrew reaches for the paper, but he can't bend low enough with the restraints on his shoulders. I crumple it in my hand, but he's already seen.

He looks at my face. "What does it say?"

I use the arm of his chair to stand up. "Nothing." I shove the paper into my pocket, next to the tigereye. "Somebody's idea of a joke."

"You should tell . . ." Andrew sounds as breathless as I feel. "Someone. I could—"

"Let it go, okay! There's nothing you can do!" When the hall gets quiet I realize how loudly I yelled. Angry, just like Ms. Vincent said. The whole hallway turns and stares at me like they're waiting for me to lose it again. I focus on Andrew. He looks like I hit him. "I'm sorry." I bend down beside him, but he pushes the control on his wheelchair and turns away. His shattered look brings back a memory locked in my brain.

"Let me tell. Let me help you."

"There's nothing you can do."

I slump against my locker. The tardy bell rings, but I don't care. I keep my books pressed against my chest to keep from trembling. I shouldn't have yelled at Andrew, but I can't tell him the truth. He'd never believe me. Even I don't believe what I'm holding in my hand. It has to be somebody's idea of a cruel prank, or revenge, something to scare me.

I'd know Trip's handwriting anywhere.

Chapter 11

The dark presses against me from all sides. My eyes hurt from the strain of searching for any speck of light. The damp is almost as thick, and heavy with the smell of saltwater and seaweed. I'm in our cave, but I don't know how I got here and I don't know how to get out. No matter how far I go, I can't find the little room with the light. I see a patch of white, vague and blurred, in front of me. I lunge toward it. Seaweed tangles around my feet and I fall forward. When I try to stand, I'm covered in it, but it's not really seaweed. It's a mass of red satin—heavy and soaking wet. It clings to me, covering my face until I can't breathe.

I tear it away, sit up, and instinctively put my hand over my mouth to keep from screaming. It isn't the first time I've had this dream. The place varies: from the cliff to the beach, to the woods, and once I even dreamed I was in my old house in Texas. I'm always running from something. I'm always covered in red satin. I'm always trying to make it to a patch of white I can never get to.

It has something to do with the accident. I'm sure of it. But I'm afraid to find out what.

Half a snore and a cough come from the floor beside my bed. Andrew. He's ended up on my floor every night this week, ever since I got the note in my locker. He hasn't said anything else about it, but I know he's worried. I can see it when he looks at me. Maybe staying in my room all night is his way of protecting me. His chair isn't with him. That means he crawled and slid himself from his bedroom, down the hall, to get to me.

His eyelids flutter open. He sits up and does his backward crawl thing. Then he pushes himself against the wall on his good side. With one hand on my dresser, he slides up the wall, takes two labored steps, then half sits, half falls onto my bed. By the time he leans against my headboard and drags himself the rest of the way up, he's out of breath.

"Tell me." His voice sounds raspy, like he's getting a cold. "Your dream."

I lean against him and squeeze his hand, but I can only shake my head. The residue of the dream clings to me like the wet satin, but I can't find the words to describe it to him.

I close my eyes, taking comfort in his bony shoulder against mine. Light filters through my blinds and chases the dark into the corners of my mind. The house is quiet except for Andrew's breathing and my slowing heartbeat.

It's Saturday. Mom said last night that she would be leaving early for work. Dad is spending today in Shelton helping an old army buddy who's having car trouble. He's probably already gone.

"Okay?" Andrew says.

"Fine." I try to smile. "Just a dumb dream." I slip from his side, but make sure my pillow is still propping him up. "I'll get your chair, and we can have breakfast."

While Andrew gets dressed, I mix up a shake for him. Some days he needs help, depending on how much time he has and how he's feeling, but today we're taking it slow, so he's okay. I do a lot of things for Andrew that most people would think were weird or gross—helping him get dressed or sometimes in the bathroom. For us it's normal—the way things have always been.

Mom left a note on the counter. "Please pick up your room and do your laundry, and keep an eye on Andrew—he's getting a cold. We'll be home late."

Mom freaks out every time Andrew has a little cough or a runny nose. It drives him crazy, but I have a hard time blaming her. He's had pneumonia a couple of times—both close calls.

I don't know what will happen if Mom comes home and finds out I didn't clean my room. It's not like there's anything else she can take from me. She's refusing to do my laundry now—that is, Dad told her not to—so I guess I should at least do that.

I kneel down on the floor and gather up the stray socks coated in fuzz and dust from under my bed. I add them to the pile of T-shirts in the corner, pull one of my bras off my desk chair, and dig a couple more socks out from under my desk. When I pick up my jeans I habitually dig through the pockets. Once last year I accidentally washed my cell phone. Trip was furious. It was an expensive phone, but I think he was more frustrated that he couldn't keep track of me for a few days until he replaced it.

In the second pair of jeans, I find a piece of paper buried in the pocket. I catch my breath when I pull it out. It's the note I found in my locker. I sink onto the bed and read it again.

We're not through.

It looks like Trip wrote the note, but that isn't possible. I stare at it for a few minutes, then I go to the closet, reach gingerly around the dress bag, and pull out the box where I kept everything Trip ever gave me—gifts, cards, wrapping paper, and all. The cards are on top. I pick up the first one:

To the most beautiful girl in the world,
Happy Birthday!

It's written in the same handwriting as the note from my locker.

I dig through the rest of the cards from Trip, comparing them one by one.

I'm sorry. I love you.

Will you do me the honor of accompanying me to prom?

Forgive me for being such a jerk.

Thanks for always being there, Love ya, Trip.

Please don't hate me. It will never happen again.

Most of the notes say the same thing, over and over again.

I'm sorry. It will never happen again.

Suddenly it feels like evidence. Evidence that everything wasn't always okay between me and Trip. Evidence that I had something to hide. My heart thumps with panic and I scan the room. After what James said to me, and the note in my locker, everything around me feels like evidence against me. Pictures of Trip and me, notes that show our relationship wasn't always perfect. A whole box of memories that condemn me.

I have to get rid of it.

I take out everything valuable: the jewelry, a digital camera, and an iPod Trip filled with our favorite songs, and put them in my top drawer, tucked safely beneath my underwear. Then I gather up every single picture I have of Trip, even the one from cotillion, hidden under a thin layer of dust on top of my hutch. I press them facedown in the box—laid to rest on a bed of tissue paper, pressed flowers, and lies.

I stop when I see the last picture sitting on top of my dresser. The one of Trip and me on the beach from the first summer we were together.

I pick it up and touch his face.

"I don't want you to leave." His breath tickles my neck and his voice makes my stomach do backflips. "This has been the most amazing summer I've ever had."

"For me, too." I lean back against his chest, soaking in the smell of saltwater and his earthy cologne.

He slips his hands under my sweatshirt and against the bare skin of my stomach. "You won't forget me, right? You'll e-mail me, like, every single day." He moves my hair away and presses his lips against my neck.

"Every minute of every day. I won't do anything all day long but e-mail you. I mean it. Nothing is more important than you."

"I wish you had a cell phone." He tightens his grip around my waist. "If I had thought of it sooner . . ." His voice trails off into the sound of the surf. "But I did get you something." One hand moves from my stomach and he pulls something out of the bag he brought with him. I try to twist around so I can see what it is, but he holds me tight. "Just a second, okay?"

I laugh. "What are you doing?"

"Hold still and smile."

"What?"

"I said smile." His hand snakes back under my sweatshirt and he starts tickling me.

In the picture my head is thrown back, laughing. My hair is blowing over my shoulder and almost in his face. Trip took the picture by holding the camera out in front of us. Then he gave me the camera so I could take pictures to send back to him. That was more than two years ago. The guy in the picture I barely recognize—the girl either. Another lifetime.

It wasn't always bad. Especially in the beginning. I remember long walks on the beach, going off-roading in his truck down narrow forest trails, the night Grandma died and he sat on the couch and held me while I cried. Even now, all I can think about is what I could have done differently. If I wasn't late all the time. If I wasn't always messing something up, or doing something to make him mad. If I had been perfect like Mom and Hannah, maybe things could have stayed good between me and Trip.

I wipe the tears away from my face hard, angry at myself for letting them escape. It's too late. I can't change any of that now.

I add the picture and the note to the top of the box. With tape from Mom's packing-supplies drawer in the kitchen, I start to seal it. With it half–taped shut I pull out the picture of Trip and me at the jetty and look at it again. Touch his face, then mine. I tuck it in my top drawer before I seal up the box.

Everyone deserves at least one good memory.

Chapter 12

A knock at my door brings me back to reality. "Allie, are you in there?" It's Blake.

What is he doing here? I scan my room, realizing how bare everything looks without the pictures of Trip. Is this worse? My getting rid of every picture of us? Does it look like I'm too ready to move on? I'm not sure what I'm supposed to be feeling.

Just in case, I pull the picture out of my drawer and set it back on the dresser. Then I dig around for one of the knit hats Mom bought me. I pull it over my hair before I answer the door.

Blake leans against the door frame. "Hey."

"Hey," I answer back, suddenly aware of the pile of laundry in the middle of the room, my black lace bra on top. He looks down at it, then quickly up again. I move closer so I cover more of the doorway.

"I thought you might like to get out of the house." He rubs his neck. "I'm heading down to Hoquiam—"

"I can't." I step forward and pull the door closed behind me. "I can't go anywhere. I'm grounded."

"So." Andrew's electronic voice comes from behind Blake. He has Mom's note in his hand. "This says 'late.' We could be back before Mom and Dad get home."

I step out of my room, eyebrows raised toward my brother. Andrew never does anything wrong. "Mom said you have a cold."

Andrew sighs then moves his hand over his communicator. "A cough and Mom freaks out. I'm a big boy."

My stomach flutters at the idea of leaving Pacific Cliffs, even just for a few hours. I try to squash the feeling. I can't go anywhere with Blake. "We can't go. Mom has the van. Dad took her car to Shelton to save on gas."

Blake looks over Andrew's wheelchair. "I bet Andrew's chair would fit in the bed of my car. We could strap it in." Blake drives a white El Camino, half truck, half car, and possibly the ugliest vehicle ever built. Somehow it fits him—a little ghetto, a little rough, still cool.

I shake my head. "It's pretty heavy, and if it rains, it would get ruined."

"Get a ramp," Andrew says, "and a tarp."

It still feels like a bad idea, but Andrew and Blake have a familiar gleam in their eyes. Maybe they need to get away as badly as I do. Maybe I should go with them, to make sure Andrew's okay. I look from one eager face to the next. "We're dead if Dad catches us, you know that, right?"

"Live a little. You need to get out of the house. I need to get out of the house." Andrew's face is full of pleading concern. I wonder if he put Blake up to this. Called him to come to my rescue.

"Okay," I say slowly, testing the way that answer feels on my tongue. Andrew's face splits into a grin. The flutter comes back, beating against the numbness in my chest. It's the closest thing I've felt to excitement in months.

"Great. Let's get going." Blake rubs his hands across his neck and smiles at me. I look away, pull my hat down farther, and follow them outside.

Blake helps Andrew out of his chair and into the seat of the El Camino. Then he finds a metal ramp in Dad's work truck and drives Andrew's chair into the back of the El Camino himself. On the way up he yells to Andrew, "Nice ride, A."

Andrew answers back, "Yours, too, B."

Blake is cool like that. He's always been comfortable around Andrew. When we were kids, Dad made Andrew a chair with big wheels so he could go out onto the beach. Unless he was sick, Blake and I never left him behind.

I retrieve a tarp and a bunch of bungee cords from the garage. Blake slides the ramp into the back of his car and works on strapping the chair in. I go back inside to put together a bag for Andrew. Then I grab my purse with the money I have left from pawning the earrings.

When I get back, Blake is inspecting his work.

"Do you think it'll hold?" I look at the lumpy mass of chords and blue tarp that fills the back of his car.

Blake plunks at one of the bungee chords. "It's strapped in pretty tight."

"You know this is crazy." I can't stop the smile creeping across my face.

Blake shoves his hands into his pockets. "You're the crazy one."

I roll my eyes, but the flutter in my stomach is back. This feels a lot like one of the adventures we had as kids. Not very well thought out, involving a lot of equipment, and something we're probably going to get in trouble for.

Chapter 13

I fight waves of panic as we drive through town. I'm pretty sure what people will say if they see me with Blake; something about me getting over Trip and moving on too fast—suspicious. I don't relax until we're almost an hour out of town. The sun comes out of the clouds and Blake rolls down his window. I lean back and breathe in ocean air and freedom. "So, where are we going?"

He sideways glances at Andrew; more and more I think the two of them came up with this plan to get me out of the house. "How do you guys feel about roller-skating?"

"Roller-skating?" I almost gasp. With my lack of coordination, roller-skating is definitely a sport that could get me killed.

"Yeah," Blake says. "There's a little skating rink I like to go to in Hoquiam. It's a lot of fun."

"But Andrew can't skate." I glance at my brother, hoping for an excuse to avoid strapping wheels to my two left feet.

Blake kills my excuse. "They'll let him take his chair on the floor. I've seen other people do it."

"Cool." Andrew nods.

"C'mon, Allie." Blake nudges me with his arm. "You aren't afraid, are you?" I used to say that to him to get him to do something crazy when we were kids. Back before I was the one who was afraid.

When we get to the skating rink, Blake untangles the mess of bungee chords and unloads Andrew's wheelchair. I watch a string of little kids carrying birthday presents into the building, but no one who looks close to our age. The skating rink must not be a big place for teenagers to hang out on a Saturday afternoon. I'm glad. Less chance that anyone from school will see us here.

After Andrew is settled, Blake pulls a bag from behind the seat of his car and slings it over his shoulder. He pats it and grins. "My blades."

The man at the counter of the rink has a shaved head, a goatee, and a bar through his eyebrow. He says, "Hey, Blake," when we reach the front of the line. "How many?"

I wonder how often Blake comes clear to Hoquiam to skate. Obviously enough that the manager knows his name. I glance at him sideways. I wonder who he skates with.

"Hey, Nick," Blake says, and tosses a twenty on the counter. "Three."

"I'll pay for me and Andrew." I reach into my purse and pull out a twenty of my own.

The manager shakes his head as he takes both bills. Blake looks hurt, or maybe embarrassed. I wonder if my paying for myself is some kind of affront to his manhood. I probably should have let him pay.

"Skates or blades?" The guy hands back my change and looks me up and down—sizing me up for looks, or skating ability, I'm not sure which, but it creeps me out. I step behind Blake.

Blake taps Andrew on the head. "Chair for this one, I have my own blades, and . . ." He looks at me. "Skates or blades, Allie?"

"What's the difference?" I immediately feel stupid. Of course I know what Rollerblades are. The guy at the counter laughs. I glance at Blake to see if I embarrassed him.

He doesn't seem to mind. He pulls one of his Rollerblades out of his bag. "Blades have all the wheels in a line, like this." He rolls his finger across the wheels.

"And roller skates are old school," the man behind the counter says. He picks up an ugly brown boot with four wheels attached. "Haven't you ever skated before?"

"No. I ice skated once, but that was a disaster." I duck my head and turn beet red. I wish I hadn't come.

"Go for skates, then." The man taps the skates. "And don't worry, even if you've never skated, Blake will take good care of you." He winks at Blake and then asks me for my shoe size.

I wonder how many other girls Blake has brought to this skating rink. On the way to the benches I ask, "So, you come here often?" I don't mean it to, but it comes out like a bad pickup line from a campy movie.

Blake shrugs. "I did some street skating in Reno, mostly boarding, but some blading, too. In Pacific Cliffs it rains too much and the sidewalks suck, so I like to come here. It's a good place to get out of town for a while."

I know what he means. It feels good to look around and not have to wonder what everyone is thinking or wonder if I'm acting the right way or doing what people expect me to do.

Instead of going out to the skate floor, Andrew heads for the snack bar. He circles the room like he's looking for something and parks himself where he can watch everyone skating. Blake sits down on the bench, takes off his shoes, and starts buckling up his Rollerblades. I sit down and stare at the skates I got from the counter. "I'm sorry. I don't think this is a good idea. Maybe I could just watch with Andrew. I don't want to slow you down."

He touches my knee. "Hey, don't worry. I won't let anything happen to you. I promise. Now let me see your foot."

Blake picks up my foot and sets it on his leg, like I was a little kid. He takes off my shoes and laces me into the skates. Then he stands up and reaches for my hands. "We'll take it slow, okay?"

I take his hand and my stomach clenches. I start looking around for someone to stare at us, or give me a look that says I shouldn't be with Blake. But here we're anonymous.

I relax for about two seconds until he pulls me to my feet. As soon as I stand, the skates want to head out on their own—in different directions. I fall forward and he catches me with his hands under my elbows and holds on until I can keep my feet under me.

I grip his arms and feel his newly earned muscles bulge under my fingers. "This is such a bad idea."

"No, it's not." Blake looks down at me. His hands are on my arms—not the death grip I have on him but light, supporting. "Just push, glide, push, glide. We'll start on the carpet first."

I feel like a complete idiot, especially when a little kid zooms past me. I fall forward and catch myself against Blake's chest—muscles again—flexing and hard under his soft T-shirt. I'm embarrassed and pull away when I catch him grinning at me.

Before I'm ready, he drags me, slipping and sliding, to the ultraslick wood floor. Andrew comes up beside me. I let go of Blake to grab the back of Andrew's chair so he can pull me around. Blake shakes his head and then takes off by himself. He's crazy good, crossing his feet when he goes around corners, skating backward, even jumping the barrier between the floor and the carpeted area. That earns him a dirty look from a mother at the snack bar and a "whoa-o!" from the little boys she's serving cake to.

After my third or fourth lap, Blake comes back and pries my fingers off Andrew's chair. He skates backward, pulling me along. "I can't do this." I'm sure I'm cutting off the circulation in his hands. "The lights throw off my balance."

"Then don't look at the lights." Blake's voice is gentle. "Look here." He brushes his cheek with my hand. I look up into his eyes, a blue green that always reminds me of the ocean. He laughs. "And smile. You're not being tortured."

I mumble my disagreement under my breath. Andrew heads back to the snack bar while Blake keeps pulling me along the floor, giving me advice the whole way. "Stand up straight, don't watch your feet," and always, "push and glide."

Left foot, right foot, stumble, glide—I'm starting to get this. Blake lets go of one hand so we're skating side by side. "Keep your eyes up. Good job. The next round you're going to do by yourself." I grip his hand to show I'm not letting him leave. "Relax. If you make it around twice without falling I'll buy you a slushy."

I try to force a flirty tone through the terror in my voice. "How about I buy you one?"

He pries my fingers off his. "Two laps."

I make it around the first lap with Blake skating beside me. I'm getting more confident, but I still feel like a complete klutz, especially when I watch little kids who can skate rings around me. Blake pulls ahead of me. "All on your own this time. You've got it."

So I push, glide, push, glide all by myself, reaching for the wall every few feet but staying up. When I finish the second lap, I go for a third. Blake gives me a thumbs-up from across the floor. I beam back at him and don't see the kid who falls in front of me. He sweeps my feet, and I go down. Hard. I hit my butt first and then bang my head against the wall.

Blake is kneeling beside me almost before I realize what happened. He cups his hand around my scar. "Your head—are you okay?"

"I'm okay." I'm dazed, either by the bump or because his face is so close to mine. "I didn't hit my head that hard." I lean forward and rub my hip. "Mostly just my butt."

Blake's face breaks into a grin of relief. "We wouldn't want to damage that either."

"My butt?" I give him a funny look. "Um, what? For a second, it sounded like you were trying to flirt with me."

Blake ducks his head and turns red. "Nah, I just—"

"You were flirting!" I try to see his eyes, covered by a lock of bangs. "And badly."

"Yeah, well." He helps me to my feet without looking at my face. "You were skating. And badly."

"Hey." I slap his arm. "You said I was doing great."

"Oh, come on, Allie, you know guys will say anything when they're trying to impress a girl." The idea that Blake might be trying to impress me feels weird, wrong, but good, too, even though I know he was just kidding around. He turns around and grabs both of my hands. "C'mon, I owe you a slushy."

"Andrew." I cover my mouth. "I completely forgot about him. He's probably bored out of his mind."

Blake laughs and points behind me toward the snack bar. "I'd say Andrew is doing just fine."

I grab on to the wall and turn myself around. Andrew is still at the snack bar but not alone. There's a flamboyant redhead perched on the table in front of him. She's holding a slushy to his mouth while he drinks out of the straw.

I stare in shock. "Who is that?"

Her name is Caitlyn, and she has dangly blue earrings, an embroidered tunic top that's retro 1970s, and neon-blue skinny jeans. She's enthusiastic about absolutely everything and thinks my freaky eye is totally cool, and her dad is a mortician. They live above the morgue. I find out all this in about five minutes, after Blake and I join them at the snack bar. I also find out that she and Andrew have been chatting online for the last couple of months. He and Blake definitely planned this.

I study Caitlyn while she talks, wondering if she could be considered pretty. Her jeans are too tight, her face is red and kind of splotchy, and she laughs too loudly, with her mouth open. She sounds like a donkey. But she has a nice smile, brilliant blue eyes, and hair the most amazing color of red I've ever seen. I'm not sure if it's her real color. In another era, Caitlyn would probably have been considered beautiful. I'm just not sure which one.

I can tell Andrew thinks she's gorgeous. She kisses him on the cheek when she leaves. Protective instincts fire like mad when I see her with him. He's never had anything close to a girlfriend before. I wish I knew more about her.

I watch her go outside and I'm shocked to see the sun going down. I didn't realize we'd been gone so long. I wonder what "home late" means for my parents. If Mom and Dad get home before we do, they'll freak out.

"We'd better go," I say to Blake. Andrew nods, but he's still smiling. It's good to see him happy, and I actually had fun. If we can make it home without getting busted, today might be okay.

Chapter 14

On the way home, Andrew falls asleep with his head on my shoulder. I'm jittery the whole way. Blake reaches over and puts his hand on my bouncing knee. "Relax," he says. I'm not sure if Blake's hand on my knee makes me relax or makes me more tense. I focus on keeping my legs still, but he doesn't move his hand.

Blake is driving fast, trying to get us home before Mom and Dad do. As we get into town I want to tell him to slow down, but I'm afraid it'll make him mad. Then I see blue lights in the rearview mirror. Blake swears and pulls over, right in front of Big J's, the only restaurant in town besides the café, and where everyone from the high school hangs out. I slide down into the seat and wish Blake had tinted windows.

Detective Weeks gets out of the now-familiar black Charger and shines his flashlight into Blake's eyes, and then mine. He takes note of Blake's hand resting on my knee. "Do you have any idea how fast you were going?" Four sophomores gawk at us as they pass beside Blake's car on their way into Big J's. I pull my hat down and keep my eyes focused on the dashboard.

Blake taps the speedometer, stuck on 100 miles per hour. "This thing doesn't work."

Detective Weeks points his flashlight at the dash. "How long has it been broken?"

"It stopped working a couple of hours ago." Blake grits his teeth. I'm sure the speedometer has been broken as long as he's had the car. Out of the corner of my eye, I watch James point out Blake's car to Randall. I slide farther down into the seat so Andrew's body is blocking me from their view.

"Uh-huh." Detective Weeks leans back and lowers the flashlight. "I don't suppose you'd mind if I took a look under the tarp in the back?"

"Do you have a warrant?" Blake moves his hand off my leg and grips the steering wheel. His face hardens. I remember that face. This is the Blake who got arrested for breaking and entering, the Blake who spent six months in juvie. I shrink away from him. I've had too much experience with personality-shifting guys.

"I don't need a warrant." Detective Weeks doesn't seem to like Blake's attitude. "License and registration, please." Blake pulls his wallet out of his pocket and then leans over me to open the glove compartment. Detective Weeks shines his flashlight on Andrew, who's still asleep with his head lolling against his chest and a little bit of blue drool, from the slushies, dripping down his chin. "Have you kids been drinking?"

"That's my brother." I say it quick, so he'll let us go. "He has cerebral palsy. His wheelchair is in the back, under the tarp, if you want to take a look."

Detective Weeks smiles and hands Blake back his license and registration without giving him a ticket. "You guys slow down, okay? The road up ahead is pretty narrow and dangerous, especially around the cliff." He looks straight at me when he says that. I grip the tigereye hard. Blake's jaw is working, like he has something he wants to say to Detective Weeks, but he holds it in.

After Detective Weeks pulls away, Randall and one of Trip's other football buddies, Dillon Mitchell, walk in front of Blake's car. Dillon pounds on the front window, then sits down on the hood so we can't leave. Andrew jerks his head up.

"Hey, Juvie, where'd you pick up this fine automobile?" Dillon yells. "You steal this one, too?"

"May be from the junkyard." Randall sits next to Dillon, and they start bouncing the car up and down.

I wish I could slide all the way to the floor. I hope they don't recognize me.

Blake revs the engine and reaches to shift into drive, but his car sputters and dies. He swears. Laughter explodes all around us.

Dillon yells, "Is that your new girlfriend, Juvie? How much does she charge an hour?" Andrew leans forward so he's blocking most of the window, to keep anyone from seeing me. Blake reaches for the door handle.

"Just drive away," I plead. "Please, let's just go home."

Blake sets his jaw and revs the engine again. This time the car lurches forward, Dillion jumps off. Then Blake puts it in reverse so fast that Randall slides off the hood. As we go by, James pounds on the roof. Blake cuts beside him so close that I think we're going to run over him.

Blake's knuckles are white from gripping the steering wheel. He keeps his eyes in front of him, but his cheeks flush red. I know he's embarrassed that I saw them harassing him.

I'm relieved to get out of town, until we get to my house. Both Dad's truck and the van are parked in the driveway. Blake hurries to unload Andrew's chair and help him in. I get the backpack and my purse. Slowly, resigned to our fate, we walk to the front door. Dad is waiting. He points at me, then Blake, then Andrew. "You three, living room! Now!"

Andrew looks at him groggily, wide-eyed and innocent. "Yes, you," Dad says. "You're in on this, too."

Andrew beams. It's been a long time since he was in trouble. I think he likes it. Blake and I perch on the couch; Andrew parks next to us—three felons awaiting sentencing.

"Where have you been?" Dad's voice booms from his chest, not yelling—more like projecting—still loud enough that Blake looks ready to bolt.

"W-we went to Hoquiam," Blake stammers. "To the roller—"

"You went all the way to Hoquiam?" Dad sounds like he doesn't quite believe that.

"With Andrew? You know he has a cold." Mom focuses her assault on me.

"Mom," Andrew moans. "Not a baby."

"It was my fault, sir." Blake's defiance to authority doesn't seem to include my father. "I dragged them—"

Dad withers him with a look. "Nobody dragged anyone.

You're all to blame for this one." His eyes focus on me and Andrew. "You two worried your mom to death, and do I dare ask how you got Andrew's chair to Hoquiam?"

"In the back of my car." Blake half stands, like he wants to escape.

"In the back of your car?" Mom repeats in disbelief. "In the trunk?"

"In the bed." Blake sinks back to the couch. "My El Camino—half car, half truck."

"It was covered," I put in.

"It had better not be damaged." Dad rests his gaze on Blake.

"We . . . I made sure it was secure." Blake tries to sound confident, but his voice is shaking.

"We used bungee cords," I say hopefully. Dad is a big fan of bungee cords.

"You." He points to me. "You're grounded. Again, or still, whatever. And you will spend tomorrow cleaning the auto shop, including the bathrooms. You." He points to Andrew, who's trying for innocence again. "Your computer time is limited to homework only."

"Dad," he moans. I know he promised Caitlyn they would chat tonight.

Dad ignores him and points to Blake. "And you. Your grandma's lawn is covered with leaves and branches and her gutters need to be cleaned out before it starts to rain again. A good project for tomorrow." It's an order, not a suggestion, even if Blake isn't his kid.

"Yes, sir," Blake answers.

"Allie and Andrew, rooms. Blake, good-bye."

I'm shocked. He yelled at us. He reinstated my grounding. But that's it. Before, Dad would have lost it if he'd caught me leaving the house when I was supposed to be grounded. He totally freaked when he caught me sneaking out before. Maybe my accident made Dad soft.

After Blake leaves, Mom follows me into my room. She must be the designated "bad parent" now. She sits down on my desk chair and I sit on the bed. She glances around; I'm sure she notices that Trip's pictures are missing, but she pretends she doesn't.

"Do you have any idea how worried I was when I came home and found you and Andrew gone?" Habitually she doesn't include Dad by saying "we." Her slippered foot taps on my floor. "You were *supposed* to be grounded." Her voice rises a notch. "You can't just go do whatever you want. Especially not with Andrew."

I want to tell her that I'm eighteen and Andrew's eighteen, and we *can* do whatever we want, but she's playing the angry/concerned mom. I don't have the energy to fight with her.

"And then there's who you were with." She shepherds a stray paper clip off my desk and into the drawer.

"Blake?" How can she object to Blake?

"Yes, Blake." She sets her jaw into a firm line.

"I don't—" I start to reach for the stone in my pocket but then grip the edge of my bed instead.

"He's not the same kid you used to play pirates with, not since that thing in Nevada." She pauses. "A lot has changed; he's changed"—pause—"and I think maybe it's better if you don't"—pause again while she picks up a pen and adds that to the drawer, too.

"You want me to stay away from Blake?"

Mom's eyes move over everything in my room—the dirty clothes in the middle of the room, the pile of gum wrappers on my nightstand, the bare walls and shelves where Trip's pictures used to be—everything but me. "I'm just saying, maybe it would be better if you spent time with your other friends."

"Other friends?" I say incredulously. More acceptable friends? Like I have any of those.

"Yes, the kids you hung out with before."

"Last year I hung out with Trip. And he's gone."

"I'm just saying, so soon after Trip's accident, people might think . . . might get the wrong idea about your friendship with Blake, and I don't want—"

Her meaning sinks into the pit of my stomach. She's thinking the same thing I've been worried about. What will people think if they know I've been with Blake? What will they say if I act like I'm over Trip's death too soon?

Mom stands up and puts her hands on her tiny waist. "You are grounded because of his poor judgment, taking you and especially Andrew to Hoquiam. And I've heard other things about him, not just the stealing, but drugs and drinking, and right now you need"—she sighs—"you need more stable friends." She brushes the gum wrappers into my garbage can. "I'm just trying to protect you. He seems to be heading down the same path as his mother. I don't want you to be guilty by association."

I grip the edge of my quilt harder. I'm so stunned I can't say anything.

"You'd better get to sleep. Your dad wants you at the shop first thing tomorrow and we both know that Dad's 'first thing in the morning' is at least two hours earlier than the rest of the world."

When she's gone, I kick the garbage can so it crashes against the floor and the gum wrappers spill. Other friends? Like the kids who were staring at us from Big J's? Or the kids who whisper about me in the halls at school?

I flop on my bed, pick up the stone, and run it across my lips. I wish it would give me the courage to tell my mom that Blake is the *only* friend I have. What's with her suddenly trying to protect me? I bite down on the tigereye. There are a lot of things I wish this stone would give me the courage to say to her.

Chapter 15

My hand snakes under the pillow, jerking the phone to my ear, even before I'm fully awake. It's an automatic reaction. Dad's home for the weekend and he's already warned me about late-night phone calls. Trip calls almost every night now, just to make sure I'm home. To make sure I'm alone.

This time his voice sounds desperate. "Allie, I need your help!"

I cling to the phone. "What happened?"

"We got stuck. We need you to go get Randall's truck and pull us out."

I strain for any sounds from my parents' room and hiss, "Where are you?"

"That spot I took you to two weeks ago, on the way to Port Angeles. Can you find it? It needs to be fast, Al. Dad has some breakfast meeting tomorrow morning he wants me to come to. If I don't make it back, he'll kill me."

I weigh the consequences of either option.

"Allie, are you there?"

I breathe out. "Okay, I'll come."

I sit up in bed as Trip's voice fades into my memory. The box of pictures and notes mocks me from where I left it, under the windowsill. Having everything boxed up is worse than his eyes staring at me all the time. I can't put the pictures back up, but I can't keep them either. A thousand insufficient ideas for getting rid of the box run through my head, but none would work. None would be soon enough. And none seem appropriate.

There's only one place to get rid of the box.

It's almost one o'clock. If I walked it would probably take me at least an hour to get to the cliff. Through the walls I can hear Andrew snoring. I listen toward Mom and Dad's room, to try and tell if they're asleep. Dad may have been soft on us when we came home from Hoquiam, but if he catches me sneaking out again, I'm not sure what he'll do. Two hours is too risky. Driving would be better, but there's no way I could start Mom's car without waking someone up.

There's only one person who might help me.

My heart pounds so loudly in my ears as I walk past my parents' door that I'm sure the sound will wake them up. I get the phone from the kitchen, carry it into my bedroom, and muffle it against my pillow. My fingers dial Blake's number without looking.

He picks up on the fourth ring. His voice is husky and groggy. I almost hang up, but he recognizes my phone number. "Allie, is that you?"

I take a breath. "Blake, I need your help."

His voice changes to sharp concern. "What's wrong?"

"Nothing, I just—" I close my eyes and press the phone against my ear. This is stupid. I can't make him come based on my paranoia. "Never mind—"

"No," he answers fast. "It's okay, I wasn't asleep." His voice softens. "What do you need? I'm here."

I look at the box again. I feel guilty for using him. "I need you to come pick me up. I need to do something. It won't take very long. I just . . . you don't have to—"

"I'll be there in ten minutes." He hangs up before I can change my mind.

I put on a bra, my sweatpants, and my sweatshirt. I tuck the tigereye in my pocket. I wait by my window. Five minutes go by, then ten.

"Where the hell have you been?" Trip's eyes are blazing.

"I came as fast as I could. I . . . I got lost."

"Get out of my way." I shrink away from him, but he still shoves me against Randall's truck on the way to get the tow rope.

A tap on the window makes me jump. I listen toward Mom and Dad's room again, and then open the window for Blake. He helps me pop out the screen, takes the box from me, and helps me through without saying anything. I turn around and slide my window most of the way closed, leaving just enough space to slip my fingers along the edge so I can open it when I come back.

We walk up the sidewalk to where he left his car, next to Randall's driveway, three houses down. I glance at Randall's pickup and remember how scared I was, sneaking into their yard, getting the keys out from under the seat, how much I jumped when the engine roared when I turned the key.

There aren't any streetlights in this part of town, the older part, away from the beachfront. The moon is blanketed by a thick haze. The neighbor's yappy little dog goes nuts when we walk past. Otherwise the street is silent except for the sound of our footsteps and our breathing.

Hazy moonlight and the shadows from the yard lights play tricks on my eyes. I see people watching us, hiding in an alleyway, behind the neighbor's fishing boat, or in the shadows behind the trees. I chalk it up to guilt-induced mind tricks but move closer to Blake anyway. We get to the car and he opens the door for me. I slide into the seat and wrap my arms around the box.

Blake starts the car. "Where are we going?"

"The cliff," I say without looking up.

"Can I ask what's in the box?"

I shake my head. "No."

I can feel him watching me, but I don't turn my head. He turns back to the front and pulls into the street. His car has a bad muffler knock. It's so loud that as we pass by my house I expect to see my dad standing at the front door, but my house stays dark.

Twice on the way up, Blake starts to say something, but he doesn't finish.

He parks by a little fence at the edge of the cliff and turns off the lights. We sit for a long time, listening to the ocean hiss and roar on the rocks below. I hold the box, squeezing it against my chest so hard that the corner digs into my thighs. Finally, I gather enough courage to open the door. Blake starts to open his, but I stop him. "Stay here."

"Allie, I don't think—"

"Please." I reach for his hand. "I'll only be a minute."

He nods but doesn't let go of my hand.

I squeeze his fingers and then climb out, clutching the box against my chest. I creep toward the guardrail. It's dented at the end, but there's no other indication that anyone has ever gone off the ledge. Everything else looks the way it's always been. Apparently, even right after the accident there wasn't much to see. Dad explained—coolly and logically—that there was no real wreckage, just me and the torn-off back bumper to Trip's truck.

There was a storm that night, and an extreme high tide that made it too dangerous for anyone to go below the cliff to retrieve the truck or Trip's body. By the time the tide went out again, there was nothing left. It was like the ocean swallowed Trip whole, truck and all.

I step closer. I wonder where they found me, where the bumper to Trip's truck was, and where Blake found the tigereye. I wonder where Trip and his truck are now; just at the base of the cliff, caught in some kind of underwater cave, or far out in the ocean where he'll never be found.

My toes curl as I lean against the guardrail. In the dim light, I can barely see the water, churning and angry below. The wind whips my hair against my face and sends chills down my back. It whistles through the trees along the ridge and makes a low mournful noise, like the ghostly moans of lost sailors, or the sounds of their widows crying. Like Trip's ghost might make. I balance the box in one arm and reach into my pocket for the stone.

"What's your problem, Allie?"

"I need to go home. I told Mom I wouldn't leave Andrew alone."

"You don't have to go anywhere. The spaz is fine."

I jerk away from him, get out of the truck, and slam the door behind me. Three steps down the path into the woods he catches me. I spin around to face him, furious. "Don't ever call him that!"

He grabs my shoulders, his fingers digging in. "I can say whatever I want." He smiles—crooked and cruel. "I can do whatever I want." He drags me toward the edge. I kick against his leg and pound my fists against his chest. He laughs.

I grab on to his arms and hold on to keep from falling. "No. Please. I'm sorry, please."

He smiles and breathes beer-breath into my face. "I could kill you, Allie. All I have to do is let go. Over the cliff. Into the ocean. No one would ever find your body. No one would ever know what happened. No one would even care."

I throw the box as hard as I can. The waves roar as it disappears beneath them. I turn, take a step, and scream.

Blake catches me as my leg slips between the ledge and the guardrail. He pulls me up, and I hang on to him, trembling. "I'm sorry, Allie. I had to follow you. I didn't think you'd jump, but I had to be sure." He steps away from the edge with me still in his arms. He holds me close. I lean against him and listen to the pounding of his heart against mine. He brushes his hand over the back of my head and murmurs into my neck, "It's okay. You're okay now."

I look up at him. The wind drives the clouds away from the moon and all I can see is Blake's face. I'm caught in his blue-green eyes. He leans forward, toward my lips. I almost let go, almost lean into his arms and let him kiss me. But something behind him, glowing white in the moonlight, stops me. I pull away. He lets his arms fall off my shoulders.

Next to the cliff is a white marble plaque, like a headstone. When I get closer, Trip's picture smiles back at me. Startled, I stumble backward into Blake. He puts his hand on my elbow to steady me. This must be the monument Angie's mom was trying to tell me about. I step forward and read the inscription: TRAVIS RYAN ISAAC "TRIP" PHILLIPS, BELOVED SON, ATHLETE, AND FRIEND. No birthday, no date of death.

I trace the letters with my finger. Trip's blue eyes and perfect teeth shine from the picture like some guy in a toothpaste ad, like he wasn't a real person, someone I knew.

The base of the plaque is covered with ghostly mementos: dead flowers, deflated balloons, a football, a teddy bear, and lots of cards. I kneel in front of the plaque and read them. "Rest in peace, buddy." "I'll never forget fourth-period wood shop with you." "To the craziest off-roader I ever met—you'll be missed."

The football has Trip's jersey number, 33, written on it in faded red marker, and every member of the football team signed it. The bear is holding a heart and has a simple but dramatic message: "To my first love—I'll never forget you.—Love, Hannah."

I lean forward with my head resting against the plaque and cover my face with my hands. My scar pounds in the back of my head. Trip meant something to all of these people, enough that they left flowers and notes and things to remember him. Then there's me, the person who should have been the closest to him, and I just threw all evidence of our relationship over the cliff. All I want to do is forget.

They knew a different Trip than I did. No one saw what I saw. He made sure of that. I made sure of that. What would it take for them to believe anything I said about him? What would it take for anyone to understand? I startle as Blake rests his hand on my shoulder. What would it take for him to understand?

I stand up with my back to him.

He breathes in. "You miss him, don't you?"

I let the tears gather in my eyes, turn around, and look up at him through damp eyelashes. I bite my lip and nod. It's better this way. Better than telling the truth.

. . . — — — . . .

I know I'm in trouble when I slide my fingers into the edge of the window frame and find it shut tight. I walk around to the side door, but it's locked and the key is missing from under the mat. By the time I reach the front door, Dad is waiting.

The good-humored firmness from last night is gone. This is the dad I remember. "Where have you been?" he demands.

"I . . . I went for a walk. I couldn't sleep."

"I saw his car." Fire lights up his eyes. "Blake's car. Your mother told you to stay away from him. He doesn't have the best reputation."

"Nothing happened." My heart races as I try to come up with an excuse. "I needed to think, needed to get away."

Mom emerges from behind Dad. Her shoulders slump and she slides into one of the dining room chairs. Without her makeup I can see the wrinkles and dark circles under her eyes. "What's going on with you, Allie?"

I lean my head against the wall. I don't think they really want an answer to that question.

"Skipping school, fighting, sneaking out at night?" Dad is so worked up that he's pacing. "You didn't used to be like this,

Allie. What changed? Was it that boy? Was it Trip?" His eyes search mine and I have to look down.

"No!" Mom breaks in, like questioning Trip is a personal attack on her. "Trip was a good kid. It's Blake. He's the bad influence."

"She snuck out before to be with Trip, too, remember?"

I close my eyes and let them argue over the top of me about last time. That I do remember. How Dad grounded me. How I told him he wasn't being fair. Then I ran to my room and cried with relief. How he was gone the night of the cotillion. How Mom made me go anyway. How I couldn't tell her I didn't want to go.

I look up and realize Dad is talking to me again. "We've tried to be patient. We've tried to understand, but you're pushing us."

Mom's turn. "I don't know what to do for you anymore, Allie. I don't know what to do *with* you. It's like I don't know you anymore."

"Know me?" I stare at her, incredulous. "When did you ever know me? When did you ever care what was happening in my life? You're so busy showing everyone how great you are and how perfect everything is that you don't know anything about me."

"Don't talk to your mother that way," Dad snaps.

I turn on him, deliberately step in front of him, anger boiling my insides. I'm in his face—challenging. "And when did you become Dad? You've been gone most of my life, and now, now you think you can just pick up where you left off? Like I'm still a little girl. Like you still have some say in my life. You don't."

Dad's mouth twitches with anger, his eyes reflect pain, but

I don't back down. His hand balls into a fist. I wait. He grits his teeth. The muscles in his neck clench, then relax. He lets out a long breath. "Maybe now isn't the time to talk about this. We're all tired and on edge. Go to bed. We can talk in the morning."

When he steps away, I realize I've been holding my breath. Bracing myself, even though I know Dad would never hurt me. I wonder if I'll always be afraid.

I can't look at him. I want to tell him I'm sorry, but I don't know how. Instead I yell at him. "You can set up the electronic monitoring collar in the morning!" I stomp back to my room and slam my door as hard as I've ever slammed it.

In a few minutes, I hear Andrew's chair in the hall. He taps on the door. "Allie, I'm sorry," he whispers. "When I saw you were gone—"

I fling open the door. "You told on me?"

"I . . . I . . . was worried."

"Go away, Andrew," I growl. "You're with them. I don't even want to look at you." I slam the door a second time. Andrew stays for a long time. I can hear his breathing, labored and raspy on the other side of the door. Finally, his chair bumps into the wall. It whirs as he leaves, and the door to his room clicks shut.

Chapter 16

"How are you doing, Allie?" His words are friendly, but his tone has an edge to it. I look up from my locker to see James towering over me, his eyes narrowed.

"Fine." I slam my locker shut and turn toward my next class.

He moves out of my way but falls into step behind me. "You have a good time with Juvie this weekend?" People around us stop to listen.

I ignore him and keep walking, but I'm in full panic mode.

"What about when the two of you went up to the cliff?"

I freeze. "I don't know what you're talking about." Blake starts working toward us from the opposite end of the hall.

"So that wasn't you with Juvie when he got pulled over, or in his car parked at the edge of the cliff?" He says it loud enough that everyone around us can hear him. Voices murmur around me. Dark looks are cast in my direction. I know what they're thinking: the ultimate sacrilege, being with another guy at the exact spot where my boyfriend died.

"No," I say. I look up. Blake is almost to us.

"That was your brother in the car, I know that was him." James is standing close enough that I can feel his breath on the back of my neck. "Seems like you got over Trip pretty fast."

I turn around and face James. All I can think is damage control. "I don't know what you're talking about. I wasn't with anyone on Saturday." I wrinkle my nose with disgust the way Angie did, and nod my head toward Blake. "Why would I be hanging out with him?"

Out of the corner of my eye I see the hurt in Blake's eyes, but he covers for me. "I wasn't with Allie. That was some chick I met from Aberdeen." Then he adds his own jab. "Why would I be with Allie?"

James looks from me to Blake. I don't think he believes either of us. "Whatever. Just make sure you stay away from her."

"No problem." Blake turns around and walks the other way.

My heart sinks as I watch him leave. Somehow I keep pushing away everyone who means anything to me.

. . . — — — . . .

Despite our joint denial and the fact that we don't even acknowledge each other at school, the rumor mill still links Blake and me together. Whispers follow me everywhere I go. I get tripped or bumped whenever I walk down the hall. I don't ever look up to see who does it. I don't talk to anyone, not even Andrew. I eat lunch in a corner by myself, with my nose buried in a book that I can't focus on anyway. The accident and my paranoia have made it impossible to concentrate on anything. My grades are worse than they have ever been, even though I spend all my time studying. There's nothing else for me to do.

I'm lonely.

In a twisted way I miss Trip. Every time someone bumps me in the halls, I miss his arm around me, shepherding me to my next class. When I go to lunch and see Angie and Randall, together again, kissing or feeding each other fries, I miss the togetherness, the feeling of being one of two. With Trip around, I was isolated from the rest of the school, but I was isolated with him for company.

Now I'm just alone.

. . . — — — . . .

The Wednesday before Thanksgiving, my locker decides to stop opening. I twist the ancient lock built into the door and jerk it hard, but it refuses to budge. Even the fixtures at school are conspiring against me. I want to slide onto the floor and cry, but instead I slam my fist against the door. The bang resonates down the hall and the thin metal quivers. Two freshman girls watch with wide eyes. Maybe since I attacked the queen, they think I'll come after them. I have this urge to growl and see if they run.

The bell rings and the halls empty out and still the door won't budge. I twist the combination, jerk harder, and when that doesn't work I pound it a second time.

"You know that's not going to help." Blake's voice behind me makes me jump.

I rub my fist. "It makes me feel better."

"Can I try?"

I'm shocked that he's even talking to me, but I step away from my locker. "Be my guest." I've already been condemned. I might as well be civil to him.

He twists the combination and then leans against the door like a thief in an old movie—listening for the tumblers to click into place. I wait for him to ask me for my combination, too pissed to volunteer that information.

The halls echo emptiness, but Blake keeps his voice low. "Cover me."

"What?"

He grabs the edge of my sweatshirt and pulls me closer. He does it so gently that I don't even flinch. When my body is shielding his hand from the rest of the hallway, he pulls a knife out of his pocket and flicks the blade open.

The glint of sharp metal makes my blood run cold. I step back, close my eyes, and lean my cheek against the locker for support.

He keeps sharpening the stick, watching the fire, and me, and sharpening the stick with his pocketknife. We're alone. Everyone else has coupled up, left the party, or passed out in Randall's parents' camper. I'm waiting for an invitation to join him on the other side of the fire, but his expression tells me I'm in trouble. I know why.

"James is a jerk when he's drunk," I finally say. I never know when it's better to speak up and try to defend myself or when I should keep my mouth shut.

Trip doesn't miss a beat in the scrape, scrape, scrape of his knife against the stick.

"It's not like I wanted to sit on his lap." Scrape, scrape, scrape. "I tripped and fell against him." Scrape, scrape, scrape. "And then he wouldn't let me go." Scrape, scrape, scrape.

"C'mon, Trip, you know I love you." I cross toward him, push his whittling aside, and sit on his lap. I wrap my arms around him and kiss his neck. He drops the stick and reaches like he's going to hold me. Instead he grabs my wrist and twists my arm behind my back. It feels like he's breaking my arm, but I don't scream until I feel the point of the knife slice into my skin.

"Maybe that will help you remember who you belong to."

"Allie, are you okay?" Blake's voice sounds far away. "You look sick."

I open my eyes and try not to look at the knife in his hand. "Why do you have that?" My voice comes out in a hoarse whisper.

"Protection," he replies. I study his face, trying to decide if he's kidding, but he turns back to my locker and concentrates on the lock. "Protection and this." He slips the blade back into the lock and wiggles it. The door springs free. "I had the locker from hell last year, so I figured out how to pick the lock."

"Oh. Thanks." I wonder how long he's carried a knife to school, and what he meant about it being protection. He traces his finger along the edge of the blade. I touch the scar on my arm through my sweatshirt. I wonder if he's ever used the knife.

Heavy footsteps of authority approach from the hall behind me. Blake closes the knife and slips it back in his pocket in one quick motion. The principal, Mr. Barnes, strides around the corner. His eyes narrow at us. "Why aren't you kids in class?"

I take a step back from Blake. "We were just—"

"Just helping Allie get into her locker." Blake smiles without any hint of nervousness. I'm sweating enough for both of us. He slips his hand into his pocket to cover the knife.

"It seems to be open now." Mr. Barnes's eyes dart from me to Blake.

"It is." Blake moves away from me. "I'd better get going, wouldn't want to keep Ms. Franklin waiting in trig." He waves with his other hand. "See you, Allie."

"Thanks," I manage to squeak.

"And you?" Mr. Barnes focuses on me.

"I need to get my books." I can feel his eyes tracing the scar on the back of my head. I try to be quick enough to satisfy his tapping foot, but my hands are shaking.

When I reach for my government book on the top of the stack, my fingers find the edge of a little piece of paper. My stomach clenches.

Another one.

I'm not as slick as Blake as I curl my fingers around the note and slide it into my pocket next to the tigereye.

"Do you have something there you want to show me?" Mr. Barnes steps toward me and I panic.

"It's just," I begin. I scrape my fingernails across the one rough edge on the tigereye. "Girl stuff. I, uh, need to go to the restroom."

"Oh." He backs away with his hands up like I said I had a live grenade in my pocket. "Oh . . . yes . . . of course."

I slam my locker shut with one hand, forget my book, decide to leave it, and walk toward the bathroom with my hand shielding the note in my pocket. As soon as I'm safely inside I pull out the paper. I'm hoping maybe it's nothing, just a random scrap of paper that got mixed with my stuff. But it has the same writing as the first note.

You'll always be mine.

I slide my sleeve up and trace the T-shaped scar on my forearm. I swallow hard twice, then turn around and get sick in the toilet.

Chapter 17

I'm trying to run away but swirls of red satin tangle around my legs. I stumble forward as claws tear and snag at the skirt. A patch of white ahead of me beckons against the gray and green all around me. If I can get to the light I'll be safe.

"Help me!" I try to scream, but there's something tied around my mouth, some sort of gag. My hands are free, but I don't pull it off.

Something grabs my legs and tears into my skin. I fall forward and wake up—my sheets tangled around my legs and cold sweat sticking my T-shirt to my back.

I touch my mouth. Why didn't I take off the gag? Why didn't I scream for help when I had the chance?

Andrew bumps my door open with his chair, but he looks like he's afraid to come inside. I've barely spoken to him since the night he told Mom and Dad I snuck out. "Are you okay?"

"Yeah."

"You want to talk?"

I should say no, but I'm so lonely that I say, "Sure."

Andrew parks his chair beside my bed. "Another nightmare? About the accident?"

I nod. I've never told Andrew that I dream about the accident, but I guess he knows.

"What do you dream?"

"A lot of running, falling, getting wrapped up in that stupid dress." I gesture toward the closet.

"The truck?" Andrew's face contorts out of control for a second.

"No," I answer. "I don't see it at all."

He reaches his hand up toward the scar on my face. "Does it still hurt?"

"Sometimes. Mostly it just looks hideous."

"Not bad." Andrew smiles sadly.

I feel guilty for complaining about my scarred face when Andrew has lived his whole life in a wheelchair, whispers and stares following him everywhere he goes.

He reaches his hand to mine and I take it. "Still prettier than Hannah, or Angie, or any other girl at school."

"Thanks," I answer, "but aren't you supposed to be like every other bratty little brother and tell me how ugly I am?"

He shakes his head.

"So if I'm prettier than Hannah and Angie, am I prettier than Caitlyn?"

He shakes his head no, hard.

"No?" I study his face, concerned. "Are you still chatting

with her?" He nods. "You really like her, don't you?" He nods again.

Fear for my brother's heart makes me grip his hand tighter. "She'd better not do anything to hurt you, or I'll go after her."

Andrews face gets sad and he looks down at the floor. I wonder if he's thinking of Trip. I study his expression, wondering how much Andrew knew about what Trip did to me.

"Sorry," he says.

I take a breath. "For getting me busted for sneaking out the other night?" He doesn't confirm that that's why he's sorry, but I let that assumption hang between us. "It's okay, little brother, you were trying to keep me safe."

. . . — — — . . .

"Allie and Blake, I need to see you for a few minutes after class." Ms. Flores looks at me for a long time before it registers that she's talking to me. To Blake and me. The rest of the class flows out the door in a wave of whispers and backward glances. Ms. Flores perches on a desk in front of us. She's tall and thin, with salt-and-pepper hair, and always has a smudge of something—charcoal, paint, flour from papier-mâché—on her face. She smiles and tugs her skirt down over her knees.

I'm waiting for the lecture about paying attention in class, turning in work, at least trying. Blake spends the whole period with his head on his desk listening to his music, and I'm not much better at paying attention.

"Kids, I need your help." Ms. Flores brushes her hand against her cheek and leaves a streak of pink chalk from today's project. "I need a committee to plan and create the decorations for the

Sweetheart Ball in February. I thought of the two of you. I was hoping you'd be willing to be part of it."

"Us?" To say I was shocked would be an understatement. I've never been a person who was "thought of" when it comes to planning a school function, and Blake is the antisocial poster child of high school events.

Ms. Flores smiles at me. "I could use your organizational skills."

Organizational skills? I always got a "needs improvement" on that section of my grade-school report card. That counselor must have put her up to this.

"And I really need Blake's artistic talents."

I look at him, confused. As far as I know, Blake has never raised his head in art, much less turned in an assignment.

"Think about it." Ms. Flores leans against her desk and smiles encouragingly. "The committee meets for the first time the Monday after Thanksgiving, during lunch. It's good for extra credit." She hands us both a tardy excuse note and then heads for the front of the room.

I walk out without looking back at Blake, but when we're a few feet outside the classroom, he stops me. "So, what do you think?"

"About the dance thing?" I shrug. "I think the counselor asked Ms. Flores to get me 'involved.' I guess you got dragged into it because she thinks—because we're friends."

"It might be good for—" Blake bumps the toe of his worn-out black Vans against the bottom of the nearest locker. Then he looks up at me. I read concern in his eyes. I look away. "I mean, it might be fun."

I don't know what to say, so I just stare at him. Helping with—even participating in—a school function is just not Blake.

"I know you don't want to be seen with me." He taps the locker with his foot again, a little harder.

"It's not that," I start, but I can't explain why I've been so mean to him. How it's for his own good.

"It's okay." He crosses his arms over his chest and then uncrosses them. "I guess I understand. But—" He looks down the hall. Hannah's friend Megan gives us a long look before she turns into the girls' bathroom. "Nothing you do is going to make them accept you. Believe me, I've tried. I just think that"—he catches me in his eyes—"maybe it's time you figured out who your real friends are."

Chapter 18

The day after Thanksgiving used to be a day for me and Mom. We'd pore over the Black Friday ads the night before and decide our best strategy for Christmas shopping. It was one of our few mother-daughter-bonding things. This year, she leaves for the resort first thing in the morning, before I'm out of bed.

Dad already has the Christmas lights up. Mom had him haul all the decoration boxes down from the attic, but we aren't allowed to put them up without her and she probably won't be around to do it until later.

I thought when Dad left the military she would spend less time at the inn. But she's always working, or on the phone talking about work, or resting because she needs her strength for some big event coming up. Mom is kind of a hostess, event scheduler, and personal assistant to Mr. Phillips. It's the perfect fit for her organizational and people skills. Maybe she should do the dance committee.

The whole idea of Christmas seems kind of bleak and gray, like the weather outside. Last week a big windstorm stripped all the trees of their fall leaves so they look like bare twigs. The constant drizzle has let up for a couple of hours, but the sky is overcast as always. Outside my window, Dad and Andrew are in the carport, lying on their backs, half under Dad's work truck, changing the oil or something. Cars are Dad's and Andrew's thing. When Andrew was little he used to lie on the ground next to Dad while he worked. Andrew would do his best to hand Dad his tools, and Dad would explain what he was doing. Andrew's brain absorbs information like a sponge. He knows any car, make and model, by sight. If he could make his hands work, he could probably fix anything he wanted to.

He loved Trip's truck, a classic 1967 Chevy. Trip made a big deal of taking Andrew out for rides in it. I know it drove Andrew crazy that Trip didn't know anything about the truck and that he treated it the way Trip treated everything else. Like it was something he was entitled to, something that was his to use and destroy.

If things were different, Andrew could be driving a truck like Trip's or maybe some project car that he and Dad would trick out together on weekends. If things were different, Andrew might be taking over Dad's shop someday.

I'm putting my laundry away when my hand brushes the iPod that Trip gave me for Christmas last year. I haven't used it in months. The earbuds are still wrapped around it. I touch the button to see if it has a charge, and it lights up.

A morbid sense of nostalgia washes over me. I put the earbuds in my ears and press play. A slow, syrupy-sweet love song comes on. I push the Next button and hear some garbage like "I'll be your sky, your earth, your air." Irritated, I shuffle through the songs, each one making me more irritated than the one before. The lyrics are full of lies. I'm ready to turn off the iPod, or chuck it across the room, when *the* song comes on. The one that came out the summer I first met Trip, the one that talks about a summer love that lasts forever.

"I requested this one for us," he murmurs into my hair. I'm floating in a sea of bloodred satin, his arms around me, his body pressed against mine. "More than any other song, this one reminds me of you."

I don't answer. I try to keep my body from becoming rigid, even as he forgets and his hand presses hard against my back, into the bruise that's hidden under my white sweater.

My hands are shaking so hard by the time the song ends that I can barely turn off the iPod. When I touch the scar above my eye, my forehead is slick with sweat. My head hurts and I feel like I could throw up. The always-closed closet doors mock me. Behind them is the garment bag; inside that is the dress from my memory.

It's the first time I've remembered something from the night of the accident.

I close my eyes and try to push my mind back there—picture myself in the red dress, dancing with Trip. Instead I come up with images from my dream, running through a tangle of thorns, my heart racing. I open my eyes. My scar pulses. The memory is there, lingering somewhere beyond conscious thought. But it feels like a new wound, too painful to touch, even if touching it might make it better.

I sit up and shove the iPod into my pocket. My room feels

too close. My house feels smaller than ever. I need to get away. I'm freezing so I put another jacket over my sweatshirt and head outside.

I pause by the truck and watch Andrew and Dad work. I'm jealous of their easy togetherness, jealous of the bond between them, jealous of their normalcy. A cold wind blows through my jacket, into my sweatshirt, and chills me to the bone.

I take a couple of breaths to calm my voice. If Dad's distracted, I might be able to tell him I'm leaving without much explanation. "Hey, Dad." I work on sounding casual and not desperate. "I kinda wanted to go shopping."

He leans out to face me. "Shopping?"

"Yeah, Christmas stuff." I press the tigereye inside my pocket, hoping he won't ask for details.

He works his hand around the wrench he's holding. I know he's trying to decide if it's been long enough for me not to be grounded anymore. "By yourself?"

"Yes, sir."

"For how long?"

"A couple of hours, maybe three or four if I find some good deals." I lean against the side of the truck.

"Just in town?"

"Town" is the last place I want to go. I bite my lip. I've learned to be a pretty good liar. Still, I'm not sure I've ever successfully lied to Dad before.

"It's still leaking." Andrew pulls Dad's attention back to their project.

"Where?" He slides back underneath the truck. "Go ahead, Al, just be back before dark."

I give Andrew a look of thanks, climb into the van, and head toward Hoquiam. I listen to the song over and over as I drive, replaying not the moment in Trip's arms, maybe the last time he ever held me, but Blake's lips against mine in the back of a damp cave.

Maybe it's time I did figure out who my real friends are.

. . . – – – . . .

The pawnshop is busier than I would have thought, people looking for bargains for Christmas presents, or maybe trying to sell stuff to get money to buy presents. The whole shop has an air of desperation. I'm nervous that someone from Pacific Cliffs will see me here. I keep my head down and scan the crowd, but no one looks familiar.

I circle the store a couple of times, check out a new laptop that would make a great gift for Andrew and an espresso maker that Mom would love. I walk over to a display of old signs, the kind Mom decorated Dad's shop with. One of them says, EL CAMINO PARKING ONLY, and it makes me think of Blake again. Maybe I could get it for him as a kind of peace offering. Trip always gave me something when he wanted to make up for things.

I pick up the sign and work my way to the counter. There are three guys making quick deals with the crowd of customers. I hold the sign against my chest. If there is anyone here from Pacific Cliffs they'll know exactly who it's for. Blake's the only person in town who drives an El Camino. When I reach the front of the line the guy at the counter to my left calls out, "Cat-Eye Girl, I knew you'd be back."

It's the guy who was here before, but I can't answer for a minute.

He nods encouragingly.

I force a smile. "Allie."

"Right, Allie. And I'm Paul."

I set the sign on the floor, reach across the counter, and shake his outstretched hand. "Hi, Paul." So now I'm on a first-name basis with a pawnshop guy. Mom would be mortified.

He trades places with the guy in front of me. "I'll handle this one. Allie's one of my special customers. What do you have for me today?"

I pull the iPod out of my pocket and he examines it. "Is there anything wrong with it?"

It was given to me by my dead boyfriend and it's filled with songs that bring back painful memories except for one that I love, but it makes me feel guilty when I listen to it. "No." I shake my head. "I'm just expecting a new one for Christmas."

"Ah, bigger and better, huh?" He turns it over. "It seems to be in good condition. This was top of the line last year. Does it have anything on it that I can play or did you erase it?"

I wish now that I had thought to erase it. "No, it still has some stuff on it."

He turns it on, scrolls down to "Allie's Mix," puts one of the earbuds in his ear, and gets a big cheesy grin on his face. "Oooo, la la. Somebody's a romantic."

I blush down to my toes. I feel like somehow I've been violated, or like I've violated Trip's memory.

He turns off the iPod and pulls out the earbud. "How much?"

"One hundred," I say hopefully.

"Try again."

"Seventy-five?"

"I'll give you fifty cash for it plus the sign you have there."

"Okay." I wasn't positive I was going to get the sign. It feels wrong to buy a present for Blake with money from selling something Trip gave me. Now I'm stuck, so I get it.

On the way out of Hoquiam, I fill up the van with enough gas that Dad won't suspect I drove this far. It makes me feel good, like I'm keeping everything under control. But the whole time at the gas station, I feel like someone's watching me. When I look up, there's a guy leaning against the outside wall. He's tall and he's wearing a jacket and baseball cap. His face is in shadow, but I'm almost sure his eyes are on me. It's enough to make me drop the gas cap and then stumble over the edge of the curb in my hurry to leave. Even though I know it's not possible, and I'm being paranoid, I check my rearview mirror for a an old Chevy truck the whole way home.

Chapter 19

The Monday after Thanksgiving I take a deep breath and go looking for Blake at lunchtime. I'm carrying my backpack with the sign hidden inside. I'm not sure I'm brave enough to give it to him, but I feel like I should at least talk to him.

Blake always spends his lunch hour in his car. I assumed—along with the rest of the school—that he was in there smoking a joint or drinking or worse. When I approach his car, he's sitting in the front seat with his head down, bent over something. Looking closer, I realize it's a pad of paper and he's sketching.

Is Blake an artist? Is this what Ms. Flores was talking about? I lean toward the window and try to see the picture

Blake sits up fast; maybe he feels me watching him. The notebook slides off his lap and closes shut before I can see what he's drawn. I tap on the window, so he thinks I wanted him to see me there, not that I was watching him in a private moment.

He glances up at me in shock and then smiles. He rolls down the window. "Hey."

"Hey." I'm suddenly shy, like Blake is a stranger and not someone I've known forever. "Were you drawing?"

He shrugs. "Yeah." His face is guarded, as if he's waiting for me to say something mean again.

"Can I see it?"

He hesitates, but then he reaches for the sketchbook and gets out. He sets it on the hood of his car and flips it open. The picture he was working on is a squirrel. It looks so lifelike that I think if I brushed my finger along its bushy tail it would feel soft. "That's really good."

He blushes and gestures toward the trees. "I fed him bits of my lunch for almost a week to get him to pose for it."

I close the book and push it back toward him. "This is what Ms. Flores was talking about. You are an artist."

He ducks his head, but he's smiling. "I started drawing in Reno. It kept me sane. For a while."

I lean close and lift the edge of the page. "Can I see more?"

He nods and starts flipping through the book. Each picture feels like a glimpse into a piece of someone I thought I knew but didn't really. Blake is an artist. How did I not know? By the sheer number of drawings it looks like he spends every lunch hour out here in his car sketching the world around him.

Alone. Like me.

Blake's eyes move between the sketchbook and my face, looking for approval. I think about what he said about trying to make the kids at school like him. Maybe he doesn't want to be alone either. I finger the edge of the sign through my backpack.

It seems too cheap to give to him, but maybe I can do something else as a peace offering. "I was thinking, you know that dance, the Sweetheart Dance or, um, Sweetheart Ball?" He raises his eyebrows. "I mean the dance committee, the one that Ms. Flores wanted us to do. Do you want to?"

Blake looks confused. "Do I want to what?"

"Be on the committee . . . with me?" I don't think it's ever taken me so long to say one sentence to Blake.

His expression is guarded anticipation. "Do you really want to do it?"

Here's my chance. Honestly, there are a thousand reasons for me not to be on the dance committee, but, for whatever reason, Blake wants to do it. And I'm kind of hoping this will be his chance to be a part of something, to show the school what he can do, and maybe Mom, too. Not for me. My chance is already gone. I swallow. "Yeah, it might be fun. Besides"—I look up at him with what I hope is an eager smile—"it might be our only chance to show this school some class."

His smile makes this almost worth it. "Isn't the meeting right now?"

"Yeah, we're late." I'm hoping he'll say we can wait until the next meeting, after we talk to Ms. Flores.

"Then we'd better hurry." He tosses the sketch pad back in his car, grabs his backpack, and slams the car door.

Outside Ms. Flores's room, my heart sinks. I can hear Hannah's fake-sweet, high-pitched voice. "So the student council has approved a three-hundred-dollar—"

Hannah is in the middle of her speech, but Blake doesn't even pause at the door. I follow him, tugging at my hat, not looking at anyone. Blake sits on a desk in the back of the room and says, "Sorry we're late."

"Blake, Allie, great. Glad you could join us." Ms. Flores nods. "Hannah, go ahead."

Hannah's face is frozen halfway between the I'm-in-charge look she was wearing and a face that looks like she ate something that tasted really bad. I sink into a chair opposite Blake and behind Randall. He's huge—broad and tall, and the center on the football team, but I don't think he's big enough to hide me from Hannah's glare. She looks down at her notes and breathes through her nose. "As I was saying, the student council has approved a three-hundred-dollar budget for the dance. That's for decorations, music, and food."

Angie in the front row waves her hand. "Didn't we have like five or six hundred dollars last year?"

Hannah stares right through Randall to me. "Last year Mr. Phillips made a generous contribution to the student-body fund. I don't think that's going to happen this year."

"You're in good with that family," Blake challenges her. "Why don't you go and ask him if he would be willing to make another donation?"

Her glare shifts to Blake. "Under the circumstances I don't think that would be appropriate."

"I agree." Ms. Flores adjusts her perch. "Besides, a smaller budget will force us to be creative, and luckily our committee is full of creative people." She smiles at Blake. He beams back at her, like he's her prize pupil.

Hannah shuffles her notes, looks at Blake, then manages to find me behind Randall again and says, "I thought all members of this committee had to be approved through the student council."

"No," Ms. Flores says. "This is a voluntary committee, so as long as a student's GPA is high enough, or they receive administrative approval, anyone can be a part of it."

I have a feeling I was on a "special case" list that the counselor gave to the principal.

"Well," Hannah says. "It would appear this committee has *plenty* of members. And since I'm swamped with my other student council stuff *and* my Beachcomber's responsibilities, I won't be able to be in charge of this. And so"—she pauses for dramatic effect—"I nominate Allie Davis to head the Sweetheart Ball Committee."

"I second it," Blake pipes up. I freeze and the blood drains from my face.

"Anyone else want to be the head of this?" Ms. Flores looks around.

I sweep the room, looking for help, but none comes. "I nominate Blake," I say in desperation.

"I think that's a great idea," Ms. Flores says, clapping her hands together. I relax for half a second before she adds, "Allie and Blake as joint chairs. This job is certainly big enough for two." Blake grins at me. I shoot what I hope are deadly darts at him with my eyes.

Hannah picks up her stack of papers, walks right past Blake's outstretched hand, and slaps them on my desk. "Good luck." She smirks. She has a hot-pink Barbie Band-Aid on the back of her hand. I wonder if anyone at school honestly believes Hannah's hand would take this long to heal.

Before Hannah is even out of the room, Blake scoops up the papers and walks to the front. "Okay, first order of business—theme." He winks at me. "Allie, do you mind taking notes?"

Ms. Flores hands me a piece of paper and a pen, but I shake my head. "I can't." If I try to keep notes, it will come out jumbled because my hands are shaking. I'll look like a complete idiot.

"I'll do it." A perky freshman with short brown hair—I think her name is Kasey—crosses the room and takes the paper and pen from Ms. Flores. Kasey parks herself in front of Blake. The way she looks at him sends a strand of jealousy down my throat. It wraps around my heart and squeezes my chest. I try to push it away. I don't deserve him.

Blake takes over the meeting and I sit in dumbfounded amazement at this Blake I didn't know. The artistic one. The one who takes charge of things. The one who stands up to Hannah George.

Chapter 20

After school, I pull out my literature book and a piece of paper drifts to the floor like a wounded seagull, stained with slanty-sharp bloodred letters.

Another note.

I will myself not to look at it, to leave it on the floor, unread, to let it be swept up with the other trash when the janitor comes by. But I'm afraid someone will see it so I hesitate only half a second before snatching it up.

You'll never be alone.

I want to laugh it off, or throw it away, but it feels like whoever is sending the notes is reading my mind. I glance around the hall, but for once nobody is watching me. I shove the note in my backpack and then touch the tigereye in my pocket. Just a stupid joke. Let it go. I pull my out notebook gingerly, afraid of what else might fall out of my locker.

"Hey."

I spin around and drop my backpack on the floor. My books spill out and the corner of the note taunts me from the bottom of the pile.

"Sorry, didn't mean to scare you." Blake leans his face toward me. "Are you okay?"

"Fine." I drop to my knees and start scooping the mess back into my backpack.

Blake bends over to help me. "Here, let me—"

"I've got it," I answer fast. I straighten up and jerk the zipper closed. "I need to hurry or I'll miss my bus."

"Oh." Blake backs off like he's waiting for me to say something to insult him again. "Um, I was kind of hoping we could go into town and look for some stuff for the dance. But we don't have to."

"Another time." I sling my backpack over my shoulder and start toward the bus line. Blake ducks his head and goes the other direction. Halfway down the hall I see Mr. Phillips coming in the front door. To get to the bus I have to go past him. I turn around and go the other way.

Blake is almost to the back door, so I trot to catch up with him. "Actually, today would be okay."

"Cool," he says. He leans against the back door and opens it for me. I glance over my shoulder, but I can't tell if Mr. Phillips sees us.

Blake is talking about stuff for the dance all the way to his car, but I'm not listening. His car is at the back of the parking lot. We have to pass James and Randall, leaning against Randall's truck, and the spot where Trip used to park—left vacant in homage to his memory. I keep my eyes on the ground, but I know they're watching me as I climb into Blake's car.

Blake is oblivious. As soon as he gets in, he hands me his sketch pad. "I came up with some ideas for the decorations. I drew these during sixth period." He starts the car and points to the map he made of the gym.

Over his shoulder I can see James watching us.

". . . so I was thinking I could do some giant paintings depicting the town's history. There are some rolls of old canvas at the fertilizer plant, the stuff they used to make the bags out of, we could put them on frames to look like sails. That was a great idea, by the way."

I force my gaze back to his face. "Huh?"

He looks out the window at James glaring at us across the parking lot. Then he turns back to me. "Forget him for a minute, okay?" He sounds irritated, with me or with James, I'm not sure.

I look down at his sketch pad. "Sorry."

"I've known James my whole life. He's a jerk, but he's all talk. Not worth worrying about."

"Right, sorry." I let out my breath. Forget James. Forget the note in my locker. Let it go.

Blake pulls out of the parking lot. "Now about the dance. I want to go by the library and get some books about the town to get some ideas for the paintings. And we need to go to the hardware store for paint, and maybe we could run out to the fertilizer plant and see if my boss will let me get that canvas I was talking about. And we need to figure out something for the frames." Blake's eyes dance with excitement.

"You want to do all of this tonight?" I'm worried about what will happen if Blake and I are seen together in town, what will happen if I'm late getting home, and what will happen if Mom knows I've been with him.

"Well, not everything." Blake grins, half-sheepish. "You came up with such a brilliant idea that I want to get going on it right away."

"It wasn't really me." I shrug.

"You're the one who got everyone to stop arguing." He brakes at a stop sign. "And Historic Pacific Cliffs is a great idea."

"Historic Pacific Cliffs" came out during a heated discussion between the three guys in the room—Blake, Randall, and Marshall Yates who's lobbying to have his band play at the dance—and most of the girls. The guys wanted a dance that didn't include a tux rental. The girls wanted the one girls'-choice dance to be formal. Angie suggested a costume ball. Ms. Flores shot that down because of dress-code concerns. Randall said matching T-shirts, Angie rolled her eyes. Through the whole conversation I kept my mouth shut, but I could see the sign WELCOME TO HISTORIC PACIFIC CLIFFS through the window in Ms. Flores's room. When Blake asked for my opinion, I said historic costumes without thinking. The idea snowballed from there. The girls loved the theme and Blake sided with me, so my idea won. I was shocked.

Blake stops at the library first. I feel eyes on us as soon as we walk in. Every time we pass someone, whispers follow. Even the librarian gives me a disapproving look when she hands Blake a piece of paper and points us to the historical section. We check out *Pacific Cliffs, a History* and *Pacific Cliffs, a City Reborn*—two old books full of black-and-white pictures and glowing history from our town.

We go to the hardware store next. Blake spends a lot of time looking over the shelf of "wrong tint" paint cans. He explains that he's going to use the rejected house paints to do his sail paintings. "They're cheap, there's a lot of paint, and they'll usually retint them for free."

I hide in the corner and pretend to look at paint swatches while Blake is talking to the paint guy. I'm not exactly trying to pretend I'm not with him. I'm just tired of everyone staring.

Beatrice, of Beatrice's Famous Chocolates, a little shop in town, comes over and grabs my hand. "Allie. It's good to see you."

Over her shoulder Blake is finishing up at the counter. I will him to stay where he is, but he comes toward us.

"Such a horrible thing to have to go through so young." She squeezes my hand. It's getting slippery with my sweat. "And Trip was such a nice young man. He used to come into the shop just to see how I was doing. He loved my dark-chocolate raspberry truffles. He always paid me twice what they were worth and said I should charge more. He got a few boxes of candy for you, if I remember right."

Blake stands behind me, a gallon of paint in each hand.

Beatrice raises her eyebrows at him and keeps talking. "The two of you were the best-looking couple at the cotillion." I can feel her eyes on my scar. "Such a tragedy." She shakes her head toward Blake and releases my hand. "Well, I should get going."

She disappears around the corner while Blake says, "You ready to go?"

I wipe my hand on my jeans and nod.

We're almost to the checkout counter when I hear Beatrice again, talking to one of the cashiers, ". . . with Joyce's grandson, can you believe it? After everything he's done? He's taking advantage of her grief, that's what I think." The cashier mumbles something and Beatrice huffs, "I still say that boy looks like Donald Shelley. Spitting image."

I look up at Blake to see if he heard her, but she was talking so loudly there's no way he could have missed what she said. Donald Shelley was the drama teacher who Blake's mom ran away with just before graduation. Whether or not he's Blake's father has been a popular debate in Pacific Cliffs, probably since before Blake was born.

I want to duck out the back of the store, but Blake keeps going. He smiles and sets the paint cans on the counter. "Actually, Phoebe—I mean, Mom—told me that my dad wasn't Mr. Shelley, but that he was from Pacific Cliffs. His name was . . ." Blake pretends to be thinking hard. The two ladies lean forward, eager for this bit of gossip. "Tom, or was it Bob?" I have to stifle a laugh when I remember that Beatrice's son is named Tom and the cashier's husband is named Bob. "Hmm, I'm not sure. I'll have to ask her again." Blake smiles at them politely. "Have a nice day." He pays for the paint and leaves them with their mouths hanging open.

Chapter 21

After the hardware store Blake takes me to his house. It's still weird for me to come here and see condos where my grandma's house used to be. Grandma died of a heart attack two months after we moved to Pacific Cliffs. I wanted to sell the house we had just bought so we could live in Grandma's house, but Mom said it wasn't practical for Andrew. In typical überefficient Mom style, she had Grandma's house cleared out and sold within two months.

Blake leaves the paint cans on the porch, grabs two apples from the kitchen, and heads upstairs to the attic. The house is empty. Blake's grandmother, Grandma Joyce, must be at her shop. She makes natural body-care products. She sells them in town, and every room at Pacific Cliffs Inn is stocked with her soap and little jars of her homemade lotion.

He sets the library books on a table in front of a pair of french doors that open to the widow's walk and a great view of the ocean. He starts flipping through the pages. The sun glints on his hair and a chunk of his bangs slips over his eyes. "What about this one?" His voice startles me. I realize I was watching him instead of looking at the book.

I lean closer so my arm almost touches his. The black-and-white picture shows a group of men in suspenders and hats staring back at the camera with stern expressions. In the background is the lumber mill that employed most of Pacific Cliffs before it shut down about twenty years ago.

"Good historical moment?" Blake asks. When he turns his head I have to step away because I was leaning so close to his face.

"Yeah, but there's a lot of detail." I reach to brush my hair back before I realize it doesn't fall over my shoulders anymore. "The crane, the logs, the little dog." I put my finger on a shaggy white mutt—the only creature in the picture who looks like he's smiling.

Blake clears his throat. "You don't think I can do it."

I lean back farther. "I didn't say that. I know that I couldn't do it."

"You've never seen any of my paintings," Blake says. I can't tell if it's a question, a comment, or an accusation.

I shrug. "You never volunteered to show them to me."

"Maybe I didn't know you'd be interested."

"I am," I say firmly.

He looks like he's waiting for the punch line. "Really?"

"Really."

He goes to a corner of the room where a big divided shelf holds four racks. He pulls a stretched canvas off the rack. The image is blurred, like something out of a dream, with all the colors—muted grays and blues and greens—running together. Still, I can tell it's the entrance to our cave. There's only one bright spot in the picture, something red hanging from a rock on the side of the cave. It reminds me of the red jacket I lost when I was eight.

I reach toward the painting but pull back, afraid to touch it. "It's beautiful." He ducks his head and slides the picture back into the rack. "Can I see more?" I look at him shyly.

He reaches into the rack and pulls out a picture of his El Camino, tricked out with blue racing stripes and custom wheels.

"Cool," I say.

He shrugs. "It's just a dream." He slides the painting back into the rack and I reach for the next one. "Not that—" He tries to take it from me, but I've already seen what it is: a painting of me, half-done, from before my accident, the scar over my eye missing.

I blush and look away.

"That one's just a dream, too," he says quietly, replacing the painting in the rack.

The weight of a thousand things I should say to him hangs over me, but I let the silence speak instead.

"Blake, you home?" Grandma Joyce's voice floats up the stairs. I breathe again and step away from him toward the corner.

Blake clears his throat. "We're in the attic."

"We?" Grandma Joyce huffs as she climbs the last stair. "Oh, hi, Allie. Good to see you." She put her hands on her hips and evaluates me. "You look a lot better than you did last time I saw you." I touch my scar. The last time I remember seeing Grandma Joyce was when I was in the hospital. "You still look a little pale, though." She steps forward and peers at my face from behind her glasses.

"How's your shop doing?" I ask to get off the subject of me.

"Great, actually, if I can keep up with the holiday orders." She sits back on a chair and looks me over. I'm waiting for her to say something about my hair or about my being too thin. Instead she asks, "I've been thinking about hiring someone to help me out." She raises her eyebrows. "How would you like to work for me?"

I take a step back farther into the corner. "I can't—"

"Not in the shop." Grandma Joyce's voice is coaxing. "I know you aren't comfortable with that sort of thing. But I could use your help here, filling orders. I could show you how I mix things up."

"I don't know." I look around at the array of glass bottles, measuring equipment, and jars filled with the ingredients that go into Grandma Joyce's natural body products. If any combination is explosive, I would be the one to find it. I touch the stone in my pocket. "I don't think I can."

"Yeah, you can." Blake's eyes shimmer with the same excitement I saw when he was talking about the dance. "You could work for Grandma and we could do the project at the same time. I mean"—he looks down at the floor—"if you want to."

"It would be fun to have you around here again." Grandma Joyce's face crinkles into rows of wrinkles that frame her eyes, bluer than Blake's but the same shape. "I could really use your help. Blake makes beautiful paintings, but when he tries to help me in the shop . . . let's just say he doesn't have the right touch."

"Maybe I don't either." I glance at Blake, but he's still staring at the floor. I think about the painting of me on the rack behind him.

"Only one way to find out." Grandma Joyce reaches for an apron behind the door. "Let's get started."

Chapter 22

Two days later there's a note stuck to the bulletin board. This one is signed, "Mom," but it scares me worse than any I've gotten so far.

Detective Weeks called. He would like to meet with you on Friday right after school.

I'd like to think that my being seen with Blake has nothing to do with my appointment with Detective Weeks, but I know better. I was with another guy, in public, not playing the good widow. And not just any guy, it was Blake "Juvie" Evans, the town delinquent. The dark cloud of *if* Detective Weeks is going to question me turns into *when*.

Mom says she can't get off work to go with me. She's busy preparing for the holiday travel season, like Pacific Cliffs is a big winter destination. Dad says he doesn't want me to go alone. He takes the afternoon off from the shop to drive me. We get there about ten minutes before my appointment.

Like most of Pacific Cliffs, the police station struggles to be quaint and nostalgic but barely pulls off small and insignificant. The building is red brick and white trim, with a wide front lawn and a flag waving patriotically in the breeze. The lobby is filled with portraits of hero cops, most of whom attained their status merely by sticking it out in Pacific Cliffs until they were old enough to retire.

The receptionist/dispatcher takes our names, even though she knows exactly who we are, and tells us, "Please, sit down. Detective Weeks is still in another meeting."

Dad sits calmly and picks up a six-month-old copy of *Field and Stream*. I work on making the rough spot on the tigereye smooth. With any luck, I look as messed up as I feel and Detective Weeks will take pity on me. More likely he'll take my face as a sure sign of guilt and lock me up on sight.

I've tried to convince myself that he'll only ask questions about the night of the accident. I won't have to lie because I still don't remember. That he won't go into the dark abyss of *before*. Dad has been bugging me to concentrate, to try to remember *something*. "Maybe if they know what happened that night, Trip's mom and dad can find some peace."

I doubt that anything I could tell Trip's parents about their son would give them peace.

The walls of the police station are supposed to be bulletproof or at least soundproof, but I can still hear his voice. Loud. Demanding. Terrifying. Dad looks at me, but I don't think he knows who is in Detective Weeks's meeting. I've heard that voice and that tone too many times before not to know. I recognize it from the times I cowered in Trip's truck while the walls of his house shook with one of Mr. Phillips's episodes.

Trip hated going to his house. Hated it. I hated it, too, because after a fight with his dad I could never predict whether Trip would be needy or just angry.

The argument moves into the hall between the lobby, the offices, and the little holding cell in the back. I don't look, but I can picture Mr. Phillips's face, beet-red and sweating, like when Trip dinged the side of his truck on a gas station pillar. "If you were doing your job, you would have something more concrete by now."

The next voice is more muffled, Chief Milton saying something about calming down and trying to get to the bottom of things.

Mr. Phillips yells back, "I know the district attorney and the attorney general. If you can't make things move forward, I'll find someone who can."

Dad discreetly raises his magazine. I don't have anything to hide behind so I get the full brunt of Mr. Phillips's glare. This time he doesn't offer to have me over for dinner or pay for my college or reinstate my cell phone. I shrink into the fake leather chair as his eyes strip my fragile covering of secrets and find their way to my vulnerable core. Being seen with Blake must have officially pushed me across some invisible line from sympathy to suspicion.

Mr. Phillips storms out and leaves a trail of smoldering brimstone. Chief Milton follows him to the door but doesn't go after him.

Detective Weeks shakes his head. "I guess that leaves me with you, Miss Davis."

My dad stands up and walks with me to Detective Weeks's office. They shake hands, cordial, like the yelling in the hall never happened.

They exchange pleasantries: "How is your business doing?" "What do you think of the Seahawks' chances of getting into the play-offs?" "I hear we're going to have an unusually wet winter." That sort of thing.

"This shouldn't take too long," Detective Weeks says.

"That's fine," Dad replies. They shake hands again. "I'll be waiting outside if you need anything." Dad leaves me to the mercy of an overzealous detective and my own Swiss-cheese memory.

Detective Weeks's office reminds me of Ms. Vincent's; an afterthought—some kind of storage area repurposed for my benefit. It has a desk with a laptop, a bookcase, a file cabinet, and a hard chair for me to sit on. The walls are bare and the bookcase holds a couple of boxes and no books. It doesn't look like he's planning to be in Pacific Cliffs very long.

He sits and gestures for me to sit in the chair opposite him. I sit. He pulls a pile of papers from the file cabinet and shuffles through them. I wait. He sets the papers down, leans over the desk, and looks at me. I hold my breath.

"I should have sent this directly to the judge, but I'm sure you just forgot. With everything going on, it must have slipped your mind. I'd hate to have to throw you in jail for something so trivial."

My heart races wildly as my scrambled brain grasps for

some meaning in what he's saying, but I come up with nothing. I stare at him blankly.

He slides a copy of the ticket he gave me across the desk. "You were supposed to have this paid by the end of the month."

"My traffic ticket?" I pick it up with fingers that have gone numb.

"Like I said, I could have turned that over to the judge and had a warrant for your arrest put out. But I know your memory isn't the best." He catches me in his blue eyes, and I read double meaning there.

I want to ask him if that was supposed to be a threat, but I just say, "Thank you."

He stands up. "Grace can take care of you out front. Just don't let it happen again."

I stand and wait for him to open the door, but he doesn't.

"So you just brought me in to remind me about the ticket?" As soon as the words are out of my mouth I regret them. I shouldn't have said anything, shouldn't have opened up a space for him to ask more questions.

"For now, yes." His voice is casual, but his eyes are hard and intense. "Is there anything you would like to ask me?"

"Why are you here?" I blurt it out before I can stop myself. I'm not sure I want the answer to that question.

"Why did I come to Pacific Cliffs?" He leans against the desk. "I'm really not at liberty to say." He could stop there, but he doesn't. "I don't think there's any way you could have missed what Mr. Phillips said on the way out. He's right about having friends in high places. And I guess he has money to throw around."

"So you were hired by Mr. Phillips?"

"No," Detective Weeks says firmly. "He may have the influence to bring me here, but he doesn't have any influence over my investigation." He picks up a pen and starts tapping on the desk. "Mr. Phillips seems pretty upset. I guess, given the situation, that's understandable." He sets the pen down and his forehead wrinkles. "Have you ever seen him lose his temper like that before?"

I slide my fingers along the edge of the stone in my pocket, but I answer truthfully. "Yes."

"With Trip?"

I feel myself getting into dangerous territory. I grip the tiger-eye hard. "Yes."

"Can you tell me anything about Trip's mental state before the accident? Not just the night of the accident, but before. Was Trip depressed at all?"

I swallow. Moody, violent, arrogant, but not depressed. "No."

"Are you sure? Sometimes it's hard to tell, even if you're close to someone."

My head starts to hurt. I should have left when I had the chance. "I don't think so."

"Did he ever drink or do drugs?"

It feels like a betrayal, but I answer, "He drank."

"A lot?"

"No. Sometimes. About the same as everyone else."

"Were you guys drinking the night of the accident?"

"I don't drink." That's the truth. It was hard enough to defend myself against Trip when I was sober.

"That's not exactly what I asked. The toxicology report on

you showed no alcohol in your blood, so I know you weren't drinking. Was Trip?"

My stomach clenches. "I don't remember."

"Without a body, that's not something we can determine, but if someone saw him consuming alcohol that night—"

"I still don't remember anything." I try to sound sure, hoping that that will be the end of his interrogation.

"That must be kind of unnerving, to have a block of time when you don't know where you were or what you did."

My blood chills. I want to ask him what he means by that, if he's accusing me of something. The truth is, it's a thought that keeps haunting me, too. I don't know what I did that night. I don't know what really happened.

"But I guess no one can blame you for not being able to remember. You took quite a blow to the head. You seem to be doing okay now, though." He smiles. "You even have a new boyfriend."

My throat goes dry, like I swallowed a mouthful of sand. Now the real reason he brought me here comes out. Because I was seen with Blake. "Blake's just a friend."

He raises his eyebrows. "Just a friend? Are you sure he feels the same? He seemed pretty protective of you when I pulled him over."

"We've been friends for a long time."

"Are you sure you want to be friends with a guy like him? Blake has a bit of a record, doesn't he? Some problem in Nevada?"

I should tell him that's none of his business. That it was a long time ago. I should defend Blake, but I don't even know how to defend myself. I step toward the door. "If we're done here, my dad's waiting. He needs to get back to work."

Detective Weeks doesn't move. "Your dad's a mechanic, right? Owns that new shop in town?"

"Yes." I say it slowly, trying to figure out where he's going with this.

"He ever teach you anything about cars?"

"No." I keep my voice even. "Dad just got out of the Army. Before that he was gone all the time."

"What about your friend Blake? Does he know cars? That thing he drives, that old El Camino, probably needs a lot of maintenance, right? Does your dad help him with that, or does he do it himself?"

"I don't know." My head is spinning, and my scar tightens. I'm not sure where Detective Weeks is going with any of this, but it feels bad, bad for me and bad for Blake.

"Funny thing about the accident report." He riffles through some papers on the desk. I wonder if the accident report is sitting on the desk beside him. I wonder what it says. "It didn't say how fast Trip was going when he hit the corner. Usually they measure skid marks to figure that out." I stand next to the door, frozen. "Do you know why they couldn't figure out how fast the truck was going?" His eyes bore into my soul.

I don't answer.

"Because there weren't any skid marks."

Chapter 23

I have to stay away from Blake.

The realization hits me like an icy wave as I walk down the lobby to the front of the police station. How could I have not seen it before? Hannah's voice screams in my head. "*You poison everyone and everything that gets near you.*" She was right, but I was too stupid, too selfish, to see that I was poisoning Blake just by being near him. Now Detective Weeks thinks he's mixed up in whatever happened the night of the accident. And I can't even remember enough to keep him out of trouble. Not even enough to keep myself out of trouble. Guilt by association.

"What did Detective Weeks want?" Dad's voice interrupts my thoughts. I forgot that he was waiting for me.

I hold up the ticket meekly. "I forgot to pay this."

"Your ticket? That's what he wanted?" Dad doesn't look like he believes me. "You were in there a long time."

"He gave me a big lecture about what could have happened. He said he could have had me arrested."

"He's right. You need to be more careful." Dad takes the ticket from me. I wonder if "you need to be more careful" means something more. "Do you have any money to pay for this?"

"A little." I shake my head. "Not enough."

Dad pulls out his wallet and pays the ticket. He's quiet all the way out to the car. Finally he says, "Did Detective Weeks ask you anything about the accident?"

I open my mouth to lie. Then I see his face, the face of a man who ten months ago was interrogating insurgents in a war zone. Lying to him is impossible. "Yes."

"And what did you tell him?" Dad's voice stays even.

I trace the edge of the tigereye in my pocket. "That I don't remember anything."

"Is that true?" his interrogator voice asks.

I shake my head, no and yes, and say, "It's all a jumble. Images that don't make any sense. Dreams."

Dad touches my arm. "Maybe if you went back to that counselor. Maybe you have post-traumatic stress disorder or something like that. A lot of guys came back from the war with that stuff. Maybe if you had someone to talk—"

"No!" I say it too quickly, and then back off. "All she did was tell me I was angry, that I should hit my pillow."

"Instead of Hannah." Dad's voice lightens a little. He squeezes my arm and then starts the car.

I lean my head back.

"Maybe you just need time."

I nod. My head hurts.

"I just hope they're willing to give you time."

My eyes flutter open. "Who?"

Dad breathes in. "This town is too small. People talk too much." He looks at me hard.

"What have you heard?" Like I don't know. Like I don't know that they're all talking about me, and about Blake, and why we're together so much, so soon.

"Some people are saying that the accident was suspicious and if they're paying for a new detective, he should be doing some investigating." He pulls out of the police station and heads for home.

I think about what Detective Weeks said about there being no skid marks. Would Dad know why there wouldn't be skid marks? Could I ask him? What would he think if I did?

"You seem to be the missing piece in all of this." He turns and looks at me. "Because you were the only witness, I worry that people might take some of their suspicions out on you. If they had a clearer picture of the night of the accident. If you could remember . . ."

My head hurts. "You're not helping. I said I couldn't remember!"

"Right." He touches my leg. "Sorry."

He's silent for the rest of the way home. He parks in the driveway and looks at me again. "Blake's grandma came into the shop today. She's having problems with that old Buick again. She mentioned that she had asked you to work for her."

"She did," I answer. "But I wasn't—"

"I told her I thought it would be a good idea. It'll give you a way to pay me back, and I do expect you to pay me back." Dad ıes his eyebrows. "It might be good for you to be out doing something."

"I don't think I should." For Blake's sake.

"Try it for a while. At least long enough to pay me back." It kind of feels like Dad is ordering me to work for Grandma Joyce. "You're eighteen. In less than a year you'll be going away to college. It's time you took some responsibility for your life."

I lie in bed that night, trying to figure out what Dad meant about taking responsibility for my life. Another veiled reference to trying to remember the accident, or something else? I've been living in survival mode for so long that anything in the future feels vague and far away. If I go away to college, will I be able to escape everything that happened here? Can I hold out that long?

I think about the painting of me that Blake has in his attic. A dream. A dream I shattered for both of us a long time ago. I rub the tigereye across my lips and try to remember what it felt like to have his lips against mine. After all I've done, I don't deserve him, but he's willing to give me another chance.

The rest of the town isn't willing to give either of us a chance, but if the accident investigation were closed, if Detective Weeks went away, then would the town forget? Would I be able to be with Blake?

Everything Detective Weeks said churns inside of me. Why were there no skid marks? Did he mean Trip went over the cliff on purpose? Was that where Detective Weeks was going with the whole "depression" thing?

But Trip wasn't depressed. Everybody loved him. He had everything. He was great at sports. He was gorgeous. He had plenty of money. He had me to control.

Maybe he was just too drunk to make the corner.

I close my eyes and press the tigereye against my scar. It would be easy. All I'd have to say was Trip was drinking that night. That he was drunk when he went around the corner. That I jumped to save myself. The case would be closed. People would stop looking at me like it was my fault. No one would question Blake. No one would care if we were together.

I'd seen Trip drive drunk plenty of times before. The night before the accident, when I snuck out to rescue him, he was drunk. I tried to get him to let me drive him home.

"You need to let me drive. Just give me the keys, okay?"

"You don't know what you're talking about. Don't tell me what to do!"

"Trip, please, you're drunk. I don't want you to—"

He turns on me so fast I don't have time to avoid his fist crashing into my shoulder. I fall backward, my back slamming against a jagged stump on the way down.

James and Randall look the other way.

The thought hits me almost as hard as Trip's fist. I sit up in bed. James and Randall both saw Trip hit me the night before the accident. They both know.

I lie in bed for hours thinking about it. When I finally fall asleep I dream that Trip hits me and that I fall backward and hit my head on something hard. The whole town is standing around, but no one acknowledges me. No one acknowledges what he did. No one helps. They just leave me there, lying in a puddle. I'm wearing the dress from cotillion. And the puddle is red.

Chapter 24

"Excellent, Allie," Grandma Joyce says as she leans over my shoulder. Three lessons into this and I'm getting better at keeping my hands from shaking, or at least hiding it from Grandma Joyce.

"She just made a striped vanilla candle, perfect texture, without burning anything or ruining the pan." She raises her eyebrows, like that should mean something to Blake. He grunts back.

Grandma Joyce shakes her head. "Blake isn't really here right now."

I've already learned that when Blake is into his art, the whole world could explode and he wouldn't notice. Right now he's studying a black-and-white picture, a charcoal pencil in his hand and a big piece of paper on an easel in front of him. He has a smudge of charcoal on his cheek and his knuckles are smeared with black.

I smile back, glowing from her praise. Being freaked out about making a mistake has actually been a good thing. I seem to be getting better at this.

"What are you working on, B.?" Grandma Joyce crosses the room to Blake and studies the picture. "Ah, the mill." She leans over and brushes the hair out of Blake's eyes.

This wakes him up from his trance. He pulls away from her. "Grandma."

"Scruffy again, Blake." She shakes her head.

"I like his hair long," I say without thinking.

Blake blushes, grins, and rubs his throat, leaving a streak of black there, too.

"Thanks, Allie," Grandma Joyce says. "Now I'll never get him to cut it." She leans closer to the picture beside Blake on the desk. "This was the mill during its heyday. Before it shut down, most of the town worked there. If it wasn't for Mr. Phillips revamping the inn and bringing in tourists, Pacific Cliffs would have probably died out completely."

She flips through the book. "Allie, have you ever seen this picture of your mom?"

I set the candle mold down and join her across the room. The page she's looking at has rows of beautiful teenage girls in varied styles of formals and big updos.

"Yeah. I've seen that picture before." I try to keep the bitterness out of my voice. Mom's official Beachcomber's picture: her gold-blond hair piled on top of her head, a sequined blue gown draping over her hips, her smile perfect—as always.

I remember how hard Mom tried to convince me to do Beachcomber's, filled out the application for me and everything.

Trip didn't like the idea of my parading in front of a bunch of other guys. And how could I wear the fitness outfit, shorts and a short-sleeved T-shirt, my bruises on display for everyone? Mom was more than disappointed. I think it was her dream for me to follow in her footsteps.

"Beachcomber's Queens—look at the lot of them." Grandma Joyce slides her finger down the page. "Your mom, and this is Patty George, Hannah's aunt. That should have been Phoebe's year. If she hadn't run off, it would have been. Just like her dad—ran away when things weren't going her way."

Blake's face twists. I think it hurts him when his grandma talks like that about his mom. I study the pageant queens so I don't have to see his discomfort. Hannah's aunt is wearing a strapless red satin dress, bloodred like my dress from cotillion. It looks so familiar that it makes my head hurt. I close my eyes. Angie's high-pitched voice fills my head.

"That's a fabulous dress, Allie. I don't know why you keep it covered up."

I pull the white sweater closer to my body. "I'm cold."

"It's like eighty degrees in here; how could you be cold?"

"Allie's always cold." Trip drapes his arm over my shoulder and starts fingering the neckline of my dress. "But maybe I can convince her to take off that jacket later tonight, after I give her her birthday present."

I elbow him away, and then wait for his subtle retribution—fingers digging into a bruise he knew was there, or a look that tells me I'm in trouble for making him look stupid in public—but it doesn't come.

"Everybody bow down." Angie rolls her eyes. "Here comes the queen."

I follow her gaze to what distracted Trip from punishing me. Hannah, standing in the doorway in her sash and crown, on the arm of some trophy date—always hot but never good-looking enough to overshadow her. Trip's eyes travel every inch of her emerald-green dress, from the deep neckline to the slit at her hip. She watches him, too.

My stomach twists with remembered jealousy. Grandma Joyce flips the book back to the page Blake was working on. She doesn't notice me gripping the edge of the table for support. The blood pounds through my scar and into my ears.

"A lot of history in this town." She pats Blake's shoulder. The men standing in front of the mill in the picture swirl to gray. "I know you'll do a great job." She turns to me. "Would you like to—" She looks at me. "Blake, get her!"

The whole room spins. My mind slides into a dark abyss of Trip's eyes, my bloodred dress, and green-satin jealousy.

. . . — — — . . .

"We're having a party after the dance. You're all invited." Hannah's eyes are on Trip. I'm sure if she could figure out a way to keep me from coming, she would.

Trip pulls me against his chest, but he keeps his eyes on the diamond cutout in the front of Hannah's dress. "We're not going to the party with you guys. I have to give Allie her present." He turns and I tip my face to his and accept a long kiss—public affection, for Hannah's benefit. "The limo's dropping us off at Allie's house. I left my truck there. We want to be alone."

"Allie, can you hear me?" Grandma Joyce's voice sounds far away, at the end of a long, dark tunnel.

My heart sinks. I don't want to be alone with Trip. The limo and all of his friends were supposed to be my shield tonight. Randall's dad insisted on the limo. To keep us safe . . .

"Allie, please wake up." I try to open my eyes, but Blake's pleading morphs into Trip's voice, breathless and desperate.

"Wake up. Do you hear me? I said wake up! You can't leave me. I'm not going to take the blame for this."

"Please wake up."

I force the memory out of my head and concentrate on the sound of Blake's voice. Slowly his face emerges out of the fog around me.

"Are you okay?" He's cradling my head in his lap. Grandma Joyce tucks a pillow under my feet.

"I think so." My heart pounds in my ears. The forgotten images swirl around my brain, trying to force their way into some meaning. Part of me wants to keep them from slipping away again. Part of me doesn't want to know what they mean.

"She skipped lunch today." Blake brushes my hair off my forehead. I turn toward his voice and see worry in his eyes. "We had a committee meeting."

"I'm okay." But I don't sound convincing. My face feels hot and I'm not sure I remember how my legs work. I try to get up.

"Sit still," Grandma Joyce commands. "I'm going call your mother."

"No." I sit up fast and my eyes start to fog over again. I lean back against Blake. "I mean, you can't. She's at work."

"You'll probably be okay," Grandma Joyce says at last, and touches my forehead. "Just stress, lack of food, and maybe some smoke from the melted wax. That attic is pretty warm today."

I nod, glad to accept her easy explanations. "I feel better already." With Blake's arms around me, it's not entirely a lie.

"Take it slow," Grandma Joyce says.

I try sitting up again, slower this time. Blake slides forward to support my back. I lean into him and let him hold me up. His fingers leave black charcoal streaks on the sleeves of my sweatshirt. After a few minutes I let him help me to a chair by the table. The book is lying on top, closed.

Grandma Joyce brings me a mug of herbal tea. "Rest for a while. When your color looks better, I'll have Blake take you home. Get some rest, and if you're up to it, you can come back and work for real in a couple of days. Just make sure you leave the window open for some fresh air."

"No. I'm okay." I stand and Blake scrabbles to help me. I have to lean on him to stay on my feet.

"Make sure she eats tomorrow," Grandma Joyce says as Blake gathers up my backpack. "I'm counting on you to watch out for her."

"I will," Blake says seriously. He grips my arm like I might slip out of his grasp and fade away.

Chapter 25

"Do you have the receipt Angie turned in from the store?" Blake leans close to me, waiting for my answer. We're sitting with Andrew in the library, trying to figure out the rest of the budget for the dance. "Are you okay?"

I pull myself out of my endless maze of thought—Trip and I were going to be alone, his truck was at my house, why was he trying to wake me up? Or was that because Blake was trying to wake me up? "Yeah, just a second, it's here somewhere."

"You look pale." Blake touches my arm. "You aren't going to pass out again, are you?"

Andrew looks up, alarmed.

I give Blake a dirty look and flip through my notebook. A piece of paper with red writing on it makes me stop.

I'm watching you.

I try to shove the note back between the pages, but Andrew has already seen it. "What is that?" His real voice is hoarse and breathless.

"Nothing. Just a scrap of paper." I flip the notebook's cover closed.

"Please." Andrew's communicator voice is even and electronic, but the hurt look in his eyes stops me.

Blake glances between Andrew and me. "What is it?"

Andrew stares hard at my notebook.

Blake holds out his hand. "Let me see it." Something about the worry I see in both of them, or maybe just my own exhaustion from bearing the weight of all my secrets, gets to me. I open the notebook and hand him the paper.

His forehead wrinkles and his hair drifts into his eyes as he studies the note. "Is this the first time you've gotten a note like this?"

I say, "Yes."

Andrew says, "No."

"How many?" Blake asks, but he's looking at Andrew.

I let it out with a breath. "This is the fourth one."

"Were they all like this?" He turns the note over and fingers the edges.

Andrew reaches for it. Blake holds it out for him to see. After studying it, Andrew types furiously. "Cut out of a card."

"You're right," Blake says. "It looks like it was cut out of something else. Maybe with a razor blade?"

It's surreal, the two of them playing detective, figuring something out for me.

"Do you have the other ones?" Blake asks.

I open up my backpack and pull out the other notes from the pocket in the side. Except for the one I sent over the cliff, I kept them. I'm not sure why, as evidence or something.

"It's Trip's handwriting." I swallow hard. "I'd know it anywhere."

They examine them one by one. Pointing out things I hadn't noticed before. The notes all look like they were cut out from a bigger piece of paper. The words were written first in black or blue ink and then traced over with red marker. One was cut out just around the words and glued on to another piece of paper. Why didn't I look at them closer?

"Let's see. Who would have a bunch of notes with Trip's handwriting on them?" Blake scratches his head for emphasis.

I'm thinking Mr. Phillips, or maybe Trip's mom, but Andrew comes up with a different answer. "Hannah."

"Hannah?" I gasp and then feel stupid. Of course Hannah. I remember the box I threw into the ocean. Every card, every flower, every scrap of paper Trip ever gave me. I saved them all. Hannah must have done the same thing.

Blake shakes his head. "That twisted little b—"

"—you have to tell someone," Andrew says.

"I can't." I look down at my hands. The tigereye appeared there almost without me knowing it. "I mean, it's not worth it." Not worth bringing the accident back into the forefront of everyone's minds. "Now that I know where the notes are coming from, I can just ignore them, right?"

"You should tell," Andrew insists.

"No, Allie's right. It's not worth it. Telling the principal something like this would just bring up a bunch of trouble for her. We can take care of Hannah George." Blake's face is hard and angry, like when he got back from Reno. His expression scares me. I glance at his pocket, wondering if he has the knife on him now.

"No. Just forget it. She's looking for attention or whatever. We don't have to give it to her." I try to force a laugh, like all of this is a big joke.

"I still say we should—" Andrew looks from Blake to me, but I know he won't tell if we decide not to.

"Allie's right. It's better to forget it." Blake crumples up the notes, walks to the corner of the room, and pushes them deep in the garbage can. The bell rings and Blake gathers up his books. "See you after school, Allie." His voice is forced casual.

Andrew glances at the garbage can with its buried evidence and then gives me a long look before he leaves the library.

"You have to tell someone."

I close my eyes and know I've heard him say that before.

Chapter 26

"Do you think your grandma will need me after Christmas is over?" The thought has been nibbling at me so long that I break the usual comfortable silence between Blake and me.

He looks over at me from his canvas and rolls his paintbrush between his fingers. "I don't know. I hope so."

Blake's attic has become my refuge. It's the only place I can get away from the behind-the-back whispers at school and the backward glances I get whenever I go into town. And here I don't have to deal with the betrayed/hurt/concerned looks I get from Mom, or Dad's subtle attempts to get me to remember something about the accident: "Do you remember who was with you at the dance?" "Do you remember getting in Trip's truck?"

It's the only place I can pretend that the last two years never happened, that I don't have to see the looks James gives me when I walk down the hall, or the pictures of Trip smiling from the trophy case.

I love everything about the attic: the sound of the ocean or the rain on the roof: the smells of flowers and nuts and fruit from the lotions and candles I make; the view through the window; and my quiet, comfortable alone time with Blake.

I like to watch him—lost in his art. His face contorts in concentration, not like what he's doing is hard but like he's focusing on something he loves. I memorize the way the light plays across his face, the way his forehead furrows, the way he bites his bottom lip when he's thinking hard, the scratch of his pencil or the quiet of his brushstrokes.

"If Grandma doesn't need you, there'll still be dance stuff to do," Blake says.

"Yeah, for a few weeks." I strain to reach a jar on the top shelf. He walks over and pulls it down for me. "Thanks," I say. I'm not sure when he got so much taller than me.

He goes back to work, but I catch him looking at me, a lot. And he keeps dropping stuff. I'm worried that he's thinking about the notes in my locker and how to get back at Hannah, but he doesn't say anything.

He's quiet until he takes me home. Then he starts talking fast. "I'm leaving tomorrow morning to spend Christmas break with Phoebe. She's doing really good, been working, local commercials and stuff." He takes a breath and starts up again. "She's dating this guy who produced one of her commercials. He has a condo at Lake Tahoe and we're spending Christmas there. She likes him a lot. I think she's hoping I like him and he likes me."

Blake drums his fingers on the steering wheel as he drives.

I can tell he's nervous about going to meet his mom's new boyfriend. I should say something that would help, something like, "Of course he'll think you're great. Who wouldn't?" But I don't say anything.

He grips the steering wheel. "I want you to come with me. Mom said I could bring a friend for a few days. I would pay to fly you down. Like the day after Christmas so you could still be with your family."

I'm already shaking my head, but he keeps going. "I could teach you how to snowboard—I mean, I've only been once, but we could learn together. It would be great, I mean fun, if you were there." Blake clears his throat. "Nothing weird, just as friends."

I shake my head harder, and my scar starts to hurt. "Me, snowboarding?" I force a laugh, trying to keep it light. "Now that is a truly horrible idea. I'd probably break my leg just trying on the boots. I'll never even make it to the mountain, and if I did, I would totally humiliate you."

Blake stops at the one red light in town and looks at me seriously. "What happened to you, Al? When we were kids you weren't afraid of anything. Now you're like, I don't know, scared to try."

I'm half-hurt and half-offended, but I know he's right. I try to cover it with a joke. "Maybe I've finally figured out that I'm a hazard to myself and others."

Blake turns back to the road. "And you're always putting yourself down. I hate that."

I tuck my hand into my pocket and cup the tigereye. "I've always been a klutz. You know that. Remember when I tripped on the cliff and almost went over the edge? Or when I slid down the sand dunes on my face? It's kind of a miracle I made it to eighteen."

"I did that kind of stuff, too, lots of times. You aren't any clumsier than I am." He pulls into my driveway and looks at me, his green eyes pleading. "Please come with me. It would take a lot of pressure off me if you were there. Mom really likes you."

I've met Blake's mom twice. Both times I got the impression that she was too out of it to register who I was, but I'm not going to tell him that. "I can't. Even if I wanted to." I know it stings him when I say that—I mean it to. "There's no way my parents would let me go."

"You went with Trip's family last summer when they went to Florida," Blake points out.

I shiver at that memory and grip the stone in my pocket. "That was different. Dad wasn't around and . . ."

"And it was Trip." Blake hits the side of the steering wheel, not hard, just enough so I can see his frustration.

I hate that he's right about that. Mom would freak if she knew I was in Blake's car now. Going away for the weekend with him would be impossible. I open my door quickly. "Thanks for the ride. Have fun in—"

"Wait." Blake reaches behind his seat. "Since I won't see you over Christmas, I'll give you this now." He pushes a flat, rectangle-shaped package into my hands. It's wrapped in white plastic.

I look down at it. "Do you want me to open it now?"

"Yeah." He leans back, then rubs his neck. "I mean, if you want to."

"Okay." I slide my fingers under the plastic and realize they're shaking.

Blake is watching me. "It's really not much. I just—"

"Oh," I gasp as soon as the cover is off. It's a painting—three kids, a girl and two boys, digging a moat around a sand castle with the ocean in the background. It's muted and shadowed with blues and grays, like all of Blake's paintings. Even the sand castle is gray, the way a sand castle on our beach would be, and not the sunny yellow that picture-book sand castles are. The bright spot in this picture is the long braid of yellow down the back of the little girl's head. I slide my finger over it.

"It's us," Blake says.

"I know," I breathe. The painting makes me happy and sad at the same time—something about seeing myself painted that way, young and innocent, before . . . before everything.

Blake is looking at my face while I trace my finger over the swirls that the paint makes on the canvas. "Do you like it?"

"I love it," I say, and feel tears pricking the corners of my eyes. I have to bite the inside of my mouth to keep them from slipping out.

He leans over, and I can feel his breath on the back of my neck. "I tried to do Andrew's chair, but I couldn't make it work. It just didn't seem right."

"It's perfect." I trace Andrew's face. "Just the way it is."

Blake's face splits into a grin. "It was really hard to keep this hidden from you. You've been at my house so much lately, not that I'm complaining, but I really wanted to surprise you."

"It's the nicest present I've ever gotten." As soon as the words are out of my mouth I know how cheesy that sounds, but I also know it's true.

Blake gets red and looks at his hands. "It's nothing, not like the stuff Trip used to—" He covers his slip with a cough.

I clutch the painting to my chest and avoid looking at Blake. I think about the stupid sign I bought him. It seems so cheap after what he just gave me. "I don't have anything for you. I'm sorry." I don't think he knows how sorry I am. Not just sorry that I don't have a present for him. Sorry for the way I've treated him for the last two years. Sorry that I can't even tell my mom that I've been hanging out with him. Sorry that I don't have anything to offer him that's worth having.

"It's okay," he says. "I'm just glad you like the painting."

"I'd better go in." I slide my legs around and out of the car.

"Yeah, I need to pack." Blake reaches over and gathers up the plastic sheet that I left on the seat in the car.

"Have fun in Tahoe. Don't break anything important. We need you to finish the paintings for the dance." I try for the joke, but I can hear the loneliness in my voice. Two weeks without Blake suddenly seems like a long time.

"I'll miss you, Al," Blake says. He leans toward me but stops short of touching me.

I slide off the seat and stand up. "Yeah, you, too. Good-bye." It sounds abrupt, but I have to get inside before I start to cry.

Mom meets me at the door. Dad must have her car, because I didn't see it in the driveway. "When were you going to tell me?" she demands before I even get inside. "Or better yet, when were you going to ask me?"

"Ask you?" I stammer.

"Ask me if you could spend every day after school alone with Blake at his house." She raises her voice. "I went into Joyce's shop today looking for you. She said you've been working at her house this whole time. You let us believe you were working at her shop."

I clutch Blake's painting against my chest. "I'm eighteen," I mutter, and try to go around her.

"You still live here." She moves so I can't get around her. "You still have to listen to me."

"Why?" I turn to face her, defiant. "You've never listened to me."

She steps back. "Allie, I've done the best I can with what—"

"With what you were given?" I finish for her. "With the clumsy, stupid, not-perfect daughter you got?"

"I didn't say that. Stop trying to make me into the bad guy." She crosses her arms. "I'm trying to help you. I don't think you understand how much you're judged by who you hang around with. I want to make su—"

"You don't have a clue, do you?" Frustration, anger, pain all comes out. "You don't even know that I've never had any friends. Not here, not anywhere. No one but Blake, and you want to take him away, too."

"Allie, you're overreacting." Mom sighs like she's trying to be patient with me. "You have a lot of friends. People who care about you. You just have to stop pushing them away."

"Acceptable people, right, Mom? People like Trip?" The words are out of my mouth before I can stop them.

Mom's face washes with fear. She breathes in and speaks quietly. "What about Trip?"

I said too much. "Trip is dead, Mom. He isn't coming back, no matter how much you want him to." I flee for my room.

I throw myself on my bed and let my anger build toward

Mom, remembering how close I came to breaking up with Trip for good.

Mom stands at the door to my room, her hand on her hip. "Trip's here. He's waiting in the living room for you."

"I told you I don't want to see him."

She comes in, sits on my bed, and brushes her fingers through my hair. "He's sent roses for the last three days. Called I don't know how many times. Texted you day and night. And I think he has something for you now. Don't you think he deserves another chance?"

I press my hand against the bandage on my arm hidden under my sweatshirt. Would she still say that if I showed her what he did to me?

"At least talk to him. Mr. Phillips said he's never seen Trip so upset. What happened between you two, anyway?"

I slide my fingers under the cuff of my sweatshirt and take a breath, trying to decide how much or what I can tell her. "Mom, I—"

"I know whatever you guys fought about seems like a big deal now, but think about what you're giving up. Trip's a great guy and his family is really important here." Her eyes are pleading with me. I know how much she likes Trip, and how great she thinks it is that I'm dating the son of the richest man in her hometown. "Things are going good for us here, with my job and with you and Trip."

She touches my arm, accidentally brushing the cut, but she doesn't notice when I flinch. "I'd hate for you to let a little argument mess that up. At least talk to him."

I tug the sleeve of my sweatshirt back toward my wrist. "Okay, Mom, I'll talk to him."

Chapter 27

Christmas is quiet and strained. I get a new cell phone and luggage, a message somewhere between "stay in touch" and "it's time to go." Mom and I pretend everything is normal, but there's a wall between us. Not because of what we said to each other. More because of what I can't say. Still, it's better than last year when I was walking a tightrope between being with Trip and being home. Dad was with us for almost the whole winter break, so he thought I should be with my family. Trip thought I should be with him. Being around Dad made Trip nervous. I don't think Dad trusted Trip. Maybe he saw something that no one else did. It didn't matter. After winter break Dad was back to Fort Lewis, finishing up the six months before he retired. Even though he was only a few hours away, it was like he hadn't really come home.

The day after Christmas, Mom and Dad go back to work. I'm going stir-crazy, so I head to Andrew's room looking for something to do. At the door I stop, because I hear a voice, a girl's voice. Andrew with a girl in his room? No way. He must be playing with his communicator again. But as I lean my ear against the door to listen, she laughs, very unelectronic.

After a couple of minutes of eavesdropping, I decide that the girl isn't in Andrew's room, but that it's someone talking to him over the computer. Then Andrew says, "Caitlyn."

I back away from the door. Caitlyn? Now I recognize the laugh. He's still chatting with her? He laughs, one of his infectious little-boy giggles. He really likes her. He sounds so happy that it makes my heart ache worse. Jealousy, selfishness, all the horrible blackness inside of me, churns like inky dark water below the cliff. It should make me happy to hear him happy. But it doesn't. It just makes the hole inside my chest bigger. Maybe for the first time, I'm jealous because Andrew can do something that I can't, because he's free to be with the person he wants to be with, and I'm not.

But if everyone could forget . . . if I could forget. I wander back to my room and look at the painting Blake gave me. I paid Dad back and bought presents for my family with the money I earned working for Grandma Joyce, but I haven't gotten anything nice for Blake.

I let myself get excited about shopping for him. I know what kind of art supplies he uses. Or I could get something for his El Camino. Or a new jacket, something nice. I gather up all the jewelry that Trip gave me and look up pieces of jewelry that are similar on the Internet and write down the price, so I'll know what's fair. I yell to Andrew that I'm going shopping. Then I take the van to the pawnshop in Hoquiam.

Paul is the only one here this time. I spread out the jewelry in front of him: a gold bracelet to make up for the time Trip gave me a black eye and I had to hide in my bedroom for a week with the "flu" so Mom wouldn't see; the silver and jade necklace for the "T" on my arm; an expensive watch, just because I was always late; and a heart-shaped silver pendant, the first gift Trip ever gave me.

Paul whistles through his teeth. "So you didn't like any of your Christmas presents? You are the highest-maintenance girl I've ever seen. Glad you aren't my girlfriend."

I smile at his joke, but I can feel my heart crumbling. Laid out before me is everything I have left of my relationship with Trip. I convinced myself that I was ready to move on. I should be happy to see it go, but it still makes my heart ache a little.

"How much do you want?"

The haggling takes longer this time. He wants everything in one big chunk, but I make him give me the price piece by piece. Each time we decide on a price, I feel like I'm sacrificing a piece of my heart. Finally all that's left is the heart-shaped necklace.

"Trip, this is a surprise," Mom says from the doorway.

I go to see, because I can't quite believe it—Trip Phillips, here at my grandma's house.

"I came to see Allie." He smiles at me standing behind Mom.

Mom moves out of his way. "Won't you come in and have some cake. We're celebrating the twins' birthday."

Trip follows her in. "I know, that's why I came."

I'm embarrassed to have him see my grandma's little house and our pitiful little birthday party—just me, Mom, Andrew, my grandma, and Grandma Joyce. I feel guilty for thinking it, but now I'm glad Blake's in Nevada.

"I can't stay very long." He produces a little white box from his pocket. "Just long enough to give Allie this."

Mom has to nudge me forward to get me to take it. I open it with trembling fingers. Inside is a sterling silver, heart-shaped pendant. I have to take a breath before I talk. "It's beautiful." Mom and Grandma crowd to see. Grandma Joyce doesn't move.

Trip takes the necklace from me. "Let me help you." He slips it around my neck.

"Thanks."

"I'm glad you like it." Trip sets an envelope on Andrew's lap. "These are tickets for the Mariners game tomorrow night. I was hoping Andrew and Allie would come with me."

I pick up the necklace and remember how I felt the first time Trip slipped it around my neck and the fluttery, butterfly excitement mingled with disbelief that Trip Phillips was actually interested in me.

"Thirty-five is my final offer for this one." Paul's voice brings me out of my trance.

It's worth more than that. I know it is, but I'm suddenly very tired. I lay it back down on the counter. "Okay."

Paul counts out my money. I start to leave, but he stops me. "I wasn't sure if I should tell you this." He rubs his chin. "I don't want to scare you, but I guess you have a right to know. A guy came into the shop a little bit after you left last time. He wanted to know what you were selling."

The tiny box that's the space I can breathe in closes tighter around my chest. I thought I was just being paranoid, but maybe someone is following me. Detective Weeks? "Was he a cop?" I ask before I think to stop myself.

Paul looks at the stuff I just sold. I'm waiting for him to ask if it was stolen, but instead he shakes his head. "Not a cop, at least he didn't show me any credentials, and I can usually pick them out even if they don't. He was pretty young."

I reach into my pocket and rub the tigereye. "What did you say to him?"

"I didn't think it was any of his business, so I didn't tell him anything. He got mad and stormed out of the shop." Paul rubs his chin. "The way he talked I was kind of wondering if he was your ex-boyfriend."

"That's not possible." It comes out breathless. My heart pounds against my chest.

"Are you sure?" He leans forward.

Rain pouring over the windshield. Flashes of lightning. His hands, white-knuckle grip on the steering wheel. The engine roars, moving us faster and faster toward the cliff. As we round the corner, he turns, his eyes meet mine. Shock, then terror. The door behind me flies open and I'm falling.

Free.

"I'm sure."

Somehow I take the money from him. Somehow I make it back out to the van before I completely fall apart. I open the door, cross my arms over the steering wheel, and sob and sob. The image of Trip's eyes, the last time he looked at me, the last time he looked at anyone, is burned into my brain. He looked at me like he was afraid of me, like he was looking at a ghost.

All this time, I've wondered what happened that night, how I got hurt, how Trip ended up going over the edge. Now every heartbeat pulses one question.

What did I do?

Chapter 28

"Allie, you look beautiful." Dad smiles from the doorway to my room. He's wearing a suit that must be new. I don't think I've ever seen him dressed up in anything but his army dress blues.

I look in the mirror and turn my head so I see only the side of my face without the scar. From this angle, I look almost normal. I turn the other direction. The image of the younger me from Blake's painting, hanging on the wall behind me, provides a sharp contrast to my reflection in the mirror. The little girl in the painting is beautiful, innocent, and unmarked. I'm hideous, guilt-stricken, and scarred.

"Are you ready to go?"

I want to scream, "No!" I want to tell him that I will never be ready. That I don't want to go. Instead, I answer, "Almost."

Every New Year's Eve, Mr. and Mrs. Phillips throw a huge party at the inn. The whole town is invited. My stomach ties in knots, and my scar pulses every time I think about it. The last place I want to be is at the inn. The last person I want to see is Mr. Phillips. But Mom bought me a new outfit, a red beaded top and a black skirt. And Dad's all about me getting out of the house. And it might look bad if I didn't go.

"Let me help you with your hair." Mom slips past Dad and picks up my brush. Her shimmery blue dress reminds me of Trip's eyes. I look away. Everything reminds me of Trip's eyes.

Since the day at the pawnshop, his eyes have haunted me. I've spent a lot of time thinking about what I remembered—nothing I didn't know before. I was with Trip in the truck heading toward the cliff. Somehow I made it out before he went over the edge. But how? And why was he looking at me that way, like he was afraid of me?

Mom brushes my hair up on top of my head. She struggles to hide my scar and the places on my scalp that are still thin from the shaved-off strip. She secures it with a rhinestone clip and covers me in a cloud of hairspray so thick that if I smiled, the expression might actually stay frozen on my face for the whole evening. Then she steps back and evaluates me in the mirror. "I have some makeup that will cover the smudges under your eyes and maybe lighten up your scar, and a hairpiece that you could wear on top to make it look like you have more hair."

Through the mirror I see Dad checking his watch. Mom smiles at him patiently. "It will only take a second. Beauty takes time, dear, you know that."

I glance at the picture behind me. I don't think there's enough time in the world to make me beautiful again.

By the time she's finished, my face feels like plastic. Mom coated so much makeup over my scar that it feels like if I smile or laugh my face will crack.

"Perfect." She steps back from the mirror. I hazard a glance. I look like some twisted, made-up zombie, not real, not really alive. I guess the look fits the way I feel right now.

. . . . — — — . . . .

The ballroom at the inn is draped in swoops of red, green, and gold. Boughs of pine and holly cover the walls. Mom smiles and nods and accepts compliments on her choice of décor as we make our way through the crowd. Dad tugs at his collar and shakes hands. Andrew looks nervous. His whole body is trembling and he keeps scanning the room, like he's looking for someone. I keep my head down and pretend not to hear the whispers that follow me.

Mom and Dad keep moving through the crowd. I find a corner to stop and look around the room. The tables are set up the way they were the night of the cotillion. I can almost pick out the one where we sat while Trip watched Hannah walk in. I close my eyes and try to remember.

"We're not going to the party. We want to be alone."

". . . alone?" I open my eyes and realize the woman standing in front of me is talking to me. She works at the post office and went to school with my mom, but her name slips into the cracks of my memory.

"What?" I don't mean it to sound abrupt, but it does.

She smiles sweetly. "I asked if you came alone."

"No." I look for my family, but they've deserted me.

"Oh." She peers around like she's searching for my companion. "Where's your date?"

I get what she's fishing for. I want to tell her that Blake isn't here, that he's snowboarding in California. I want to tell her that I'll be joining him there, even though I won't be, but I force a smile and say, "No date. I came with my family."

"Oh." She looks disappointed. "Well, you look—" She stops. Her eyes widen as her gaze travels over my shoulder. "Who is that with your brother?"

I turn around. Caitlyn is in the middle of the dance floor, sitting on Andrew's lap, running her fingers through his hair. Her outfit is even more colorful than it was the first time I saw her—a sequined green miniskirt, purple leggings, and a purple sweater covered in silver bows that match the one in her brilliant red hair.

All eyes are on them. I pick out Mom from across the room, horrified. Dad looks somewhere between shocked and amused. Other expressions vary from pity to disapproval to nods of acceptance. For once, no one is looking at me. I suddenly like Caitlyn a lot more.

"Her name is Caitlyn," I answer, but don't think the woman is listening to me.

I take the opportunity to back toward the door. I'm about ready to break for the bathroom, thinking I could spend the whole evening hiding there, when I hear a terrifying sound. "Allie." Mr. Phillips isn't yelling like he was at the police station, but his voice makes my blood go cold. "I was hoping you would be here."

I look up and see Mr. Phillips and his wife, always within

arm's reach. Mrs. Phillips is wearing a fluffy white fur coat and dangly silver earrings. I meet her eyes and have to turn away. They look just like Trip's.

"We had hoped to give this to you earlier." To my horror Mr. Phillips holds out a little box wrapped in gold paper and tied with a red satin bow. "But we've been away visiting relatives in Florida. As you can understand, Christmas at home would have been unbearable this year."

I try to keep my gaze on the box, but my eyes drift to Mrs. Phillips's eyes, now brimming with tears. I shake my head. "You didn't need to—"

"Oh, but we wanted to." He presses the box firmly into my hands. "We wanted you to know how much you still mean to our family."

While they watch I untie the bow and slide the lid off the box. Inside is a pair of earrings. Diamond earrings. I swallow hard.

"They're real diamonds. Please try to be careful with them. I'd hate for them to get lost," Mr. Phillips says pointedly.

I try to force "Thank you" from between my lips, but it comes out more of a hoarse whisper. I try again. "Thank you." I back toward the door to the restroom. "I was just—"

"Of course." Mr. Phillips smiles, but his eyes stay hard. "We'll see you later. Enjoy the party."

I push through the restroom door, breathing hard, looking for a refuge, but Hannah's voice from around the corner stops me. "—the most hideous outfit I have ever seen. I can't believe she would even show her face here at all."

I back out again, flee for the hallway, find a dark corner, and sink onto a red velvet bench, still clutching the little box in my hands. They could have been any diamond earrings, but they're not. They're the ones I pawned two months ago. If Mr. Phillips knows about the gifts I pawned, what else does he know? What else does he think he knows?

Chapter 29

"There you are." Mom's voice starts out sharp, but then it softens. "Why are you hiding out here?"

"I have a headache." I lean my head against the cool window, but it doesn't help the throbbing in my scar. "Could I please just go home?"

She sits down on the bench beside me. "Okay, maybe it wasn't fair of us to bring you here. I'll go tell Dad I'm taking you home."

She comes back in a couple of minutes. We get our coats and I follow her out to the van. The wind and rain have picked up, like the night of the accident. All the way home I keep my face against the cold window, watching the rain slide down the glass, remembering the way it covered the windshield of Trip's truck.

"Are you sure you'll be okay alone?" Mom asks as she pulls into the driveway. "I could stay if you want."

"No." I manage a weak smile. "Dad would never forgive either of us if you left him at the party alone."

"Yeah." She laughs. "Parties really aren't Dad's thing." I start to get out, but she stops me. "What do you know about the girl Andrew was with?"

I shrug. "Her name is Caitlyn. He met her when we went to Hoquiam. I think he's been chatting online with her ever since."

"She's a little . . ." Mom hesitates.

"Weird," I supply.

Mom shakes her head and smiles. "Yeah. That might fit." She leans over and brushes a piece of hair back over my ear. "I guess I never thought we'd have to worry about girls with Andrew, but here she is. I wish I knew if this is a good thing for him or not."

"I do, too," I admit. Seeing her concern for Andrew makes me wonder what would have happened if I had told her everything about Trip. Maybe I should have.

She sits back in her seat and sighs. "I'd better get back so I don't miss the big countdown. Are you sure you'll be okay?"

"I'm fine. I'm just going to go to bed."

"Okay. Make sure you keep the door locked."

I try to laugh off her concern. "It's Pacific Cliffs, Mom. What could possibly happen?" But as soon as I get in the house, I twist the deadbolt and check the back door to make sure it's locked.

I take a long shower to wash out the hairspray and the thick layer of makeup from my face. I put on my pajamas and go to bed, but I can't sleep. Everywhere I look I see Trip's eyes, watching me. The house feels too quiet. I go into the living room, turn on the TV and curl up on the couch. My lack of sleep catches up to me and I doze off to the sound of the "New Year's at the Needle" celebration in Seattle.

My head jerks up and my senses are immediately alert. I know that I heard something outside before I'm even fully awake. I listen, but the only sound is the TV, the rain splattering against the side of the house, and the wind howling like a chorus of lost souls. My scar prickles and I reach for the stone, but I left it on the dresser in my bedroom when I got ready for bed.

Then I hear it again, a bump on the front porch. The hair on the back of my neck and around my scar stands on end. A squirrel or a raccoon, I reason with myself, or Sasha wanting to come in out of the rain. But my tiger-striped cat dozes on the other chair—a sleepy purr vibrating out of her throat.

The rumble of an old pickup, like Trip's, roars down the street. Headlights pass in front of my house—slow. I sink deeper into the couch so I won't be seen through the window and wish for my tigereye. The headlights pass again, slower. I can't stop thinking of the guy at the pawnshop, the earrings—that Mr. Phillips knows I sold Trip's gifts, the locker notes, the accident, how incredibly messed up my life is.

I should go check out the noise, reassure myself that it's nothing, but I can't make myself move. I strain my ears again—silence. I reach for the remote to turn the TV up so it will drown out any other sounds. The reporter, wearing a long blue rain jacket and a wilted paper crown, asks the crowd outside the Space Needle about their New Year's resolutions. New Year's resolutions—last year it was "ten minutes early for everything, get straight As, and—"

I gasp as the flash of a face appears at the front window. I curl my fingers around my quilt and reach for my cell phone. Then there's a tap on the door and a voice whisper-yells, "Allie."

I stay still for a second, my heart thumping, every nerve in my body on edge.

"Allie." This time his voice is loud enough that I recognize it. I jump off the couch and hurry to open the door.

He's drenched, weather-beaten, and almost unrecognizable. He's not even wearing a jacket, just a black T-shirt that clings to his chest. I step aside to let him in, but he leans against me, wraps his arms around my neck, and starts to sob.

"Blake." I hold his wet and trembling body close to mine. "What happened?"

He keeps sobbing. There's something embarrassing about a guy crying. Especially when it goes on for a long time and you don't have any idea why he's so upset. I'm not sure what to do.

I pat his back as the wet from his clothes soaks into me. I move with him to the couch. When he sits down, I pull away and wrap him in Grandma's quilt. He keeps shivering and saying that he's sorry, but other than that he's not making any sense. I'm almost to the point of calling my parents or maybe even a doctor when he finally starts to calm down.

"Allie, I'm sorry." He wipes his face with the quilt.

"You already said that." I'm not sure what else to do so I stand up. "I can get you something warm to drink."

He nods and wraps the quilt tighter around himself. I heat a cup of water in the microwave and mix in hot cocoa. When I bring it back to Blake, his teeth are chattering so loudly that they almost drown out the "nine . . . eight . . . seven . . . six—" I click the TV off with the remote before the countdown hits "Happy New Year" and sit down beside him. "You want to talk about it?"

He sips the cocoa and stares across the room. With his hair

wet and plastered to his forehead, the lost look on his face, and the little bit of cocoa at the corner of his mouth, he looks like a kid. I feel like a mom trying to protect her little boy. I'm cold, too, because of the wet that soaked into my clothes from his, but I don't dare crawl under the quilt with him.

Finally he sets the mug down. "I'm sorry, Allie."

"We already covered that part, Blake. But what do you have to be sorry for? What happened?" My mind is racing in a direction I can't go—cliffs, accidents, red dresses.

He sighs a quavering, after-tears sigh, and stares at the chair where Sasha is still sleeping undisturbed. "My mom."

I relax a little and wait for more.

"Phoebe." He shakes his head. "Things were going so well this time. She was clean for at least ten months. She was happy. She was working. And Greg, her new boyfriend was—is—actually a decent guy."

He breathes in. "The vacation was fun. Snowboarding was excellent, and his condo was so cool. I wish you could have—" He trails off. "Everything was good until two days ago. I went out boarding, and when I came back they were fighting, screaming at each other. He accused her of taking some money from his wallet. I wanted to believe that he was lying, that my mom wouldn't—" Blake swallows. "But I could see the way her hands were shaking, and the red around her eyes, and I knew. It had been almost a year."

I'm rubbing Blake's shoulder, trying to keep him warm, or offer some comfort.

"He threw her out. He said I could stay, that he would put me on a plane home the next morning. But I couldn't let her be alone, and I was too pissed off at Greg to use a plane ticket he bought—stupid, I know. I took two hundred dollars with me. Grandma told me not to tell Mom I had it." He swallows. "I didn't, but most of it was gone."

I squeeze his shoulder; my heart is aching to take away his pain. "I couldn't call Grandma for more money. I couldn't let her know Mom had . . .

"Greg called us a cab, but by the time we got to the bus station, we had missed the last bus, so we had to sleep there. It was cold and the benches were hard and metal. There were these creepy guys hanging around, saying things to Mom and staring at her, but she slept like it was no big deal. The next morning she barely talked to me at all—just asked if there was enough money left for her to get some coffee.

"My car was at her apartment, and by the time we got there I was so mad that I just left. Left her standing there like some kind of stray dog—her hair all over the place and makeup smeared across her cheeks. I didn't even make sure she got back into her apartment." He buries his face in his hands.

"Blake, I—" but there isn't anything for me to say, no words—nothing that will help him.

He runs his fingers through his hair, exhausted. "My car broke down so I had to walk the rest of the way here." He stands up. "I'm sorry. I shouldn't be dumping this on you. I'll go."

I reach for his hand. "No, stay." The pain in his eyes seeps into my chest—rain on my ocean. "Please." I stand up. "You need some dry clothes. I'll go find something."

I find a pair of sweatpants and a T-shirt in my dad's drawers. Briefly I consider underwear, but that would be way weird.

He'll drown in Dad's clothes, but at least they're dry. Blake goes into the bathroom to change. I wait until he's out before I change in my bedroom. I take a long time because I'm trying to process all of this—Blake, here, his mom, and me.

When I come out, Blake is sitting on a towel on the couch and staring at nothing. He looks so lost and hurt that I want to put my arms around him and hold him until he smiles again. But I can't bring myself to get that close to him. Instead I get a pillow and a dry blanket from the linen closet.

"I think you should stay here tonight." I hand him the pillow. "It's late and I don't want to drive you home in this mess. Is Grandma Joyce home yet?"

He wraps his arms around the pillow. "Tomorrow night." He starts to stand. "I don't have to stay. I can just—"

"Sit down," I say. "We covered the 'sorry' part. You've been through a lot. You're allowed to freak out." I'm using the same words he used on me in the cave—trying to get him to smile—but mostly so he remembers how much I owe him.

"Allie, I can't—"

"Sit," I say, and to reinforce that this is a command, not a request, I push against him.

He sits down fast and I end up on his lap. He pulls me against his chest and buries his head in my neck. "Thanks for being here."

My face is burning when I pull away. I scoot to the edge of the couch and curl my legs underneath me. Then I pick up the pillow and motion for Blake to lie down on my lap. After he does, I tuck the blanket around his shoulders.

Emotion and exhaustion overcome him. In a couple of minutes

his deep, even breathing mixes with Sasha's snoring. Stupid cat slept through everything.

I can't relax with Blake's head on my lap. I have this freaked-out, guilty feeling. Like I'm in trouble. Like someone is going to catch us together.

"No one will ever love you the way I do."

I'll never forget the look on Blake's face the first time I saw him after he had spent eight months in Reno and nearly three in juvie. I was kissing Trip. I think Trip made sure that was the first thing Blake saw. The message came through loud and clear. I'd given up on him, the way everyone else in Pacific Cliffs had. I hadn't tried to write him, or call, or anything while he was gone. Instead I had hooked up with Trip. I'd been with him for almost the whole time Blake was gone.

He didn't say anything to me for nearly three months. When we passed in the hall at school his face was blank, like I wasn't even there. Then one day he caught me alone at school when I was on my way to the bathroom during class.

"I don't like the way he treats you," he blurted out, something he had been holding on his tongue for a long time.

"What?" My heart started pounding. How could he know anything?

"I said, I don't like how Trip treats you." This time every word was clipped and precise, bitten off with anger.

I ducked my head and tried to push past him. "It's none of your business, Blake."

He put his hand on my shoulder and stopped me. When I looked into his eyes, I could see concern, and pain, and frustration there. It made me want to dissolve in his arms and tell him everything. Instead I pulled away and kept walking.

"Allie," he called after me. "Don't—" That was as far as he got before Trip grabbed him from behind. That happened a lot with Trip. He'd just appear when I thought I was alone—like he was always watching me.

Trip put Blake in a headlock, choking him until Blake was coughing. "Were you touching my girlfriend?"

"Stop it!" I screamed.

Trip's eyes rested on me for a second—cold and angry. He threw Blake against a metal garbage can. Blake hit the edge so hard it sliced into his forehead. By the time a teacher came to break it up, Blake was bleeding all over the floor.

Trip told the principal that Blake had been harassing me in the hall, and I backed him up. Half the school had heard me scream, "Stop it!" Trip said that he was trying to get Blake away from me and that he tripped and fell against the garbage can. I agreed with Trip. Blake was suspended for four days. Trip got detention for three, but he only went once.

I push Blake's bangs back and I can see it, a faint pink line across his forehead—my fault—the scar he got trying to help me. I let him down then, too, let him take the blame for something that Trip did.

Sleeping like this, he looks so vulnerable.

"Stay away from him, Allie. Did you see how easy it was for me to hurt him? Next time I'll smash his head in."

I press my hand against my right eye and answer the voice.

"You can't hurt me anymore. You can't hurt him."

I wish I could believe it.

Chapter 30

"What the hell?" Dad says when he walks through the door and sees Blake sleeping with his head in my lap. "Is this why you wanted to leave the party?"

I slide out from under Blake carefully, so he doesn't wake up. "Shhh," I say when I reach the door. I explain what happened briefly and with as few details as possible.

"How could any mother do that?" Mom says.

I try to hush her up, but Blake's eyes flutter and he sits up. His hair is mashed on one side and standing straight up on the other. He blinks a couple of times like he's not sure where he is.

Dad walks over and sits on the couch beside him. "Where did you leave your car, son?"

Blake clears his throat and looks around for a minute like he's still disoriented. "Just before Taholah, underneath that big casino billboard."

Mom and I look at each other. That means Blake walked over ten miles in the storm.

"Why didn't you call someone?" Dad says.

"My phone's dead." Blake brushes his hand through his hair like he's embarrassed.

Dad goes into mechanic mode. "What kind of noise was your car making? What happened just before it quit? How old is the battery?"

Blake struggles to answer Dad's questions. I think of my conversation with Detective Weeks. It makes me feel better that he seems to know less about cars than I do.

Finally Dad lets it go. "You can stay here tonight. We'll see if we can figure out what's wrong with your car tomorrow." He stands up. "I think we all need to go to bed, including you, Allie."

. . . — — — . . .

After Mom and Dad go to bed, I sneak into Andrew's room. "We need to talk." I try to look stern. He goes for innocence, but his computer is on his lap and I'm sure he's chatting with Caitlyn. "Why didn't you tell me she was going to be there?"

"You were . . . you've been . . . ," he tries.

"Busy? Preoccupied?" I reach for his laptop, but he holds it away from me, so I ruffle his hair instead. "Never too busy for you, little bro." I sit on the bed. "So, you and Caitlyn?"

He blushes, ducks his head, and types, "So, you and Blake?"

I shake my head. "We're just friends."

Andrew raises his eyebrows. "You don't have to be just friends."

"I do." I trace the edges of his quilt. "It's complicated."

He shakes his head. "You worry too much about what people think. Blake needs you. You need him. You should be together."

I shake my head. "It's not that easy."

"Allie, Andrew, bed!" Dad's voice booms through the wall.

"I'd better go." I stand up, grateful to have a reason to stop talking about this. "We'll talk tomorrow, and I'm expecting details."

I'm almost to the door when Andrew says, "Allie." I turn around. "You don't owe him anything."

Outside Andrew's room I lean against the wall and close my eyes.

"I can't go, I . . . Dad'll be home tonight. I need to stay here."

"You owe me, Allie, for flaking on Christmas." He's in my face, his body trapping me against the wall.

"She doesn't owe you anything." Andrew's voice from the doorway to his room surprises me. I didn't know he was home.

Trip turns around. "What did you say, spaz?" He takes a step toward Andrew.

Andrew stands his ground, but his hand is shaking. "She . . . doesn't . . . owe you—"

"Forget it, okay? I'll come." I put my hand on Trip's shoulder, pulling him away from my brother. Trip clenches and unclenches his fists. Next to him, Andrew looks like a rag doll.

"Allie . . . don't. You don't have to—" Andrew's eyes plead with me.

"You stay out of this!" Trip yells.

I try to ignore the look Andrew gives me. I wrap my arm around Trip's waist. "Let's go."

On the way back to my room I take a detour and watch Blake sleeping. He's lying on his stomach with his arms stretched out under his head. His breath is deep and even. My heart bubbles into my throat just watching him.

I wonder how long until I'm allowed to be happy again.

Chapter 31

When we go back to school after winter break, things have changed between me and Blake. We're still just friends, but the barrier between us has disappeared. It might have started melting before, but now it's completely gone. Other people treat him differently, too. He takes charge in the dance committee meetings and everyone listens. There's a group of freshman girls, with Kasey at the head, that makes a point of talking to him after every meeting and every time they see him in the halls. I watch him laugh and joke with them and wonder if I missed my chance again.

I get another note in my locker.

You'll always be mine.

I try to shrug it off and not let it bother me—Hannah's pitiful attempt to get to me. But it feels too much like the truth.

. . . ▬ ▬ ▬ . . .

I'm not as alone as I was before. I spend every lunch with Blake and Andrew, working on dance committee stuff. Because of the committee, I find myself working with and talking to people who would never have talked to me before: major-attitude Marshall Yates, always perky Kasey, and even consistently oblivious Angie.

The only one I don't talk to is Randall. I can't look at him without remembering that he saw Trip hit me, and he didn't do anything to stop him. With Blake he's actually friendly, but he still won't look me in the eye.

A couple of weeks before the dance I end up with Angie at the beach, filling up bags with sand to act as weights for Blake's sail paintings. It's weird to be alone with her. Technically we have hung out, but only in the our-boyfriends-are-friends sort of way. I always thought she was an airhead, and when I was with Trip, I didn't really talk to anyone.

Dating Trip wasn't quite the social in at Pacific Cliffs that I thought it would be. He may have been the most popular guy at school, but he was good at keeping me isolated. The girls were loyal to Hannah because they had known her since forever, and no guy dared say a word to me with Trip around.

At first I thought it was cool: I was the center of his world and he was the center of mine, and I was flattered by his jealousy. But being the center of Trip's world was exhausting. I never knew what kind of mood he would be in or what would set him off. Things would be great for weeks and then I'd do something wrong and he'd lose it. I could never predict what it would be.

"Ugh! The guys should totally be doing this." Angie misses the bag and fills her shoe with sand for about the fourth time. She takes it off and shakes it. "This was their idea. 'Sand, ladies, it's free. What better way to anchor the sails?' " She puts her shoe back on. Her imitation of Blake makes me laugh, and then I feel guilty for it.

"You know guys." I tie up another bag and add it to our pile. "They're all about the building part—power tools, sharp objects—there has to be danger involved. Women always end up with the dirty work—dishes, laundry."

"Having babies, periods." She rolls her eyes. "At least this dance is girls' choice, so we don't have to do all the work and then sit around and wait for a guy to ask us."

"So you have a date?" I misjudge the distance to the bag and dump half a shovelful back on the ground.

"No," she sighs. "I can't decide who to ask."

"What happened between you and Randall?" I want to add "this time," but I resist the urge.

She shrugs. "I'm not sure anymore. We fight all the time when we're together. But when we're not"—she screws up her face and pushes her blond-red hair out of her face—"I kinda miss him."

"You make a cute couple." They do, even if they fight a lot. I never got Angie and Randall's relationship. They always have these big fights in public. Not like me and Trip. All of our fights were in private and usually one-sided.

"Do you think I should give him another chance?" Angie brushes the sand off her rolled-up jeans. "I mean, we are kind of great together."

"I don't know." I'm not up to giving relationship advice. It's bizarre that she would even ask me.

"No one's asked him to the dance yet." She stops filling bags and looks at me. "Are you going?"

I drop the bag I was trying to tie and the sand spills out. "No."

"No? Not with Blake?"

I shake my head and bend closer to refill the bag.

She looks out toward the cliff. "I guess if my boyfriend died I wouldn't go, either. Just kissing another guy would freak me out. I mean, what if Trip were a ghost or something? Would he come back and haunt you if you were with another guy? Especially a guy like Blake."

The look I give her, I hope, portrays that that is the stupidest thing I've ever heard. Even so, when the wind blows against my head and my hair ruffles around my scar, a cold chill runs down my back. Trip doesn't need to haunt me in person. His circle of influence stretches way beyond the grave.

She goes back to filling the bag. "Blake is kind of cute in that 'bad boy, rebel without a cause' sort of way. What do you think Randall would do if I—"

Someone yelling and a vehicle tearing across the sand stops her before she finishes her sentence.

"There's the guys," Angie says. For a second I think she said, "There's our guys."

Blake and Randall are driving toward us in Randall's pickup. Blake is in the back, hanging on to a frame made out of metal tubes. It looks like Randall is trying to shake him out.

"Hello, ladies." Randall slams his truck into park and jumps out almost before it comes to a complete stop. I'm afraid that Blake is going to be thrown out, but he's grinning as he jumps out behind Randall.

"We cut metal with fire." Randall beams like a little boy.

"Brilliant." Angie looks at me and rolls her eyes. "See?" I can't believe I'm sharing a private joke with her.

"So the good news is, you can stop all of this, because my friend Randall here"—Blake slaps Randall's back—"has engineered the frame so it won't tip over, even without weights."

"So we've been doing this for nothing." Angie throws her shovel down and glares at Randall. "We've been out here in the cold wind, with sand blowing in our faces, getting dirty, and busting our butts, so you guys could tell us 'never mind.'"

"I thought you'd be impressed." Randall drapes his arm across Angie's shoulders and makes a broad gesture toward the frame in the back of the truck. "Isn't it cool?"

She pulls away. "Like I said, brilliant. You couldn't have called when you figured out we didn't need to do this?"

"Maybe I don't have your phone number," Randall says.

"You used to have my phone number and it hasn't changed. In fact, you used to have me on speed dial and that picture of me on the front of your phone." She steps closer to Randall. "I wonder whose picture you have there now."

Randall claps his hand over his pocket, but Angie is too quick for him. She grabs his phone and takes off across the beach. He chases her, but she's pretty fast. It takes me this long to get that she's flirting.

Blake turns to me. "Sorry you had to do all this work for nothing. What do you think of the frame?"

I study the metal structure. "I thought we were going with wood because it was cheap."

"Yeah, but Randall's dad had a bunch of metal pipe that he said we could use. And it will be sturdier. And—"

"And you got to cut metal with fire."

"Yeah, that part was cool," Blake says.

"It looks kinda metallic and new." I look up quick, in case I insulted his work. "I'm sure it will look a lot better with your paintings hanging on it."

"We do need to age it a bit." Blake runs his hand across the frame. "With black paint or maybe brown. We can work on that this weekend." He drops his hand and says softly, "Just two weeks until the dance."

Dread creeps into my heart like fog. I don't want the dance to come, mostly because it means the end of my excuse to hang out with Blake. After New Year's Eve, Mom said it was okay if I kept working for Grandma Joyce, but she's had fewer orders lately, probably because the holidays are over.

"How's the last painting coming?" I say.

"Finished it. Last night. I was up until like two o'clock." He yawns.

"You finished the last one?" I feel like he left me out of something important. "I didn't even get to see it."

"I know," Blake says. "I want it to be a surprise, for the night of the dance."

I look away from him and toward the ocean and Angie and Randall. They seem to be patching up their relationship again, chasing each other in front of the waves, with the glow of the setting sun behind them—like something out of a movie. I turn back to Blake because the scene is so familiar that it hurts to watch. "I guess I'll see the last painting when we set up the day before."

Blake brushes his hand across his neck. "I was thinking about that." He clears his throat. "It would be stupid for us to do all this work and then not even go to the dance."

I look down and draw circles in the sand with my toe. "I'm surprised Kasey hasn't asked you yet. I heard she was going to."

"Actually, she did." He draws a circle next to mine with his shoe. "She put a big poster over my locker a couple of days ago."

Jealousy hits my chest—cold and sharp. I fight it. "Oh, I guess I missed that."

"You didn't see it because I took the poster down fast. I didn't want her to be too embarrassed when I said no."

My heart leaps. "Why did you say no? Kasey's really nice and cute and—"

"I told her I already had a date." Blake steps closer to me—so close I can feel his breath on the scar over my eye. "I told her I was going with you."

I step back and my eyes travel over his shoulder to the cliff road and the rocky surf below.

"Stay away from him."

"I can't." I'm trying to work up tears by concentrating on the image of Blake in Kasey's arms. "It's too soon. I'm not—"

"Too soon for who?" Anger flashes in his eyes and I step back, instinctively moving to protect myself. "You or the kids at school? You or the people in town?" He kicks at the sand.

I squeeze my eyes shut as real tears burn behind them. Now I don't want him to see me cry.

He stops. "Allie, I'm sorry." He wraps his arms around me and pulls me against his chest.

"Don't." I try to resist his embrace, but he won't let go. I start to melt and let him pull me close. His arms around me feel nice—strong enough that I feel safe, but not so tight that I feel trapped.

"I'm sorry," he says into my hair.

I grit my teeth to keep from crying and shake my head against his shoulder to show him he has nothing to be sorry for. I don't trust my voice. As soon as I open my mouth, I'll start bawling and then who knows what will come out.

"I just want you to be okay. I just want you to be happy again." He smoothes my hair over the top of the scar. "It doesn't matter how long it takes."

I can't answer so I lean against him. My head fits perfectly under his chin, between his neck and his shoulder. When Trip held me it never felt this right. He was so tall that my head got buried in his chest, and it wasn't soft—not like the tenderness I feel in Blake's arms.

We stay still, breathing together. My mind fills with the memories of a dozen summers here with him. Exploring the cliffs. Building castles in the sand. The kiss in the cave. And everything since then. Bringing me my homework. The night I threw the box of bad memories over the cliff. Roller-skating in Hoquiam. Him crying on my shoulder on New Year's Eve.

I think about what Andrew said.

What do I owe Trip?

What do I owe this town?

What do I owe Blake?

The wind sings through the cliffs, the waves crash on the beach. It's all muted by the sound of his heart thumping against mine, and a tiny, long-silent voice in the back of my head asks, "What do I owe myself?"

Angie's giggle crashes into my brain like the sneaker waves that used to knock me into the cold surf when I was a little girl. I step away from Blake—quick, embarrassed. Randall is standing behind Angie with his hands on her waist. His eyes are filled with something that looks like disapproval.

"Maybe you guys should double with us." Angie giggles again.

Blake clears his throat, "We aren't—"

"No, thanks." I slip my hand into Blake's. "We already have somebody to double with." I stare back at Randall, making him look me in the eye. Remembering that he saw Trip hit me and didn't try to stop him. I keep my eyes locked with his until he looks away.

Chapter 32

The next day when I come into the kitchen for breakfast, Blake is sitting at the table, eating a bowl of cereal with Andrew and Dad—the sugared kind, the kind that his grandma won't let him eat.

"Hey," I say, dropping my backpack.

"Hey." He grins back. "I thought you might want a ride to school."

"Means I don't have to wait for her," Dad says as he pushes out his chair and kisses me on the forehead. "Have a good day."

"You ready to go?" I ask Blake.

"What's the rush?" he says. "Andrew's bus hasn't even got here yet. Sit, have a bowl of cereal."

"Sounds good." I sit in the chair next to Blake and pour myself a bowl of the sugary stuff, too. Sitting together, the two of us crunching on sugared cereal, reminds me of when we were kids. It feels good.

All the way to school we talk Sweetheart Ball plans—not dance committee stuff—our own plans. Andrew told me he asked Caitlyn so we're doubling with them.

"So what do you want to do for costumes?" Blake asks as we turn into the school. "We don't have very much time."

"Caitlyn invited me to go costume shopping with her on Saturday. She said her sister manages a vintage clothing/costume shop in Aberdeen." I'm a little worried about shopping with Caitlyn. Based on her regular wardrobe, I wonder what kind of costume she's going to come up with.

"Saturday's not good for me. I have to work." Blake pulls into the school parking lot and turns off the car.

"She doesn't want you and Andrew there anyway. She said it's girls' choice so we get to choose." The idea of picking out a costume for Blake without his input makes me nervous. What if he hates it? "But if you have any ideas . . ."

"I trust you." He turns off the car. "Vintage clothing, huh? Sounds cool."

"Yeah, I have a feeling that Caitlyn buys most of her clothes there."

Blake looks at me like he's surprised. "What's wrong with Caitlyn's clothes?"

"They're a little weird. Don't you think?"

"She has her own style. That's cool, right? Like you and your hats." He reaches over and tugs at my beret. I hold it down so he doesn't see the weird mass that my hair has become. I'm trying to grow it out so it really covers my scar.

Blake climbs out, shoulders both of our backpacks, and reaches for my hand. I glance behind him, to see if anyone is watching, but I take his hand and hold on as I climb out of the car. Thanks to Angie, the whole school probably knows we're going to the dance together anyway.

I'm kind of floating across the parking lot when I hear a shrill voice screaming in our direction. "You broke into my house!" It's Hannah. This feels familiar, but the last time Hannah freaked out on me, we were in the cafeteria, not in the parking lot. "Both of you." She points a long, red, manicured fingernail at me first, and then at Blake. "You were in my bedroom."

My heart flutters like a bird trying to escape from my rib cage, but Blake stays calm. He grips my hand. Maybe he thinks I'll go after her again. "What are you talking a—"

"You stole it. Right out of my bedroom. Because you were jealous." Her voice quivers. "Jealous because he loved me more."

The other kids in the parking lot make a loose circle around us, looking for another chick fight—Hannah and Allie round two. But I'm not going to lose it this time. I scrape the edge of the tigereye with my chewed-off fingernail. "What exactly do you think I—"

"—everything, everything he ever gave me. It's all gone." Instead of lunging toward me she flops onto the curb and bursts into shoulder-shaking sobs, the kind that get hard to watch after a couple of seconds. The circle evaporates, kids looking at each other, shrugging, and shaking their heads as they walk away.

She looks so pitiful that part of me wants to comfort her. I look around for Angie or Megan, but they aren't here. I walk toward her and reach for her shoulder. "Han—"

"Don't touch me." She bats at my hand and I step away.

"Break it up!" Mr. Barnes yells. The circle reforms as he

steps between me and Hannah. He looks from me to Blake then to Hannah—a sobbing, gushy mess on the sidewalk. He backs away like he did when I mentioned feminine supplies. "Maybe we should take this to Ms. Holt's office."

Between the three of us we get Hannah into the health room. She's blubbering about calling Detective Weeks because we broke into her house.

"What was stolen?" Ms. Holt asks calmly. The nurse's office is crowded with me, Blake, Mr. Barnes, Ms. Holt, and Hannah. It gets worse when the bell rings and Ms. Holt has to shut her door because of the long, curious looks from the hallway.

"I had a little scrapbook," Hannah sniffs. "I kept everything in it that Trip gave me when we were dating. I wanted to look at it last night. I was just missing him or something. But it was gone."

"Are you sure you didn't just lose it?" Mr. Barnes sounds condescending, the way adults do when they don't get how important something is.

"Yes!" Hannah looks at him incredulously. "I always kept it in my top drawer."

I almost want to ask her if that's her underwear drawer, to see if we are really that much alike.

"And you're sure it wasn't just misplaced?" Ms. Holt is gentler than Mr. Barnes, but Hannah is just as vehement.

"Yes!"

Blake and I exchange a glance. If Hannah's book was really stolen, then maybe she wasn't the one leaving notes in my locker. But she could have made up the whole thing to get us in trouble. The last note is still in my backpack. If I pull it out now, does it look like I *did* break into her house? Blake is watching me. I press the tigereye and pick up my backpack.

"Maybe it's better if both of you go to class," Mr. Barnes says.

This is my moment to escape, for both of us to escape. I don't want to get Blake into trouble. I hesitate for a second, but I unzip the pocket and pull out the note. I show it to Hannah. "Was this part of one of your notes from Trip?"

Her eyes widen and she snatches the note from me. "What did you do to it?" She looks at Ms. Holt and Mr. Barnes. "This proves she stole my book. Stole it and destroyed it. She cut it into pieces." Hannah covers her face with her hands, now completely devoid of the marks I put there, and starts sobbing again.

Blake looks nearly as shocked as Hannah does. He probably hates me for bringing out the notes, because somehow he'll take the blame.

"Where did you get this?" Mr. Barnes barks at me, his half-patient, coaxing tone gone.

"I found it in my locker"—my voice falters—"last week." Blake reaches over and takes my hand. "It wasn't the first one."

Mr. Barnes looks from Blake to Hannah to me. He nods to Blake. "Do you have anything to add to this?"

He grips my hand tighter. "I saw the other notes that were in Allie's locker." He clears his throat. "But I threw them away."

"Is there anything else I should know," Mr. Barnes says slowly, "before I call the police?"

"Andrew saw the notes, too," I answer. At least we'll all go down together.

He licks his lips. "I see."

With the addition of Andrew and Detective Weeks, the nurse's office is overflowing. Mr. Barnes sets up chairs outside so we can come in one at a time for questioning. Hannah goes first. She tells Ms. Holt that she has a headache, so Detective Weeks questions her while she lies on the little bed with a cold cloth on her head. Then Hannah's mom comes to picks her up. She spends a few minutes in Ms. Holt's office, then leaves with Hannah. Both of them look very pale.

Andrew is shaking and coughing when he goes into the office. I'm sorry I dragged him into this, but his interview is short. He gives me a weak thumbs-up and goes back to class. Blake's is longer. I'm dying to press my ear against the door and listen, but there are too many people around. I get the full brunt of the whispers and stares as the other students pass by on their way to class. I hear words like "jealous" and "crazy" and "juvie."

Blake finally comes out. He looks okay, and he smiles and squeezes my arm when I pass him on my way into the office.

Detective Weeks is at the desk in the little closet that was Ms. Vincent's office. That counseling session seems ages ago. He looks serious when I sit down. Then he starts firing off questions. "When did you get the first note?" "Who has access to your locker?" "Have you given your combination out to anyone?" "Does Blake have it?"

I answer as honestly as I can, but I don't tell him about Blake's knife. I don't tell him Blake doesn't need the combination to get into my locker.

His last question is the hardest. "Why didn't you tell anyone?"

I struggle for an answer. I didn't think anyone would believe me. I didn't want anyone to think I was crazy. I didn't want everyone to be thinking about Trip and the accident again. I finally come up with "I don't know."

He shakes his head and lowers his voice. "If someone is threatening you, I need to know. I'm on your side, Allie. I'm just trying to find out the truth. Now, is there anything else you want to tell me?"

I think about Mr. Phillips, and the diamond earrings, and what pawnshop Paul told me. I wonder if there's any way Detective Weeks would believe me if I said someone was following me. Not a chance. Then I think about the secret, above everything else that I have to keep. My secret. Trip's secret. Everything else could just be my imagination. That at least I know was real. I have the scars to prove it. I swallow. "No, sir."

He shakes his head. "And I suppose you don't remember anything more about the accident, either?"

What do I remember? Being jealous of Hannah, being afraid to be alone with Trip, seeing his eyes just before he died. Things that make me even more confused about what really happened that night—that make me wonder if somehow I'm responsible for Trip's death. I can't tell him that either. "No, sir."

"That isn't good enough anymore, Allie." He stands up, frustrated, angry. I shrink toward the door. "I have something at my office I want you to take a look at. Something that might jog your memory. I'll expect you there after school on Monday. That'll give you a couple of days to think about it."

Chapter 33

"My sister isn't here yet." The woman standing behind the counter in front of the vintage clothing store takes me by surprise. She's tall, model thin with all the right curves, and impeccably dressed. The only hint that she's related to Caitlyn is her hair. It's long and red, not as flaming as Caitlyn's, and swooped into gentle, effortless waves that probably took her hours to achieve. Standing next to her I feel like an ugly dwarf. I self-consciously tug at the scarf on my head. She reaches a long slender hand out to me. "I'm Mel. I set some ideas aside for you two in the back room." A chunky gold bracelet slides down her arm as she sweeps her hand toward a door behind her. "You can go look if you want to. Caitlyn's always late."

"Thank you." I don't know what else to say so I push through the door. The back room is full of boxes and racks of clothes, neatly organized by size. To one side is a pale green-and-gold,

old-fashioned settee piled with garment bags. I try to shake a feeling of dread when I look at the bags. They remind me of the one in my closet. And of body bags.

My interview with Detective Weeks has me terrified. Anything I remember condemns me, and I'm not sure if I'm a good enough liar to make him believe something I made up. It would probably go something like this:

Me: "We drove up the cliff, to celebrate my birthday. Trip brought a couple of bottles of champagne. He drank them both himself."

Detective Weeks: "Why did you let him drive if he was drunk?"

Me: "Because he would have beaten me up if I didn't."

I can't say that. Nothing I come up with works.

My head hurts. I pick up a gray-and-black-plaid garment bag, thinking about the one I have in my closet.

"You came!" Caitlyn's voice startles me so bad that I drop the bag and it slides to the floor. She sounds genuinely surprised. She walks over and throws her arms around me. I stiffen, but she doesn't seem to notice. "This is going to be so fun." She's wearing an orange silk top, red jeans, and a thick gold chain. Her hair is done up in a thousand fiery red braids. "I've never had a girls' day out like this before. Never even been shopping with anyone except my mom and my sister, and Mel hates to shop with me." She picks up the bag I dropped. Inside is some kind of red cocktail dress. She holds it up to herself and then offers it to me.

I shake my head. I am not wearing anything red to this dance. "I haven't ever been shopping with anyone but my mom, either."

She stops unzipping the next bag and looks up in surprise. "Really?"

I shrug. "Yeah."

"But you're so . . . I don't know, gorgeous." She sounds sincere. I should acknowledge her compliment, but right now gorgeous is the last thing I feel. I shake my head and adjust the scarf over my hair. She finishes unzipping the bag and takes out a ruffled blue hoopskirt. "I'd think someone like you would have tons of friends."

"We moved around a lot, so it was hard to make friends." I lean forward and reach for another bag so she doesn't see the stab of pain hit my face.

"My problem is, I live above a mortuary and my dad's a mortician. People either think that's übercreepy or just gross." Caitlyn measures the hoopskirt against her waist, sighs, and hands it to me. "People are so weird about death. I mean, it happens to everyone, right? So what's so weird about it?"

I take the skirt and set it aside as a maybe. "I guess people don't like what they don't understand." I think that could explain why Catilyn doesn't have any friends, but I'm starting to like the way she's open about everything and not afraid of what people think. I wish I could be like that.

"Death isn't so hard to understand. Your body stops working for whatever reason, so your soul leaves. Simple enough." She walks over to the corner where a scented candle sits on an antique dresser. "It's like this." She licks her fingers and then uses them to put out the candle. It hisses out and smoke curls up from where the flame had been. She gestures to the smoke. "The fire isn't really gone, it's just different. People don't disappear, either, they just change into another form." She lights the candle again with a box of matches sitting next to it. "Mel hates the smell of dust and mothballs."

"Maybe she shouldn't be working in a place like this, then."

"Maybe, but she's trying to work her way through beauty school." Caitlyn unzips another bag and pulls out, ironically, a black velvet dress that looks like it belongs at a funeral. "Yuck, I hate black." She tosses it aside. "I've felt them, you know."

"Felt what?" I wonder if there's something in the conversation I missed.

"People's souls," she says nonchalantly.

The hair all over the back of my head stands on end, and I check in with the stone in my pocket. I can't decide if Caitlyn is trying to scare me or impress me. But she's so casual about it that it doesn't seem to be either.

"They stick around for their funerals, to see where they're being buried, and to say good-bye to their family." She pushes aside a pioneer-style dress, also black. "The sad thing is, I don't think their families even know that they're hanging around, because they're too sad. But I can feel them."

"That's kind of creepy." Goose bumps rise all along my arms.

"Not really," Caitlyn says. "Most people are pretty decent, so their souls are pretty decent, too. It's not a bad feeling when I know someone is in the room that no one else can see. It's just different."

Of all Caitlyn's eccentricities, I'm having the hardest time wrapping my mind around this one. What kind of person views death and ghosts so casually?

"Like you, for example," Caitlyn says. "Andrew told me that

your boyfriend was killed in an accident, where you got that." She points to the scar above my eye. "So do you ever feel like your boyfriend is with you, even though you can't see him?"

Not just my scar, but my whole body prickles. I'm pressing against the stone in my pocket so hard that it's digging into my leg. "No," I answer firmly.

"Andrew didn't like him very much." Caitlyn picks at a loose string on the edge of the settee.

"Who?"

"Your old boyfriend."

"I don't know. Trip used to take him out in his truck once in a while. Andrew liked that." It's a lie, but lying to defend Trip is a habit I haven't broken yet.

Caitlyn is shaking her head. "No, Andrew didn't like Trip at all. He told me that Trip didn't treat you very well. Andrew said that if he were strong like your dad, he would have thrown Trip out."

I'm not sure how to answer her, so I force a laugh. "I guess no guy likes his sister's boyfriend."

"You're probably right." She picks up a tie-dye flower dress. "Oooh, I like this one, I'm going to try it." She disappears into the dressing room.

"Heard you fighting." Andrew's voice trembles with anger. "Heard what he called you. He shouldn't . . . shouldn't talk to you that way."

"It isn't like . . . you don't understand." I pull my sweatshirt tighter around me, glad he can't see what's underneath.

"I'm stuck in this"—he gestures at his chair—"not deaf."

"It's his dad. Trip's under a lot of pressure. He says those things. He

doesn't mean it." I can't meet Andrew's eyes, can't let him see my hurt. "He'll be sorry tomorrow."

"He'll bring you something, so it will be okay." His bad hand shakes wildly. "But it won't be."

I trace the scar over my eye, thinking of the look on Andrew's face, trying to remember how many times he might have seen me and Trip fighting. Andrew told me once that people forgot he was in the room, because of his chair. I didn't think I did, but maybe I was wrong.

"Haven't you tried on anything yet?" Caitlyn's voice brings me back to the shop. "Let me help you."

The next bag she opens has a tan-and-gold spandex jumpsuit with tiger stripes and feathers at the wrists. "Isn't this cool?" She holds it against my chest. "And it matches your cool cat-eye."

I'm already shaking my head. "What era is that?"

"I don't know, disco? Seventies?" She holds it to her own chest. "I wonder if it would fit."

Probably not, but I don't say that out loud. I'm trying to imagine what Mom would say if Caitlyn showed up at our house wearing that.

"Maybe not." Caitlyn opens the next bag—a fringy leather dress. "What do you think—Sacagawea?"

I smile. "I can just see Andrew in a coonskin cap."

"This is so much fun," Caitlyn says. "I've never had a friend like you before." She squeezes my arm.

I swallow and regret every bad thing I ever said about Caitlyn. She's met me twice, she barely knows me, but she's willing to accept me as a friend. And I've never had a girls' day like this before either. I need to enjoy it. It might be the only one I get. I reach for the next bag. Inside is a vintage World War II soldier's uniform. "I think this is a guy's costume."

Caitlyn grabs it out of my hands and squeals, "Andrew would look so gorgeous in this. Mel wouldn't have put this here unless there was a matching girl's costume. Help me find it."

We keep digging, piling what I'm sure are expensive antique costumes on one side of the settee, until Caitlyn finds what she's looking for. She gasps and pulls out a soft white blouse and a red swing skirt. There's a pair of white gloves, a black hat with a long red feather, and a Red Cross armband.

"It's gorgeous," I say. "Try it on."

"Okay, but this time you find something, too."

I pick up a few dresses that I liked—the ruffled hoopskirt, the pioneer dress, and the Sacagawea costume—and follow her into the dressing room.

I change into the hoopskirt first and step out, drowning in ruffles. Caitlyn is turning back and forth, looking at herself in the three-way mirror. I almost gasp. She's beautiful. The creamy blouse makes her pale skin glow pink. It emphasizes her trim waist and big chest, while the swing skirt makes her legs look great. She has piled her braids back under the hat. She has the same high cheekbones that Mel has.

"Let me see," Mel says from the front of the room. "Do a spin." Caitlyn twirls around and the skirt flows out and then swirls around her legs. Mel steps around her, looking at her critically. "Not bad. You look almost normal." I'm guessing from Mel that this is high praise. "Some cute shoes, a pearl necklace, and I could do something with that hair." She touches Caitlyn's braids and shakes her head.

"I love it." Caitlyn beams in the mirror. She looks so sure of herself, so confident that she looks good; I wish I felt that way.

"Do you have any more like that?" Liz, a girl I recognize from Pacific Cliffs, says from the front of the shop.

"Sorry, this is one of a kind," Mel answers. I see a gleam of pride or at least approval in the way she looks at Caitlyn. Then she turns to me. "No. Way too many ruffles."

I try on the other outfits but none seem to work. Caitlyn is in the front of the store, still in her dress, trying on necklaces. Finally she comes to the back and stands by the dressing room. "Did you find anything? I'm starving."

"No," I answer pitifully. I'm discouraged and hungry, too. "Maybe we should just give up."

"No way," Caitlyn says brightly. "Give me a second."

When she comes back to the dressing room she has a fringy green-blue flapper dress. I've already looked at it a couple of times but decided against trying it on. "I can't wear that."

"Why not?" Caitlyn shakes it so the fringe moves. "It's cute."

"It's sleeveless." I automatically reach to pull down the sleeves of my sweater.

"It's not even cut low." Caitlyn pushes the dress toward me. "Let's see what it looks like."

Panic rises in my chest. "I can't wear sleeveless."

"Why not?" Caitlyn says.

"I . . . I . . . get too cold."

"We'll be in the gym and you'll be dancing," Caitlyn insists. "Just try this one. It's fabulous. There aren't very many costumes left to try, and I'm starving." She shoves the dress around the curtain and into my hands.

I'm sweating as I slide the flapper dress over my head. When

I try to zip it up, the zipper gets stuck in the fringe and then slips out of my damp fingers.

"Let me see, let me see." Caitlyn is whining from outside the curtain.

I tug the zipper up hard. The excuses are already forming in my mind. It didn't fit. It has a rip in it. I force myself to face the mirror. The glow of the fluorescent light makes my arms and shoulders look pale and sickly, but that's it. I run my fingers down the delicious bareness of my skin. I haven't looked at my arms in months, afraid of what I would see. But here they are, bare and gloriously unmarked, except for the scar on my forearm. All this time I stayed covered, hiding the bruises that have disappeared, bruises that are never coming back. I laugh out loud.

"Allie, I'm coming in." Caitlyn pulls the curtain and stops with her mouth hanging open. "You look amazing."

"Let me see." Mel steps toward me. "Come out into the light." In the brighter light of the store, the dress shimmers and the fringe changes from green to blue, depending on how the light hits it, kind of like Blake's eyes.

"Totally you." Caitlyn is beaming as much for me as she was for herself. "Try the headband." She hands me a green sequined headband with a peacock feather in the back.

I put it on and smile at my reflection in the mirror. I feel pretty again, sexy even, but most of all, free. I shake my shoulders in a little shimmy, to make the fringe sparkle, just because it feels good.

Mel looks at me critically. "Fishnet stockings, green heels, a long necklace, and you're set. I have a cool pinstriped suit with a white-on-black tie and a black fedora that your date could wear."

"So you're good, right?" Caitlyn says.

"Yeah." I run my hands down my arms again.

"Go change." She gives me a little shove toward the dressing room. "I'm ready for lunch."

I'm reluctant to take off the dress. It feels so good. I still haven't changed when Caitlyn pokes her head in. She hands me a fuzzy blue wrap. "Mel told me if you're worried about being cold you could wear this, but hurry up."

I take the wrap from her and slide it over my shoulders.

"Let me see the dress without that sweater." He reaches across the seat and tugs at the sleeve playfully. He's in a good mood, excited about his surprise.

"I'm cold." I pull away. I'm never sure how he'll react to seeing the evidence of what he does to me. Sometimes it makes him remorseful, but just as often it makes him mad, like it was my fault. "Where are we going?" I concentrate on making sure I have the right level of excitement in my voice and snuggle up against him. "C'mon, tell me."

"You'll just have to be patient." His eyes sparkle, even in the dim light of the truck. He grips the steering wheel with one hand and puts his arm around me with the other, pressing into the bruise on my shoulder.

Dread pours into my stomach. He's been planning my birthday surprise for weeks. Dropping hints and telling everyone. What happens if I don't come up with the reaction he's expecting?

My stomach tightens with the memory of living in the uncertainty of Trip's emotions. Always feeling like I was walking on the edge of a cliff.

Cliff.

In my memory we were driving up the road toward the cliff. But why?

"Are you still in there?" Caitlyn shakes the curtain.

What if we weren't going to the cliff? What if he was taking me somewhere else, somewhere beyond the cliff?

"Allie?"

I keep thinking about it while I get dressed. Trip hadn't taken me to the meadow for ages. Why would he take me there the night of the dance?

"You need to do something about your hair." Mel's voice slams into me as soon as I step out of the dressing room.

"What?" I reach up and adjust the scarf over my head.

Mel puts her hand on her hip. "Your hair would look better if it weren't so shaggy."

I duck my head and step away. "I've been trying to grow it out."

"Allie used to have the most beautiful hair," Caitlyn says. "Down to the middle of her back. Andrew showed me pictures."

"Well, right now it just looks bad." Mel's words sting, like they were coming from Mom, or even Trip. "You should let me cut it."

I try to adjust the scarf so it covers my hair better. I want to cry. When I put on the dress, for the first time in forever, I liked what I saw, and now Mel is telling me how ugly I am.

"Ooo, let her cut it." Caitlyn is almost clapping her hands. "Mel is great with hair and makeup. Sometimes she helps Dad out."

I have to look up to make sure I heard her right. I can't imagine sophisticated Mel working on dead people.

"I have an idea." Mel pulls off the scarf before I can stop her. She ruffles my hair like she's evaluating it. "But you'll have to trust me."

“I don’t know.” I try to smooth it over the scar.

“You need to cut it.” Mel’s voice is almost commanding. “Anything is better than what you have now.” She walks over and puts a BE BACK IN AN HOUR sign over the door. “We can go to my apartment.”

“Now?” Caitlyn asks. “I’m starving.”

Mel rolls her eyes, but she gestures to her purse. “We’ll get takeout on the way. I’ll buy.”

Before I have a chance to back out, I’m sitting in the middle of Mel’s tiny but tastefully decorated kitchen with wet hair, wearing a plastic drape, while Caitlyn texts Andrew and eats Chinese food.

I cringe at every snip and rub the tigereye under the drape. Mel works fast, not even hesitating when she pulls the comb over the scar on the back of my head. When she’s done with the scissors, she runs some kind of gel through my hair and fluffs it with a cold hair dryer. She pronounces me done and Caitlyn brings over a mirror.

I gasp at the reflection. My hair is shorter than it’s ever been, even shorter than it was after the accident. It’s so short that the ends turn up in little curls.

“Wow, you look like Andrew. I love it.” Caitlyn hugs my head.

I touch the curls to make sure they’re mine. Then I run my fingers through what’s left. I wonder what Blake is going to say.

“I could help you with makeup.” Mel studies my face. “I have something that would cover your scar, so you’d hardly know it was there.”

I touch the ridges over my eye. “Okay.”

Caitlyn and I go into the bathroom while Mel retrieves

what looks like a silver tackle box. Inside are jars and tubes and rows of every color makeup possible. Mel mixes a couple of thick foundations on her wrist, holds it up to my forehead, mixes some more, and then starts smoothing the mixture over my eye. She puts foundation over my whole face, and then brushes it with powder. She adds eyeliner, mascara, and a light pink lip gloss before she turns me around to look.

It looks like someone else staring back at me. But it is me—only I look like a younger, more innocent me. Like the picture Mom has in the living room of me with fluffy blond hair and a little blue sundress, or the picture that Blake painted. I touch the place over my eye. I can feel the scar, but in the mirror, it's gone. It looks natural, not like what Mom tried to do, and my face doesn't feel like plastic.

I want to cry with joy or relief, or what, I'm not sure. Caitlyn hugs my head again and beams at me.

"I could show you how to do that, if you like," Mel says. When she smiles I realize that she does look like Caitlyn.

I smile back. "Thanks, that would be great." For the first time in a long time I feel beautiful.

Chapter 34

My hands tremble as I try to duplicate what Mel did with my hair. I've already given up on covering the scar, I'm too nervous I'd make it look worse. Twice I put on a hat, then a scarf, and then took them off again.

Dad loves my haircut. Mom thinks it's "nice, but weren't you trying to grow it out?" Andrew says we finally look like twins.

Blake hasn't seen me yet. I'm almost as worried about his response to my hair as I am about my meeting with Detective Weeks later today.

I'm ready when he comes to get me for school, but I linger in my bedroom, listening to him talk car stuff with Dad. The El Camino is running okay, but Dad says there's still a lot of work that needs to be done. He's helping Blake through the repairs, not charging him for them.

"Allie, you're going to make Blake late," Dad yells through my door.

I come out holding my breath. Blake takes my backpack and says, "Hey, ready to go?"

"Sure." I study his face, looking for a reaction, but he walks away.

He doesn't say anything the whole way to school. Hardly looks at me, even. As we wait to turn into the parking lot I'm thinking *he hates it, he hates it, he hates it* with every ding of his turn signal. Suddenly I don't feel beautiful anymore. My head feels too bare without my hat. My scar feels too exposed. If only I'd been able to do the makeup the way Mel did.

I stay in the car when Blake gets out, trying not to cry. I'm waiting for him to yell at me for cutting my hair, to tell me how much he hates it, to tell me that I look like a freak, to tell me how ugly I am.

He opens the door for me and I turn my legs around and step down, but I can't make myself stand up. I stare at the gravel that covers the parking lot and rub the stone in my pocket. "I'm sorry," I finally say.

"Sorry," he says. "Sorry for what?"

"It's just hair." I bite the inside of my cheek to keep from crying. "It will grow back."

He squats down in the gravel in front of me. "Allie, what are you talking about?"

"My hair." Tears burn behind my eyelids. "I'm sorry I cut it. Caitlyn's sister just—"

He laughs, which makes me feel worse. Then he stops. "You think I don't like your hair?"

I look up, but instead of facing him, I look over his shoulder to a group of freshman girls, including Kasey. They're watching us. *Don't make a scene.* "It's okay if you hate it," I whisper.

"Hate it?" Now he looks worried. He rubs his neck. "Allie, I . . . actually . . . I mean I'm sorry. I didn't even notice you cut it until just now."

I stare back at him, shocked. "You didn't even notice?"

He clears his throat. "I was thinking about my car and the dance meeting today. I'm sorry, I just—"

"So you don't hate it?"

He takes both my hands and pulls me to my feet. "You're beautiful with short hair and beautiful with long hair. You'd be beautiful bald." Someone behind us snickers. "In fact . . ." He slides his fingers through my hair and cups the scar on the back of my head. I look in his eyes and they go tender. "You are the most beautiful, incredible, amazing girl I've ever met."

He pulls me toward him and our lips touch for the first time since the day in the cave. The freshmen snicker again. A few seconds into his kiss, I stop caring who's watching.

He pulls away. "Better?"

I can't speak so I nod.

He presses his forehead against mine. "Anytime you need that, you know—"

Someone behind Blake catches my eye. James is leaning against his car watching us. I stare back at him hard. I'm tired of being afraid. I turn my lips toward Blake's ear. "I'll probably need a lot of those." For a second, even my interview with Detective Weeks doesn't seem so bad.

Chapter 35

My dad picks me up after school and goes with me to Detective Weeks's office a second time. They exchange pleasantries.

"Just looking for some basic information and clarification. You can certainly wait until she has a lawyer present if that would make you more comfortable, but she isn't being accused of anything." This from Detective Weeks.

Dad glances over at me, maybe a little longer than he should. Is he wondering if I'll need a lawyer? Finally he says, "No. It's fine. We intend to cooperate fully. We want you to find out who's harassing Allie with those notes." He looks at Detective Weeks hard, like he's giving him an order. They shake hands again. He turns to me and touches my shoulder. "I'm going to walk back to the shop. You can pick me up there at six."

Detective Weeks's office is still pretty bare. A couple of books and maybe a new box or two are on the shelf. It still doesn't look like he expects to make Pacific Cliffs a permanent home.

He re-explains what he told Dad about information and clarification, and lawyer, but I can't shake the feeling that I'm about to be interrogated, especially when he turns on a little recorder and says the date and has me say and spell my name.

Then he gets down to business. It's almost a relief. "I want you to tell me anything you remember about the night Trip Phillips died."

"I don't remember anything." I touch the tigereye, then squeeze my hands together in my lap.

"Nothing before the dance or getting ready?"

"Get out of the way, Andrew. I have to get my purse. I have to go."

"Don't go. Stay with me. It's our birthday."

"You don't understand. I want to. I just can't, okay. Trip would be furious. He's been planning tonight forever."

I clench my hands, remembering how hard Andrew tried to get me to stay home that night. It feels like something I shouldn't tell Detective Weeks so I say, "No, sir."

He leans toward the tape recorder. "It should be noted that Miss Davis is suffering from memory loss due to injuries sustained in the accident that killed Trip Phillips." He riffles through some notes. I brace myself for something bad. "The cotillion fell on the night of your eighteenth birthday, correct?"

I nod. He gestures to the tape recorder, so I say, "Yes," in a voice more mechanical than Andrew's communicator.

"You attended the dance with Trip Phillips, who died in a car accident later that night."

It's not a question but I answer, "Yes."

"What were you and the deceased Mr. Phillips's plans after the dance?"

"I don't remember."

"According to the report, your mother said you were supposed to come straight home after the dance, that you had been grounded?"

"Mom said you have to come home right after the dance. No exceptions."

"I will, if I can."

"Promise me. Straight home."

"I guess so." I shake my head to clear the voices that are flooding my brain. He raises his eyebrows. "Yes," I say into the recorder.

"Do you remember why you were grounded?"

"You're lucky I'm letting you go to the dance. Your dad said absolutely not."

"I snuck out of the house."

"To do what?"

I take a breath. I have to remember something or he'll get suspicious. "To pull Trip out of the mud. He and his friends went four-wheeling and got stuck. You can ask James and Randall. They were there." If he did ask James and Randall, I wonder what they would tell him.

"Where were you and Trip Phillips heading after cotillion that took you up the cliff road?"

"Just a short drive. So we can be alone. So I can give you your birthday present. Your mom will never know. It's not like the spaz is going to tell on us."

Trip's face floods the space behind my eyes, and his voice, not coaxing, just sure, so sure, that I would go wherever he told me to go. Do whatever he asked me to do. Why was he taking me to the meadow?

"He wanted to be alone so he could give me my birthday present," I answer.

Detective Weeks looks surprised that I actually answered. "Do you remember what that present was?"

Something else works its way forward.

"I want you to wear it. Forever."

"No!" I realize I answered the voice in my memory, not his question. Detective Weeks pauses like he's analyzing my outburst. I push back against the voices, sweat sliding down my back. "I mean, no, sir, I don't remember."

He shakes his head and continues. "Was Trip Phillips drinking the night of cotillion?"

I breathe in. Here's my chance to make it all go away, to tell him that Trip was drunk, but I answer, "I don't remember."

He leans back. The scar above my eye pulses with every heartbeat, but I don't dare move my hand to rub my head. "So you maintain that you remember nothing about the accident that killed Trip Phillips?"

"No . . . I mean"—scrape the tigereye for little flecks of courage—"yes. I don't remember anything." Nothing that doesn't incriminate me.

"Let's try something else. What can you tell me about Blake Evans?"

I force the swirls in my head to stop. "Blake?"

"Yes, Blake Evans. You were with him the night I pulled him over for a speeding infraction on November fifth of this year, correct?"

"Yes."

"And what is your relationship with Mr. Evans now?"

I pause, but this isn't something I can lie about. "Blake is my boyfriend."

"So you two are romantically involved?"

"Yes."

"And how long has that been going on?"

I should say forever, but I stick to "A few weeks."

"I see, and before that, what was your relationship with Blake?"

"Friends." I say it firmly.

"And how long have you and Blake been friends?"

"Since we were little, like four or five."

"I see. And did you maintain that friendship when you were dating Trip Phillips?"

"No."

"No?"

"Blake was gone for part of it, he was—" I swallow hard.

Detective Weeks shuffles through the papers and pulls out one to read. "Serving time in a juvenile detention facility in Reno, Nevada, for a breaking and entering charge."

Everyone knows, but I feel like I'm betraying Blake when I say, "Yes."

"What about after he returned to Pacific Cliffs. Were you and he friends then?"

"Stay away from him, Allie."

"Not really." I can't look at Detective Weeks or the recorder. "I didn't see him that much, and Trip didn't like me to—" I stop myself.

Detective Weeks leans forward. "Trip didn't like you to . . . ?"

"Trip didn't like Blake."

"I see, and how did Blake feel about Trip?"

"I don't like the way he treats you, Allie."

"I don't know. I didn't really talk to him then."

"What about the night of cotillion? Did you talk to Blake that night?"

"You don't just have to go with him wherever he wants. He doesn't own you."

Panic grips me. I didn't remember until now that Blake was at cotillion. I keep my voice calm. "I don't remember."

"Did you have an argument with Blake that night?"

"I don't remember."

"Did Trip and Blake have an argument?"

"You don't learn very fast, do you, Juvie? She's mine. She'll always be mine."

"I don't remember."

Abruptly, he says, "I don't think I have any further questions at this time. We'll be in touch with you later if there is anything else. Thank you for coming in."

I'm really confused, but I give him a formal "You're welcome."

He turns off the recorder. "I want to show you something, Allie, off the record." He turns around and fishes something out of one of the boxes behind him. It contains a piece of white fabric coated in dark brown stains. "Have you ever seen this before?"

I nod. "Yes, sir. It's the sweater I wore to cotillion."

He takes another plastic bag out of the box, something else that could have once been white, but it has the same brown stains and it looks like it might have spent time buried in mud.

He touches the other bag. "What about this?"

I shake my head no.

"It's a T-shirt. A vagrant found it hidden under a log in the woods behind the cliff and brought it to my attention." He picks up the bag with the sweater inside. "Do you know what the brown stains are all over this sweater?"

"Blood." My stomach knot tightens. "My blood."

"Right. So what do you suppose the brown stains are all over this shirt?" He touches the other bag.

"Blood?" I guess.

"It is blood, but the question is, whose blood?"

I wait for him to answer that question, but he acts like he wants me to answer it.

Finally sighs. "I haven't got the lab results on that one so I can't answer that for sure. But my guess is it's the same blood that's on the white sweater. Your blood."

My scar throbs in time to the clock ticking behind him. I can't figure out where he's going with this. "Why would my blood be on—"

"This shirt is too big to be yours. Too small to be Trip's. But if my hunch is right, and your blood is on this T-shirt, it means someone else was there the night of the accident, with you, with Trip." He narrows his eyes and leans forward. "There might even be some of his blood on the shirt."

I'm not sure if he means blood from the shirt's owner or Trip's blood. If Trip died going off a cliff why would his blood be anywhere but inside the truck or spread out over the ocean?

He puts the bags with their bloody evidence back in the box and sets the box on the shelf. "Lab results can be unpredictable.

It could be a couple of weeks, could be a couple of days. But if I'm right, there was another witness that night. Someone who might do a better job of remembering what happened."

Blake. His name, his face, flashes in my mind. Was Blake there that night? Why would my blood be on Blake's shirt? Why would anyone's blood be on Blake's shirt?

Detective Weeks shakes his head like I've disappointed him somehow. "You have to trust somebody sometime, Allie. I just hope when the time comes, you decide to trust the right person."

. . . — — — . . .

I don't go home after I leave the police station. I drive toward the cliff, but I don't stop there. Everything that Detective Weeks said swirls around and around in my brain. The spot of white, someone else there. Blake fighting with Trip. Blake fighting with me. And something else, something important. Something I can't quite remember.

I go past the cliff, up the road beyond and officially out of Pacific Cliffs, to the one place I've avoided since the accident. The place that I'm now positive Trip was taking me to.

It's a lot wetter than it was this summer. Dad's truck slips and slides but makes it up the steep trail where Trip took me off-roading for the first time. When the trail gets too narrow, I park the truck and get out. The path winds back into the woods. I push low-hanging branches out of my way and step over long thorny vines.

"Watch your head. Maybe I should just carry you."

After a few minutes I reach a clearing. A little stream flows through the middle. Huge boulders line the bank. A tall pine tree stands in the center.

"Here it is. My special place. No one in Pacific Cliffs knows about it but me."

I move toward the tree and trace my fingers over the letters. TRIP LOVES ALLIE.

"Now it's our *special place."*

He cut the letters deep, so they stand out like scars against the bark. Someday our names will probably be the reason this tree is weak enough to fall over in a storm.

I sit down on one of the boulders next to the stream.

"Close your eyes and hold out your hand."

The setting sun filters through the tress. The stream rushes by. My head is throbbing, but I grit my teeth and will the memories to keep coming.

"Do you like it? I had it designed especially for you.

"Nothing's too good for my girl."

Pain throbs in my chest and in my head. Gray swirls over the memory. I shake my head and breathe in deep to keep from blacking out. I stand up and walk into the woods while my heart slows down. A few feet in, something red, buried under the bushes, catches my eye. I squat down, careful not to get in the mud, and reach through the brambles. They snag my sweatshirt and tear into my skin, but I keep reaching until I have it in my hands. I pull it out into the light.

When I realize what it is I almost drop it again. Red, satin, high-heeled, and open-toed. It's one of the shoes that I wore to cotillion. It's barely recognizable, but I'm sure that's what it is. The red has faded in patches to more of a pink-orange. It's covered in pine needles, rotting leaves, mud, and something else.

I brush my hand along the side to clear the debris off the side of the shoe. I examine it closer. At first I think the other stain is blood, like the blood on the white shirt Detective Weeks showed me, but when I touch it, it feels greasy.

"What the hell did you step in, Allie?"

My stomach aches with remembered anxiety.

"Be careful, you're getting it on my truck."

But he was in a good mood that night.

"Keep your feet on the floor, okay?"

And I couldn't afford to make him mad by telling him his truck was leaking oil.

I lean forward to look for the other shoe, but it isn't in the bushes. I stand up and look around the woods, forcing myself to remember again.

Running, breath coming in gasps, claws grabbing my legs, tearing at my skirt.

I walk farther down the path that leads away from where I parked. I find a snag of red fabric on one of the vines. The claws were blackberry vines, roots, low bushes. I know who I was running from. What was I running to?

A white shirt, coated in blood. Too big to be mine, too small to be Trip's.

Blake's face floods my mind again. Was he here?

The rumble of a truck coming closer startles me. There are a million trails in these woods. That truck could be going anywhere, but I don't want to risk being caught here. I start back to the clearing. The sound fades and then cuts out.

A big boulder on the edge of the path stops me. I run my finger over the sharp edge, then trace the scar on the back of my head. Did I fall against a rock like this? Did Trip make me fall against it? If he did, how did I end up in the truck?

A branch cracks, then footsteps. I stop, but all I hear is my own breathing. I look around. A clearing in the clouds, something white on the path ahead of me. My stomach lurches.

I blink and realize two things: the spot ahead of me is real, not in my mind, and it's gray, not white. Tall, dark-haired, thin. Even with his back to me, I know who it is. He's blocking the path back to Dad's truck, and it's too late to run from James.

In a quick motion I throw the shoe into the woods. The sound of crackling branches when it lands causes James to turn around. I walk toward him, quick but casual, like I don't care if he sees me here.

"What are you doing here, Allie?" he demands. He's wearing his football jersey, gray with white numbers on the front.

"I could ask you the same thing." I try to keep my voice even.

"I asked first." He crosses his arms and moves so he takes up the entire pathway.

I decide to go for the widow-in-mourning approach. "I came here to think. I was missing Trip. He used to bring me here."

He shakes his head. "Don't give me that bull. I saw you in the parking lot with Juvie this morning, attached to his face. You came here looking for something."

I make my face blank. "What would I be looking for?"

"It's not here. I already looked."

"What's not here?" For the first time I think that James might know something about Trip's accident that I don't.

"The present he was going to give you for your birthday. He bragged about it all night. He didn't tell me what it was, but it must have been worth a lot. Enough for you to kill him for it." His eyes narrow at me. "I know you sold all of his other stuff at that pawnshop in Hoquiam. You only wanted him for his money."

"You've been following me!" The pieces click into place—the guy standing in the shadows, the guy who followed me to the pawnshop, it was James. "Why?"

"Mr. Phillips made it worth my while." He leans back against a tree, bold, bragging, like Trip. "But I would have done it anyway. I've been waiting for you to slip up so I can see justice done."

I think about the way James turned his back when Trip hit me. The way he wouldn't look me in the eye after that. I glare at him. "Since when do you care about justice? You didn't try to stop Trip when he—" I bite my tongue to keep from finishing that sentence.

"Go ahead, Allie. Say it. Tell everyone what Trip did to you. It just makes you look more guilty. It's on the news all the time. Women who kill the guys who beat them up."

I push past him and head toward Dad's truck.

"Keep running, Allie. Keep pretending everything is fine. It doesn't make any difference. Sooner or later you'll screw up and then we'll all know how Trip died. I'm watching you."

Chapter 36

"Where do you want this set up?" I jump as Kasey's voice brings me back to the clipboard in my hand. She sets down the box of tablecloths for the refreshment table. She's been unbelievably nice about the whole thing with Blake. She asked Marshall Yates to the dance after Blake turned her down.

I force myself back to the map that's page three of my notes. "Left corner. The long tables need to be set up at right angles, with the little round ones in front."

"Got it, boss." She picks up the tablecloths again and heads for the corner.

I can't believe I'm here directing traffic as we set up for the dance. After what happened with James, I prefer to be in a crowd, safe from his prying eyes. But being here feels surreal, like everyone's reality is disconnected from my reality, like I'm watching myself stumble around with everyone else, playing normal, while inside my mind everything is falling apart.

No one else feels it. Andrew is in the corner with Marshall, programming lighting sequences in his computer to go with the music. Randall and Blake are hanging Blake's paintings over the frames. Angie is draping fishnets and lights over the basketball hoops.

Even Hannah is here with her own clipboard in the corner of the room, pretending to supervise. Except for the missing scrapbook, the police didn't find any evidence that Hannah's room was broken into. Ever since then I've seen Hannah alone more and more. In the girls' bathroom yesterday I actually heard Megan say that she thought Hannah had put the notes in my locker just to be mean.

"You okay?" Blake whispers, and kisses me on the cheek.

"Fine." I look down at my notes and grip the clipboard harder. "Just trying to keep everything straight."

"You're doing great." He crosses the room to help Randall with another frame.

"This is really coming together." Ms. Flores steps beside me. "This could be *the* best dance this town has ever seen." She glances at Hannah and leans closer to me. "Better even than cotillion." She leans over and gives me a sideways hug. "You've done a great job."

I shake my head. "Not me, I just—"

"No, you really worked your butt off. Organized everything. Kept everyone on budget." She looks down at me and smiles. "Don't belittle what you've done, Allie."

I glance down at the papers in front of me, the map and a spreadsheet/check-off list for everything. Something that Andrew made for me on the computer, but with notes and information I gave him. Did I really do all of this?

Blake and Randall carry the last frame through the doors, sweating and grunting. "That will teach you to use metal," Angie calls from her perch below the basketball hoop.

"Watch it or I'll take your ladder," Randall says. She makes a face at him.

"So has Blake told you the good news?" Ms. Flores asks.

"No." I shake my head. "What good news?"

"You haven't told her," she yells across the room to Blake.

"Yeah, Blake," Angie yells, "why haven't you told her?"

Blake turns red and drops his end of the metal frame. It almost lands on Randall's foot. Randall swears but tries to cover it with a cough when Ms. Flores shoots him a look.

"Now is as good a time as any for the announcement." Ms. Flores crosses the room. She has a smudge of blue paint across the back of her skirt. She takes the microphone from Marshall. "Is this on?" She taps the end while Marshall turns up the volume. Blake is inching back behind the pole he was holding on to. "Thank you all for your hard work. I knew you guys could pull this dance together and make it the best in the school's history." She pauses while Randall and Marshall start whooping. "I'd like to take a minute to thank Blake and Allie." Everyone applauds. I reach for the stone in my pocket as my face burns. "I would also like to recognize Blake for the beautiful artwork he has spent so many hours creating just for this dance." She pauses and looks fondly at Blake. "I couldn't bear to have his paintings just rolled up and stored away after tomorrow night, so I showed them to members of the city council. The city is going to buy them. They'll be displayed in various public buildings around town."

The gym erupts in cheering. I walk over and wrap Blake up in a hug. Randall is shouting "Wo, wo, wo, wo," and beating his fist in the air. Andrew sends crowd-cheering sound effects over the sound board. Angie nearly falls off the ladder because she stands up and screams. Only Hannah stays still, hugging her clipboard to her chest and looking all alone.

. . . ▬ ▬ ▬ . . .

Everyone else has cleared out. Only me, Blake, and a janitor are left in the building, and the janitor is nowhere to be seen. I slide onto the floor beside the stage, exhausted. Blake finishes plugging in a couple of cords and slides onto the floor next to me.

"You missed one." I point to one canvas sail that's still tied up at the top of the frame.

"That's my surprise." His voice is full of anticipation; my stomach flip-flops, a mixture of excitement and dread. What if I don't have the reaction he's expecting? "You wanna see how everything looks?" He walks over and dims the lights, flips on the wind machine, and then pushes a couple of buttons on Andrew's computer. Blue and green lights play across Blake's paintings and they billow like sails in the breeze.

He climbs up the ladder, slices through the rope that's holding it up with his pocketknife, and the last sail unfurls. I stand up and walk over to get a better look. It's a woman, standing at the edge of the cliff, watching the waves. She's wearing an old-fashioned dress and her hair is almost covered by a gray scarf. The locks that aren't trapped are gold blond and blow in the wind. She's clutching a cross at her chest and the bright spot in the picture is a ship on the horizon. The woman is smiling—joy and relief written in her eyes.

She has my face.

"I call it *Hope*." He climbs down the ladder and wraps his arm around my waist. "I looked at so many pictures from Pacific Cliffs where the people looked hopeless—widows waiting for their husbands to come home from the sea, the loggers after the mill closed, the dock workers when the port moved south. I wanted to show that Pacific Cliffs was more than businesses shutting down and people dying in storms. I wanted to show hope." I turn around to face him. He traces the scar over my eye. "When I started to paint her, I knew she had to have your face."

I look away, beyond the painting, and think about what everyone at school will say when they see it at the dance. A painting like that will give them more ammunition to use against me and Blake, probably forever. I can see Hannah George rolling her eyes. "*Hope*? With her? Can you imagine anything more stupid?" And what is James going to say? What is James going to do?

"It's cheesy. I know"—the breathless excitement is gone from his voice, like his sails have lost their wind—"but it will be dark at the dance, and no will be able to—"

"I love it." I wrap my arms around his neck. None of those people matter, not Hannah George, not James. Not even Trip. Only Blake. Only us.

He smiles and blue-green light dances across his eyes and makes them bluer and greener. "Well, since we're being cheesy anyway, would you like to have one dance with just us, before everyone else comes tomorrow?"

I smile and nod. He walks over and types something into Andrew's computer. A slow, sappy love song floats through the speakers, not one of the songs Trip put on the iPod, not even the one about a summer love. Something new, just for us.

I lean into his arms and snuggle into the place between his neck and shoulder where my head fits so well. I breathe him in—paint and dust and sandalwood and almonds—all the smells that remind me of his grandma's attic, and him.

We're barely moving, leaning into each other, breathing together, my forehead against his cheek, his hand tracing little circles on my back. After a few minutes he pulls back and looks into my eyes, clears his throat, swallows, clears it again. "There's something I've been wanting to"—he breathes in—"something I've been meaning to tell you."

My heart beats wildly, afraid of what he's going to say. Afraid of what he might confess. I want to tell him to stop, but I can't speak.

He breathes again. "Allie, I—"

"Are you kids still here?" I jump back as the janitor flips on the lights. We both turn red. "I'm not getting overtime tonight, especially not to babysit a couple of hormone-crazed teenagers. You two get on home, or up to the cliff—somewhere I don't have to be in charge of you." He waves us away.

"Sorry," Blake whispers. I have to stifle a nervous laugh.

We're almost to his car when Blake checks his pockets and swears. "I left my knife and Andrew's computer in the gym." He hands me the keys to his car. "I'll be right back."

I don't want him to leave me alone, but I nod. As soon as he walks away, the wind goes cold. Icy chills circle the scar on the back of my head. It's more exposed because of my short hair. I glance around the parking lot and clutch my arms around my chest. My sweatshirt is gone. It feels so good to wear short sleeves again, that even though it's February, I'm not wearing a jacket. I get into Blake's car and lock the doors. It takes a couple of tries to get the engine started. The blast of air that comes from the dash is as cold as the wind outside, so I turn the heater off.

I glance around me and see someone standing between the school and the Dumpster. His face is in shadow, but I'm sure it's James. I should go say something to him, tell him to leave me alone, but I'm afraid. He makes sure I see him before he steps back behind the building.

I reach for my tigereye, but it's gone. My fingers dig through my pocket, desperately searching, but it isn't there. I search the seat and the floor of the car, but the stone is gone. I must have dropped it in the gym when we were setting everything up.

I have to find it.

I open the door and start to get out with one eye on the Dumpster. "Whoa, where are you going?" Blake blocks the door with his hand so it doesn't hit him.

"I left something inside, I have to—"

"It's locked and I didn't see the janitor's truck. I couldn't get in to get Andrew's computer or my knife. Is it something you need for the dance?"

"No." I glance back at the shadows. "It's not that important."

"It's cold out here." Blake takes off his jacket and drapes it over my shoulders. I slide back into the car, and he gets behind the wheel. He puts his hands over the air vent and shakes his head. "Heater's busted. Great, one more thing."

I snuggle against his side for warmth and comfort. "It's okay. I'll keep you warm."

He leans over and kisses my forehead. Then he slides his fingers along my cheek. I lean into his hand—rough and warm—strong enough to toss bags of fertilizer but gentle enough to paint the picture of my face. I sigh in relief, feeling safe with him here.

"I still want to—" He hits his hand against the steering wheel. "Ah, why can't I just say it?" He clears his throat. "Allie, I think I love you."

I choke on a nervous laugh. "Think?"

He turns red and stammers, "I mean, I know I love you. I've loved you since I was four and you were five." He turns away from me and grips the steering wheel with both hands. "Okay, that was stupid. Nothing like what I'd planned."

I slip my arm over his shoulders.

He leans forward. "It's okay if you don't. I understand if it's too soon . . . I just—"

I lean my lips to his ear. "I think I love you, too."

He turns to me with such a shocked look that I almost laugh. "Really?"

I nod. "Really." He pulls me close and our lips melt into each other's. It feels so good to be in his arms, to be kissing him. Let James watch. Let the whole school and the whole town watch. I don't care anymore. Blake loves me and I love him. The rest of the world can go away.

My cell phone buzzes in my pocket—Dad. I don't mean to answer, but when I try to silence it, it opens. "Allie, Allie, are you there?"

"Hi, Dad." I breathe in and hope I don't sound as breathless as I feel. “We were just—” Breathe again. “We were just heading home now.”

“Good, I’ll expect you in about ten minutes.” The phone clicks off.

“I guess we’d better go,” Blake says. “Got to keep the sergeant major happy. I don’t want to do anything that would keep me away from you,” he says.

“Don’t worry.” I laugh, but another voice echoes in my brain.

“Nothing will ever keep us apart.”

I reach for the stone, but instead find Blake’s hand. I take it and hold on tight the rest of the way home.

Chapter 37

The clock says 7:20, even though it's really only 7:00. I couldn't get to sleep last night, but I'm not tired.

Blake loves me. I love him. Nothing else matters. I said the words out loud, but they didn't feel big enough to encompass what I feel for him. Love, gratitude, exhilaration, all swirl around my chest and through my whole body.

I love Blake.

It's not like before. Not quick and exciting and giddy. Not so fast that it took my breath away. Not like with Trip.

It came on slowly, like the tide filling up the entire shore before you even realize it's coming in. So slow that I didn't expect it, didn't know I was falling in love until I said it out loud. At the same time it feels like I've always been in love with Blake. Like he said, since I was five and he was four.

It's Saturday morning, the day of the dance, finally. I wrap my grandma's quilt around me and wonder if it's too early to call him. Blake, Andrew, and I aren't leaving for Hoquiam until ten. We're going skating and then having a gourmet dinner prepared by Caitlyn's mom. Mel is going to help Caitlyn and me with our makeup and hair. I still haven't figured out how to duplicate the disappearance of my scar. I'm eager for Blake to see me without it.

My phone rings and my heart leaps. It's him. He must feel the same way I do. He couldn't wait to call.

I reach for the phone, almost giggling with excitement. "Hey, babe."

"We have a problem." Blake's voice is serious.

"What is it?" In a second my mood has changed from exhilaration to fear. I grip the phone and pray that he's kidding.

"There was a fire in the gym last night." He swallows. "Ms. Flores wants us to meet her at the school."

"Your paintings?" I wrap the quilt closer to me but all the warmth is gone.

"I don't know." His voice sounds pained. "I'll be there in ten minutes."

. . . — — — . . .

Most of the town, two fire trucks, and the entire volunteer fire crew of Pacific Cliffs are standing in the school parking lot outside the gym. It's raining—a slow, cold, drizzly rain, the kind that sucks the joy out of everything. Through the crowd I pick out Ms. Flores, wearing a long coat and rubber boots and talking to one of the firefighters. Hannah is here, too, looking like she just left the beauty salon. She must sleep in full makeup and with her hair done.

Ms. Flores waves me and Blake over. Hannah follows. We step to one side, and after giving Hannah a funny look, Ms. Flores lets her stay. "It isn't as bad as it looks," she says. "The fire suppression system put out most of the flames before the crew even got here. But I guess it's a mess inside, water and soot everywhere." She puts her hand on Blake's shoulder. "I don't know how your paintings fared."

"How did the fire start?" Hannah is eyeing me suspiciously.

"They're still doing the investigation." Ms. Flores passes her hand over her face. She has a glob of brown paint above her eye. "But it looks like a wiring issue. The building is old and the circuits might have gotten overloaded." She looks at Blake. "Did you guys unplug the equipment before you left last night?"

"No." Blake hangs his head. I slide my arm around his waist.

"It's okay. I didn't tell you that you had to. We'll know more when the chief comes out. He said we might be able to go in and see what we can salvage later today, as long as his investigation doesn't raise any questions." She looks toward the school. "It's a blessing that this happened now, when there weren't any kids inside."

It seems like forever, milling around in the cold rain with the rest of the town. The rumors fly, and people are looking at me and Blake again. We retreat to his car to get away from the rain and the gossip, but without the heater it doesn't do much good. About an hour after we get there, Mom shows up with coffee for all the firefighters. She asks me to help pass it out.

While I'm handing out coffee, I see Chief Milton and Detective Weeks in a heated discussion. I'm close enough to hear the words "arson" and "investigation." Detective Weeks keeps looking at me. I know I should say something about James standing by the Dumpster, but I don't want any more attention, and I can't prove it was him. And if I told everyone he was at the school last night, what would he say about me?

Police Chief Milton gets on the loudspeaker in his car. "The fire crew has finished the initial investigation. It looks like the fire was started by an overloaded circuit." I breathe a sigh of relief. I don't have to tell anyone about James. "You can all go home. Once the firefighters have taken out all of their equipment, we will allow a few people to go inside with the chief to get their personal belongings."

He starts to put the radio back into his truck but Mom stops him. She smiles her public-relations smile and takes the radio from him. "Mr. Phillips has agreed to have the dance tonight at Pacific Cliffs Inn, so everything will go on as planned." She beams at me like she's doing me a big favor.

It takes another half hour for the firefighters to pack up all of their hoses. In that time Ms. Flores decides to let me and Blake and Randall go inside. Hannah looks absolutely livid that she doesn't get to be one of the elite to see the destruction in the gym. The face she makes would be funny if everything weren't so horrible.

Except for a haze of smoke, the hallway looks normal, so I'm not expecting what we find when we walk into the gym. The floor is wet and the wood is already buckling. Everything is covered with thick black soot.

Blake runs his hand across one of his paintings and leaves a streak of fingerprints through the black.

"Don't touch anything!" Randall's dad, the fire chief, warns.

"Some of them are salvageable." Ms. Flores puts her hand on his shoulder. He just nods.

"Man," Randall says, "when I was a kid I always wanted the school to burn down. But this is kind of sad."

"The fire must have started here." Ms. Flores points to the corner that I've been afraid to look at. I follow her finger to *Hope* and see what I already knew. The painting of me got the worst of it.

Bits of the woman's face—my face—are left, hanging in blackened strips from the metal frame. The sail looks like a ship after a pirate attack. Her expression looks mournful instead of hopeful, and the place where the ship was on the horizon is a blackened hole.

"Doesn't look like there's much left to salvage," Randall says, "except for maybe these." He points to a staple gun and a hammer that we forgot. He kicks the staple gun and it leaves an outline in soot on the gym floor.

"Probably not." Ms. Flores has a streak of soot across her forehead. She gestures to the lump of black plastic that used to be Andrew's computer. All the speakers are burned or melted, too. "The school's insurance will probably cover your personal belongings. Allie's mom told me they still have most of the decorations from the cotillion in a storeroom at the inn. We could put up those, but we'll have to hurry."

She starts moving toward the door. I keep my eyes on the ground, searching while trying to look like I'm not searching. No one notices. They're all too caught up in the mess. Then I hear a thump and something sliding across the floor. I turn around to see Randall picking something up.

I cross the room to him. "What is that?"

"Just a rock." He slides his fingers over the tigereye and wipes a streak of soot off of it.

"It's mine," I say, holding my hand out, "for luck."

"I don't think it's working." He dumps it into my hand. When it lands the tigereye breaks apart into two pieces. I gasp when I see it. The yellow stripes inside have turned bloodred.

Chapter 38

Blake slams the staple gun through plastic green vines and into a wood frame harder than he needs to. He's in a really bad mood. I've been avoiding him since we got to the inn. Tiptoeing around like I was walking on eggshells is too familiar a feeling. I don't like it. And Roger Phillips keeps poking his head through the doorway, like he needs to supervise us. I don't dare get close to Blake while Trip's dad is watching.

The tigereye is in my pocket again. I put it back together, but every time I bend over, the pieces slide apart and the edges dig into my thigh.

Hannah is eating this up, pinning little flowers to the curtains, joking with Angie and reminiscing—I'm sure—about the happiest night of her life. Back before I stole her spotlight.

"Did we bring any more staples?" Blake snaps at me.

"I'm not sure." I nervously touch the bulge in my pocket. "There might be some in the back of your car. I could go look."

"No, I'll do it." He stomps across the ballroom and through the back door.

I'm almost happy to see him leave. Then Mr. Phillips calls me over. I set down the bow I was pinning to a tablecloth and walk over to meet him.

"Hello, Allie." He puts his arm over my shoulders. I want to shake it off, but instead I force a smile. I can still pretend everything's okay. "It's really coming together. Seeing these decorations up again is kind of bittersweet, isn't it?"

I look across the fake grass and flowers, the ugly metallic streamers, and the satiny tablecloths tied with bows. I hate everything about it.

He grips my arm. "But you don't remember the first time they were put up, do you?"

I look down at the floor, not sure how to answer that.

"Such a shame about the fire, and Blake's paintings." Mr. Phillips shakes his head, but he doesn't look like he thinks it's a shame.

"We really appreciate your letting us use the ballroom." I can even force my lips to say pleasant things.

He waves his arm. "No problem, happy to do it. In fact, I wish you would have asked me to have the dance here first, then we could have avoided the mess at the school. And"—he's still smiling, but his dark eyes are hard and intense against mine—"maybe Blake would still have his paintings."

I pull away with the distinct feeling that I'm being threatened. "I should get back to work."

He's not done. "I have something that belongs to you in my office. I've been meaning to return it, but I see so little of you now. If you'll follow me." It's an order, not a request. I wish I had the courage to refuse. I wish I had the courage to ask him why he had James follow me and what he thinks he's going to find out by threatening me. I wonder which of the things I sold he's going to return to me now and how I can possibly be nonchalant about it. I work on making my face a mask as I follow him down the hall and into his office.

Like everything else in his world, Mr. Phillips's office is clean to the point of being sterile. The bookshelf behind him is lined with pictures of Trip, including—I shudder—two of Trip and me.

He sits behind his desk, reaches into a drawer, and slides a flat black frame facedown toward me. "It was in bad shape when I got it." I touch the edge of the frame, afraid of what it might be. It's nothing that I sold at the pawnshop. "One of the guests turned it in to the office at the inn. She said she found it on the beach when she was out walking. 'Such a nice-looking couple,' she said. 'I'm sure they don't want to lose this.'" Mr. Phillips turns the picture over. I see me and Trip, standing in front of the same archway that Blake was just stapling. I'm wearing the red dress now hidden in the back of my closet. Trip is wearing a tux and his perfect grin. I look trapped.

I try to keep the horror out of my expression as Mr. Phillips runs his finger down the edge of the frame. "I could have had the photographer just make up another copy, but I knew you'd want the original." He touches the discoloration on the edges. "It still has a few water spots, but it's not too worse for the wear." He looks up at me with the same stone-cold look that Trip had. "I'm sure you didn't mean to lose it. Trip told me you were absentminded—always losing things. Like the expensive gifts he gave you."

My scar throbs and cold runs the length of my back. I can't say anything as he pushes the frame into my hands. His smile doesn't reach his eyes. "That's what I like about the ocean. It returns things you thought were lost."

Chapter 39

I stumble back to the ballroom with the picture clutched against my chest, like it was precious, instead of something I loathe. I'm afraid to see Blake, but he isn't around. I'm not sure what I should do with the picture. I can't just lay it down on the table and get back to work.

Caitlyn crosses the room to me. She's grinning like there isn't anything wrong in the world. "C'mon, Cinderella, time to get ready for the ball."

I look around the room. "I can't—"

Mom, right behind her, looks firm, but the corners of her mouth are twitching. "I called in a few favors. A group of people from town are going to finish the decorations so you guys can get ready to go. Blake's already gone."

My heart feels heavy when I think of Blake leaving without coming to find me first. Maybe it's better if he's mad at me. Maybe it's better if he stays away.

A limo waits for us outside. "Dad's, from the mortuary," Caitlyn explains. Mom and I climb in after her.

Mel is driving. "We need to get going," she says, and looks at her watch. "The dance starts in a little over an hour and you still have to do costumes and makeup."

"And eat," Caitlyn says. "Mom sent the dinner she was making down with us when we found out you guys weren't going to make it to Hoquiam."

When we get home, Mom hustles me through the door. "I'll start the tub for you. Grandma Joyce brought by some bath stuff."

"Just a second," I say. So far no one has noticed the picture in my arms.

"Be quick," Mom answers, "or the water will be cold."

I hesitate in the doorway to my room, looking around to see where I can leave the picture. I'm afraid that Trip's dad will ask me what I did with it when he sees me at the dance. I decide on its previous location, on top of my hutch. I balance on my desk chair and reach to put it there.

A sharp knock on the door makes me lose my balance. I fall backward, pulling the top of my hutch with me. The corner of the picture frame glances across my shoulder as it falls, slicing into my skin. The hutch steadies itself, but I fall hard onto the floor. The frame breaks and the glass shatters.

"Allie," Mom yells through the door. She wiggles the handle, but I locked it. "Allie, are you okay?"

"Fine," I call back, but my voice is shaking. "I just tripped and broke a glass."

"Let me clean it up for you." She wiggles the handle again. "You go take your bath."

"It's okay," I yell back. "I've got it."

A line of blood appears where the picture hit my shoulder. There's a red mark around it that will turn into a bruise soon. I wrap a T-shirt from the floor around my hand so I don't get cut when I pick up the broken frame. The print slides out and lands face-down on the floor. I gasp and nearly fall again. On the back, in Trip's sharp handwriting, are four words.

You belong to me.

I don't want to touch it, but I lean forward and run my fingers over the edge. It's another piece of a note, glued onto the back of the picture. I close my eyes and remember what the whole thing said.

I'm sorry I got so mad. I hate the thought of you ever being with anyone else. You belong to me.

The piece wasn't cut from one of Hannah's notes; it's from one of the notes Trip gave me.

. . . — — — . . .

I deserve this.

The water slides over my body and makes the cut on my shoulder sting. I shouldn't go to the dance. I should stay home. I should stay away from Blake. My hands are shaking, not from the cold water.

I'm numb as I dress for the dance. Caitlyn has enough enthusiasm for both of us anyway. Mel has to keep telling her to sit still while she shapes her hair into a forties twist with pin curls at the side.

Mel evens out Caitlyn's blotchy complexion with pink makeup. When she turns around, she's breathtakingly beautiful, like an old movie star. I finally know what era she belongs to.

Then Mel starts on me. She tightens and sprays the natural curls around my head so they're still soft but can't possibly move out of place. Then she works her magic and makes the scar over my eye disappear. I only wish that she had some magic makeup to cover the scars on the inside. That she could erase the last three years and I could go back to the day when Blake kissed me in the cave, knowing what I know now.

"Oh, Allie, you look beautiful." Mom leans against the doorway to her bedroom. "It makes me feel old to think you're a senior now." Mel and Caitlyn go past her and down the hall, but Mom stops me. She puts her arms around me and hugs me against her chest. When I pull away she has tears in her eyes. "I want you to know I feel bad about what I said about Blake, and about all of our fights. And about everything I missed last year."

I study her expression, wondering what she means by "everything."

She wipes the tears away. "Work has been kind of all-consuming. There has been so much pressure—"

"It's okay, Mom," I say, but I can't make my voice sincere, I'm so tired of her excuses about work.

"I'll try to do better. I promise." She sighs and brushes her hand across her eyes one more time. She smudges away some of her foundation, and I notice dark blotches under her eyes. She forces a smile. "Wait until you see Andrew."

Andrew in the vintage World War II uniform is dashing. There's no other way to describe him. He looks so much the part of a soldier that Dad is getting choked up—Dad. Caitlyn's Red Cross armband makes it look like Andrew's wheelchair is part of the costume. I've never seen him so happy. For his sake I plaster a smile on my face and vow to keep it there the whole evening.

Andrew can't take his eyes off Caitlyn. He kisses her in front of our parents. She sits on his lap for pictures. Then she kisses him.

Blake hates his costume. I can tell. I should have chosen something more casual for him. He keeps fidgeting, pulling at the collar. He looks like someone stuffed him into a suit without his permission, which I guess I did. He stands next to me as Dad takes his picture, stiff and trapped, the way I look in the picture from cotillion. He doesn't touch me at all.

Dad follows us in the van with Andrew's chair so he can ride in the limo with us. Caitlyn sits on Andrew's lap and they kiss the whole way to the dance. Through the rearview mirror, Mel rolls her eyes.

Blake sits by the door and looks out the window. A good six inches separates his left hip from my right one. He doesn't even hold my hand. Maybe he's finally figured out that I am poison, just like Hannah said. I feel the barrier creeping in between us again. As much as it hurts, I'm grateful. The less Mr. Phillips sees of Blake and me together, the better—for Blake.

At the dance, around everyone else, Blake acts normal. He has friends now: Marshall whose band will not be playing, now that we're at the inn; Randall and Angie; and even Kasey. I fight against a wave of jealousy, because this is what I wanted, for them to accept Blake. But more and more it seems like he doesn't need me.

Ms. Flores catches us before we even have the chance to dance. "One of the members of the city council is here," she says. "I hate to interrupt your evening, but he wanted to ask Blake about the condition of his paintings."

"Go ahead," I say. "I'll wait over at a table in the corner until you're done."

I'm hoping for an invitation to join them, but Blake nods to me and follows Ms. Flores to the other side of the room. I flop down at a table in a dark corner and watch everyone else dancing.

Andrew and Caitlyn are in the middle of the floor, oblivious to the rest of the world, making slow circles in his chair. She's perched on his lap with her arms around his neck and her head on his shoulder. I look away. At least someone is having a good time tonight.

I know I'm feeling sorry for myself, being a baby, selfish—acting like Hannah because all of the attention isn't on me. Blake worked hard for this dance and no one even gets to see his paintings. It would be great if he could fix them enough so the city would still want them.

I trace the edges of the tigereye through my little beaded purse. It reminds me of something else. The little purse I carried with me to cotillion. I trace the tigereye again. I had it in my purse that night, but if I kept it in my purse, how did it fall out? How did Blake end up with it?

I watch him from across the room and push that thought

away. It falls under "questions I'm afraid to ask." I'm too tired to let my memories get to me tonight.

A chair scrapes across the floor on the other side of the table. I look up and see James sit down. I look around for Hannah, expecting a joint assault. Angie told me they were coming to the dance together. But James is alone.

"Hey, Allie." His voice is low and friendly, probably softened with alcohol.

I ignore him and keep my attention on Blake, Ms. Flores, and the city council guy.

"Are you having a good time tonight?" He leans closer to me.

I smell beer. I give him a disgusted look and slide my chair back to leave. He puts his hand on my arm, covering the scar that was his fault. "What's your hurry? Juvie doesn't even know you're gone, and Hannah's pissed off at me for some reason. We could leave together."

"What kind of game are you playing?" I snap back at him.

I glance at Blake. He's still talking to the guy from the city council.

"Don't embarrass me, Allie."

I pull away and walk to another table, away from James and closer to the rest of the crowd. I hope that will discourage him, but he follows me. He sits down and slides his chair so it's against mine. I'm trapped between his chair and the table. He puts his hand on my knee and looks down. "Those shoes are nice, but I think I like the ones you wore to cotillion better."

My heart stops.

"So Cinderella goes to the ball and leaves her shoe behind—evidence against her." He inches his hand up my fringy skirt.

"Stop it," I whisper, and try to push his hand away.

He moves his hand higher on my leg. "Maybe I don't have to show that cop what I found."

"I said, Stop." I say it a little louder. Some of the couples on the edge of the dance floor look over at us.

"You don't have to be such a bitch." He clamps his fingers down on my leg and leans into my ear. "I could make it all go away. If you ask nicely." He turns and presses his lips against my neck.

I jump up and backhand him—hard. My chair clatters to the floor behind me. The song ends and the dance floor is quiet, so everyone can hear him when he starts swearing at me and holding his nose. Blake and the city council guy are staring at me across the room. Andrew and Caitlyn are staring at me from the middle of the floor. Everyone is staring. I want to crawl under the table. I want to run, but Randall walks over and stands in front of me, all six foot four of him.

"What's the problem?" he says.

"He—" but I can't finish. Randall isn't going to believe me over James no matter what I say.

Randall steps past me and claps his hand on James's shoulder, to congratulate him, I guess, for humiliating me, but he says, "You've had too much to drink, my friend. It's time for you to go home."

James takes his hand away from his nose, which isn't even bleeding, and sputters while Randall directs him toward the door. I'm almost as shocked as James at Randall's reaction. So shocked I can't move.

"Murderer!" James turns bloodshot eyes on me. "She killed

Trip." He turns toward the crowd like he's pleading his case. "We all know she killed him!"

"No!" Andrew is almost as loud as James. I don't remember him crossing the room, but his chair is in front of me, blocking James from coming closer.

Randall and James stop struggling, for a second as shocked as the rest of us at Andrew's outburst.

Andrew turns his chair to face him. "Don't touch her—" He's struggling for control, his whole body shaking with anger. "Stay away—" His real voice fails him. He slams his hand over his communicator so hard that it comes free of the strap and crashes to the floor. It emits a high-pitched squeal and then goes silent. After what seems like forever, Mr. Barnes steps in and helps Randall manhandle James. They disappear through the door. Blake picks up the communicator and sets it on the table. The music starts up again and the crowd drifts away, sending semihushed comments and glances in our direction.

"I'm sorry," I say without looking up. "I didn't mean to make a scene. Didn't mean to embarrass everyone." I look around for the city council guy but can't find him. He probably left as soon as he realized Blake's girlfriend was a freak and probably a murderer. "I'm sorry, Andrew, I didn't mean for your communicator to get broken." My voice trembles and I reach for the tigereye inside my purse. "Can we leave?"

"No." Andrew is still struggling to get control over his body. "Not your fault."

"You can't let a guy like that ruin your night," Caitlyn says gently. She's holding Andrew's bad hand, trying to keep it still. "You worked too hard."

"They're right," Blake says. "We worked hard for this and we aren't going to let James ruin it. Let's go dance." He grabs my hand and pulls me to my feet. His eyes snap with anger. It makes me want to shrink away from him, but I follow him onto the floor.

Blake's arms and chest feel stiff and hard against me—like Trip's. There's no comfort and no melting into his embrace. He won't look me in the eye. He looks away, over my shoulder. Like everyone else. My fault. Always my fault.

James's accusation still rings in my ears.

"*Murderer.*"

A thought that I've kept buried, even from myself, rises to the front of my mind, where I can't push it away.

What if James is right? What if I did kill Trip?

Chapter 40

After two stiff, painful dances I tell Blake that I need to go to the bathroom. As I walk out I see him cross the room toward Kasey. It hurts, but how can I blame him for wanting a girl with less drama in her life?

In the plush red bathroom of the inn I lean over the sink and splash water on my cheeks to make the blotches go away. I rub my eye and smear the makeup that Mel used to cover my scar. My scar, my freaky eye, and James's voice in my head all accuse me from the mirror.

Murderer.

I close my eyes and lean against the sink, defeated.

"Good job, Allie. You managed to screw up the dance for everyone."

I look up. Hannah is standing behind me. Her eyes are as red as mine and her expression is deadly, but she still looks like the beauty queen that she is. The light catches the emerald brooch that holds together her blue velvet nineteenth-century ball gown. "Why do you have to go after everything that's mine?"

I grip the edge of the sink.

"James told me you sold everything Trip ever gave you. That you were after him for his money."

I look at her while what she's saying registers. James told Hannah about me selling Trip's things. Panic pulses through my veins. Now that she knows, everyone else will know.

"I bet you killed him for his money. You and Juvie. You had this planned all along so you could be together." She laughs, but her laughter is filled with pain, and her eyes swim with tears. "What's so special about you? I don't know what any guy sees in you. You didn't deserve a guy like Trip. You don't even deserve Juvie."

Her words feel like fists to my stomach. Fists to my face. Like having Trip back again.

Her voice wavers. "Trip was the best thing that ever happened to me and you—"

I turn around and face her. "You didn't even know him." It comes through clenched teeth. I'm done with this, done with all of this. If I'm going to be damned, at least it should be for the truth.

"What?" She backs away from me.

"I said, you didn't know him. You think he was perfect. You all think that the great Trip Phillips could do no wrong. But you didn't know the other side of him. You don't know how lucky you are that I came here."

Hannah's eyes widen, like what I'm saying is sacrilege. "Don't you dare—"

I thrust my arm in her face so she can see my scar. "He did this to me. Cut me. Branded me. So I wouldn't forget who I belonged to."

She backs away. "That's not . . . not true. You're lying." Her voice falters, but she doesn't take her eyes off my scar. She doesn't want to believe me, but I think she does.

"Now he's gone. And you guys still won't let me forget. You still won't let me forget that I belong to him." I push past her and she cowers in the corner. I fling the bathroom door open and run down the hall and outside.

My shoes slide on the wet sidewalk and I almost fall. I pull them off and keep running. *You killed him, you killed him* pulses in my ears with every heartbeat. I should go to the police station and turn myself in, but I run past it. My fishnet nylons rip and icy spikes tear at my feet with every step I take. Eventually my run slows to a walk. I clutch my arms around my shoulders, freezing. It's raining, slow and drizzly. I don't even have the fuzzy wrap or a hat for protection. I don't even know where I'm going, home or to the cliff.

Headlights slow beside me, but I ignore them. Blake gets out of the car. "Allie!"

I don't stop.

He walks beside me. "Allie, stop."

I keep moving.

"Please stop." He puts his arm over my shoulder.

I push him away.

"I'm so sorry, Allie, I know I was a jerk tonight. I just . . . The fire and my paintings and Mr. Phillips—"

I turn on him. "What do you want from me? Didn't you

hear James? I'm a murderer. Guys I love end up dead. You need to stay away from me."

He stops, stunned, like I slapped him. I am a murderer. Now he believes it, too.

I start walking again, but in a few more steps he's beside me again. He reaches for me, his eyes pleading. "Just stop, okay. Listen to me. There are some things I need to tell you about the night Trip died, please just—"

"No!" Dread floods my body like the icy waters of the Pacific filling our cave. I don't want to hear what he's going to say.

Lights flash behind him. Chief Milton gets out. He's coming to arrest me. I'm sure of it. He shines his flashlight on me and then on Blake. "What's going on here?"

"Nothing." Blake steps away from me and tries to shove his hands in his pockets, but his costume doesn't have any pockets. "We just had a fight."

Chief Milton puts the light on my face so it blinds me. "Did this boy do anything to you? Did he try to hurt you at all?"

The whole situation is bitterly ironic, Chief Milton coming to rescue me from Blake, now, after everything. "No." I shake my head. "Like he said. We just had a fight."

The flashlight goes back to Blake's eyes. Chief Milton studies him for a long time while we stand shivering. "You'd better go. I'll make sure Miss Davis makes it home okay." I follow him back to the police car. He opens the passenger side door and lets me in. Before he shuts it behind me, I hear him say to Blake, "I'd advise you to stay away from her."

Blake stands there alone, rain dripping off his bangs, like a wet dog. Watching us drive away.

Chapter 41

Blake sends me fifty texts on Sunday. I don't read any of them.

Mom tries to talk to me, actually defends Blake. "I don't know what you two fought about, but you might want to cut Blake a little slack. There were some complaints about his grandmother's products at the inn, so Mr. Phillips had to cancel the contract he had with her. She can't support both of them with that little shop. I heard they might lose their house."

My fault, all my fault. If Mr. Phillips canceled Grandma Joyce's contract, it was because of me.

Andrew can't talk to me; he's sick, coughing, probably got pneumonia when he and Caitlyn and Mel were driving around in the limo looking for me.

My fault. I ruined the dance for everyone.

On Monday, Mom takes the van to work so I can drive myself to school. I'm late so I skip going to my locker and go straight to first period. I look around for Hannah, wondering what she'll say to me now that she knows my secret. She's probably in Ms. Holt's office now, blubbering to her everything I told her at the dance. Any minute I'll be called out of class to explain myself. Maybe it will be a relief. Finally having to tell everything Trip did to me. Maybe it will help my case when I'm tried for murder.

But Hannah doesn't show up for class. The bell rings and nobody calls me down to the office. I follow the sea of whispering students to my locker, like everything is normal.

"What is that smell?" Angie wrinkles her nose and looks at Blake, oblivious to the idea that she might be hurting his feelings. He doesn't respond. He gives me a sad, silent look, then he turns away.

Hannah comes down the hall. She manages a cold glare for Blake and Randall, even Angie. Nothing for me. I'm standing right in front of her, but she stares through me like I'm not here. I guess if I don't exist then what I said about Trip can't be true.

Randall makes a face. "Did someone leave a tuna fish sandwich in their locker?" I smell it, too, something oceany, fishy, rotten. He starts sniffing the lockers like a bloodhound. He holds his nose. "Whew! I think it's in here." He points to my locker.

Everyone gathers around while I work the lock with numb fingers. I'm afraid of what I might find. The smell is so bad it almost gags me. I don't want to see what's inside, but I open the door. A cascade of faded notes, ruined pictures, and bits of cardboard and rotting seaweed cover me. Everything that was in the box I threw into the ocean is spread out across the floor for everyone to see.

I collapse to the ground, frantic, trying to gather the notes and pictures up before anyone sees what's written on them. Blake is on the floor beside me. "No!" I push him away. "Don't look at them!" He can't see what's written on the notes.

But it's too late. Everyone has already seen. I can feel their eyes boring into the scar on the back of my head, condemning me. I melt onto the floor and a wave of black crashes over my head and sweeps me away.

Chapter 42

Dad's sitting on my desk chair beside the bed. I can't quite remember how I got in bed. I can't even remember how I got home. The only thing clearly burned into my brain is the image of my whole relationship with Trip, spread out over the school hallway for everyone to see. "How do you feel?" His voice is gentle.

My head is pounding, I feel weak, and my mouth tastes like bile. I wonder if I threw up at school. Mom is here, too. She lays something cold and wet across my forehead. I curl up tighter in a ball, like I could shut everything out. Like I could be a little girl again, home with the flu, two concerned parents standing watch over me.

"Detective Weeks would like to—" Dad starts.

Mom shakes her head at him. She leans over the side of my bed. "The doctor prescribed these"—she holds out two little blue pills. "For anxiety, and to help you sleep."

I take the pills from her and swallow them without answering.

She sits back and brushes my hair off my face. "These are just temporary fixes. I've spoken to Ms. Vincent. She thinks you should spend some time at a mental-health clinic for teens in Seattle." She draws in a breath, probably at the thought of her perfect world interrupted by a daughter in a mental institution. "Grandma Joyce and Blake told me that these incidents of near-collapse have happened before—"

Traitors.

"We"—she looks at Dad, but he's studying his hands—"we think it would be best if . . ."

I close my eyes against her words and let the blue pills carry me away to an ocean of red dresses, black pickups, and dead boyfriends.

. . . — — — . . .

The clock says 1:20, but the sun is out so it must be afternoon.

I wrap my fingers around the stone and curl up in a fetal position. The days have started to run together, but I think it's Wednesday. Four days since the dance. Two days since I found the mess in my locker. I haven't been back to school. Blake comes by faithfully every day to check on me, but I pretend that I'm asleep so I don't have to see him.

I can't wait anymore so I drag myself to the bathroom so I can pee. It's about the only thing that gets me out of bed. I don't look myself in the eye when I bend over to wash my hands.

I turn off the water. Then I hear it. A whimper, like someone crying, but trying to hide it. I slide the door to Andrew's room open slowly, but he must be at school. I shut the door and listen again. It's Mom.

Why isn't she at work? My chest fills with guilt. She must be worried about me, but I can't make myself play "normal" anymore.

Dad is home, too. I can hear him moving around the kitchen. He starts down the hall. He's almost past my door before I force myself to open it. "Dad." My voice is croaky from lack of use. "Dad."

He walks back to my room. "Hey, how are you feeling?" He says it softly, like he's afraid I'll lose it again.

"Better." I grip the stone and try to sound better.

"Would you like something to eat?"

I take in a breath. "What's wrong with Mom?"

"Oh." He won't look in my eyes. "You don't need to worry about that."

The tone of his voice makes my heart clench with fear. Like it's about more than just me. "Tell me."

He pushes past me and shuts the door behind him. He sits down on my bed and motions for me to do the same. "She lost her job."

Your fault, your fault.

"There was some problem with the books at the resort. An outside accountant came in and did an audit. I don't know what he found, but I guess there was a bunch of money missing. Mr. Phillips blamed your mom. He fired her yesterday."

"Mom would never—" I cover my mouth. "Mr. Phillips knows that." I stop. He *does* know that. If he fired Mom, it wasn't because he thought she had stolen money from the resort. It was because of me. I'm suddenly mad. Furious. Mr. Phillips is a bully. He thinks he can intimidate me into—what? Breaking up with Blake? Leaving Pacific Cliffs?

A confession?

"Yeah, he does know that, but it doesn't look good." Dad runs his hand through his hair and his shoulders slump. "I have some loans coming due on the shop, and with Mom losing her job . . ." He stands up. "But you don't need to worry about that. We'll work it out, okay? I'm heading back to work. There's food in the fridge. I made spaghetti last night."

He starts for the door, but halfway there he stops, turns around, and comes back. He sits down on the edge of my bed. The corners of his mouth twitch and he keeps rubbing a grease stain on the palm of his hand. He doesn't say anything for a long time. When he finally talks, his voice is quiet. "There are some things I wanted to clear up, just between the two of us." He traces the lines in his fingers where the black grease stains never really wash out. "Detective Weeks asked me to come in and look at some of the things that were in your locker. Some of the notes that Trip had written to you."

I try to swallow, but my throat has closed off.

"A lot of apologies. A lot of 'It will never happen again.'" The sides of his jaws are working. "I've heard those kinds of excuses before."

I close my eyes and will him to stop talking. Will the blackness to overtake me again.

"Allie, when I read those notes it made me wonder . . ." He breathes in. "Did Trip ever do anything . . . did he ever hurt you?"

I squeeze my eyes tighter to keep the tears from escaping. Crying right now would be a confession, but I don't have any words to answer his question.

"For all those years I was gone . . . when I was doing what I thought I should be doing to keep you all safe, to protect my family." His voice wavers. I can't open my eyes now. I can't face the pain I hear in his voice. "If somehow I missed something, if somehow I failed to protect you, I'm sorry."

Part of me wants to let it all go—curl up against his chest and tell him everything. But I can't let him bear the burden for something that was my fault. I can't make him think he failed, or know that I did, that I wasn't the tough soldier he raised me to be.

I don't say anything.

The silence hangs between us—the weight of so many years of his being gone presses against me. He puts his arm around me and squeezes. I grit my teeth and retreat to a place inside where I don't have to feel anything. Finally he pulls away.

"There's one more thing." His voice is grave. "The fire, and that boy at the dance, and the whole thing with your locker, has people talking. They're demanding that Chief Milton reopen the investigation into Trip's accident, none more loudly than Roger Phillips." My eyes flutter open and I watch his hands clench and unclench. "I've heard Blake's name thrown around a lot. I don't want to see this turned into a witch hunt. If you remember anything, now's the time."

Chapter 43

After Dad leaves I lean back against the pillow and keep my eyes closed. I want to take the blue pills and curl up under the covers and shut everything out. But I can't hide, not anymore. I have to fix the mess I've made. I have to face . . . whatever comes.

I get dressed carefully—brown dress pants and a blue button-down shirt, something Trip bought for me to wear to a business lunch his dad dragged us to. I don't even try to cover the scar. Today I want everyone to see it. I want Mr. Phillips to see it, because somehow, I know Trip caused it.

I get in Mom's car, take a deep breath, and head for the inn.

The smile on Mr. Phillips's secretary's face freezes when she sees me. "Mr. Phillips is in a meeting."

"I can wait." I plunk myself down on the leather couch across from her desk.

"It might be a—" she starts, but the door to the office opens.

The first man out I recognize as the city council guy from the dance. I'm guessing the next two out are also members of the city council. Marjorie Phillips comes out next, wrapped in dark brown fur. Her eyes are on the ground so she doesn't see me.

Mr. Phillips doesn't see me at first, either. He's focused on the man he's talking to. When he sees me his smile turns into a grimace. He wipes it away quick and comes across the room to me. "Allie, what a pleasant surprise." He's smiling but there's nothing pleasant about the look in his eyes.

I don't take his outstretched hand. The speech I had formulated on the way over disappears. I'm left with four words. "You fired my mom."

Mr. Phillip's face twists. "I don't think—"

I plunge forward. "You canceled the contract that Blake's grandma had with the inn. And I'm guessing"—I look around at the other people in the room, but none of them will meet my eye—"that this meeting is to discuss why displaying paintings that were done by an artist with a criminal record would be a stain on the town." The look that passes between the city council members tells me I'm right.

Mrs. Phillips speaks up. "The historical committee doesn't feel that the pictures portray the right—"

"Have you seen them?" I challenge her. She glances at her husband. Fear flashes in her eyes. "Have any of you seen the paintings that Blake did?"

Mr. Phillips reaches to put his hand on my shoulder, but this time I step away. He sighs. "Your friend Blake's criminal record aside, the paintings are amatueristic and, unfortunately, destroyed. As for the other matters, my contract with Mrs. Evans is none of your business, and this is neither the time nor the place to discus your mother's indiscretions." He leans closer, so only I can hear him. "You have no idea who you're dealing with."

I answer like everyone in the room heard his last statement. "No, Mr. Phillips, I know exactly who I'm dealing with. I went to seven different schools. I know a bully when I see one."

I look around the room. "How much money did he offer to throw at some civic project if you didn't display Blake's paintings?" One man coughs and looks away. A woman pretends to check her watch, another brushes some lint off her sleeve. I make sure I make eye contact with every one of them before I turn and walk away.

I maintain my dignity until I get back in Mom's car. Then I collapse onto the seat. I press the stone as alternating waves of triumph and dread pass over my body. Mostly, the triumph wins out.

. . . ▬ ▬ ▬ . . .

Mom is sitting at the table in her bathrobe, no makeup, hair straight and flat, stirring a cup of coffee when I get home. She barely answers my greeting. I could tell her everything that happened in Mr. Phillips's office and it probably wouldn't register. I could tell her everything that Trip did to me while we were dating and she wouldn't even blink.

I go into the bathroom, wet down a washcloth, and press it over my freaky eye because my scar is threatening to explode.

Voices from Andrew's room stop me. It sounds like arguing. Andrew is upset. I can hear him stammering. I lean my head against the door as a fit of coughing stops whatever he was trying to say.

Caitlyn is yelling at him through the computer, cussing him out. The urge to protect him races through my blood. I push the door open with the idea that I'm going to stop her before she really hurts him.

"Caitlyn, what's your problem?" I burst in. Andrew's still coughing, doubled over in his chair.

"Allie, thank goodness," Caitlyn says. "I need you to talk some sense into him. Doesn't he sound terrible? I told him he needs to go to a doctor, I told him—"

"Baby me," Andrew sputters. "Like Mom. I'm not a baby. I'm tougher—" He breathes in hard. "Tougher than you think. Any of you."

"Talk to him." Caitlyn sounds really worried. "His cough keeps getting worse."

"Can take care of myself." Andrew waves wildly with his good hand. "Mind your own business."

"Andrew, I—"

He does the impossible, hangs up on Caitlyn. Then he turns his chair around to face me, fire blazing in his eyes. "No one tells me," he breathes, "anything! Mom's job! Dad's shop! And you!" He starts coughing again. Caitlyn's right. He does sound bad. He breathes in a wheeze. "You all think I'm helpless, you all think I can't handle anything."

I walk over and put my hand on his shoulder. "I didn't mean to—I didn't know a lot about anything, either." Andrew coughs again. I bend over him—concern for my brother erases everything. "You sound bad."

He leans forward in his chair. "Just"—he wheezes—"stress. Everyone. School, family, and Caitlyn on my back. I'm fine. A stupid cough. Mom has too much now. Don't tell. I'm an adult. I can—" Breathes hard. "You don't have to take care of me."

"You're right." I kneel down so I'm next to him. "But we take care of each other, right? You've taken care of me plenty of times."

He smiles a sad smile and reaches to touch my hair, gets his fingers caught in my curls, and pulls away. "Not now. Too much for Mom. If it gets too bad, I'll see a doctor. Promise."

"Okay, I'll wait. But call Caitlyn back. She's just worried because she loves you."

His face lights up. "Do you think?"

I rumple his hair. "Yeah, little brother. I do."

Chapter 44

I'm drowning in a sea of red and green—satiny red against my skin, swirling green covering my legs. Getting in my way. And all around me more green—shapes moving and blending together. I'm trying to run, but the shapes reach for me, fingers grasping at my dress, pulling my hair, tearing into my arms. I push past them, my blood pounding in my ears, my lungs burning. A spot of white in the middle of the green. Someone is there.

"Help, please help me!"

But the wind tears my voice away before it reaches him. I turn and look behind me. Something grabs my leg. I'm caught. I jerk against it and fall. Spikes dig into my legs and my hands as I try to claw the vines away from my legs to stand. But it's too late. I feel hands on my shoulders dragging me to my feet.

I wake up with a jolt. My scar throbs. I sit up slowly and try to come out of the dream. This time I want to remember. I'm missing something important. I know I am. I rub the scar over my eye. The fingers were tree branches. My leg was caught in a blackberry vine.

I know who I was running from.

I'm almost sure I was trying to get to Blake.

My whole body goes cold. I slide out of bed and cross the floor to my closet, like I'll find the answer there. The garment bag is in the back, where Mom hung it. I haven't touched it since cotillion. I hook my fingers under the hanger and pull it out. I forgot how heavy the dress was, long and full, tight on top, and suffocating.

I carry it across the room and lay it on my bed. I hesitate. I've dreamed so many times that it contained Trip's body that I'm afraid to open it. I breathe in and force my fingers to move. The zipper sounds loud in the quiet room. The red satin looks gray in the pale light of almost dawn. I reach above my bed and turn on the light. Slowly, hesitantly, I touch the dress.

"Do you like it? It's to wear to the dance."

I trace the lacy patterns on the front.

"But it's not a birthday present."

I slide my fingers around the edges of the dress and slide it out of the bag. Spread it out on the bed so I can see everything. The skirt is snagged and ripped. A strip of the underskirt is torn off and hangs below the hem. The lace in front is spattered with little brown spots. When I turn it over, the back is covered in bigger splotches that are the same color as the ones on the white sweater. My blood.

My scar throbs.

"I'm saving something special to give you on your birthday."

I pick up both pieces of the tigereye from my nightstand and press them into my hand.

I close my eyes, breathe in deep, and will myself to remember.

"Close your eyes and hold out your hand."

The blood rushes around in my head.

"Do you like it? I had it designed especially for you."

"It's so beautiful. The swirls of gold and silver remind me of waves."

"That's what I wanted you to think. The main diamond is two carats. The side stones are a carat each. And look, tigereye. Like your eye. I always felt bad that I didn't buy you that necklace at the fair."

"This must have cost a fortune."

"Nothing's too good for my girl. I want you to wear it. Forever. It's an engagement ring."

The dawn filters through my blinds. I press my fists into my eyes to shut out the tears and the colors that blend into one another. My head is throbbing, pulsing between the scar over my eye and the one in the back of my head. I grit my teeth and will the memories to keep coming.

"No." My answer slips through my lips with a tiny wisp of courage.

He looks at me in utter disbelief. "What did you say?"

"I said no." My voice gets stronger. "I won't marry you. I won't live like this anymore."

"What?" His eyes snap. "I've given you everything you ever wanted. Spent all that money on you." He shakes his head hard. "You can't say no to me."

I know I am pushing him to the edge. But I don't back down. I don't even look away. "I just did, Trip. I'm done with this."

"But I love you, Allie. No one will ever love you the way I do."

Blake's face flashes in my mind; he's standing outside the inn, telling me I don't have to leave with Trip, telling me that Trip doesn't own me. I grip the tigereye through my purse. "You don't love me. If you loved me you wouldn't do the things you do to me. You wouldn't hit me. You wouldn't ever hurt me."

He stands up and jerks me to my feet. "It's Juvie, isn't it?"

I look him right in the eye. "No. This isn't about Blake. It's about me. I deserve better."

I saw the lightning in his eyes and I knew I had pushed him further than I had ever pushed him before. I had to get away. I made him think I threw the ring into the bushes so he would be distracted, so he would let go of me. But I kept it. Even after he started chasing me. Even when I knew he was going to kill me. I kept the ring.

I set the tigereye back on the nightstand and pull the dress all the way out of the bag. I search through it, inside the folds of the skirt, pick it up and shake it out. Then I dig around the bottom of the bag. The little white purse that I took to the dance isn't here. I slipped the ring inside it as I ran.

I pick up the tigereye again and press it into my hand so the two pieces slide apart and it cuts into my palm. I had the tigereye with me that night, too. I kept it in the white purse.

Blake.

Sickness washes over me and fills my throat and heart. I can't breathe, like I'm drowning. He brought it back to me. If he found the tigereye, he must have found the ring. Nausea, anger, and fear mix together in my stomach.

What happened to Trip after he caught me? I know he caught me. I know he's responsible for the scar on the back of my head and the one over my eye. I've always known. And Blake was there that night. A white T-shirt, my only hope, my bright spot in a sea of green. I was running toward him.

Detective Weeks has his T-shirt, covered in my blood, or maybe someone else's.

I think about the knife Blake keeps with him.

Protection.

What if there was a fight? What if Blake saw Trip do something to me and he tried to protect me?

I press the tigereye until one piece slips through my fingers and bounces onto the carpet. What if Detective Weeks knows about the ring?

What will happen if he finds out that Blake has it?

Chapter 45

The dress goes back in the bag and to the farthest corner of my closet. I get dressed as fast as I can. I stuff all the money I have from my pawned goods in my bag and go in for breakfast.

Dad looks at me, surprised, but he says, "Glad to see you're going to school today." I eat breakfast and then brush my teeth, like everything's okay. I get my backpack while Dad clears his bowl and puts the dishes in the dishwasher. I've never seen him so slow. Every move he makes takes forever. Finally he picks up his coffee mug. "Do you want me to take you to school or do you want to take Mom's car?"

"I'll take Mom's car." I grab my backpack and head for the door.

The short drive to school is excruciating. I have to keep telling myself, don't speed, don't speed. Detective Weeks is watching me, waiting for me to slip up and so is James.

Maybe I can get to Blake before he goes to class. We can run away. Leave Pacific Cliffs, forever.

My heart drops as soon as I get to the parking lot. Detective Weeks's black Charger is parked in front of the school. I try to stay calm as I get out of the car. Maybe there's something else in my locker. Maybe he came for me. My head pounds and the crowd of students heading into the building are too close, but I push inside.

All hope drains out of my heart when I walk in the building. The crowd makes way as Blake walks by, his head down, in handcuffs. He looks past me, like he can't see me, but I see the pain in his eyes. It tears my heart out. Behind him, Detective Weeks is all business, but I catch the look he gives me when he walks by—triumph.

I start to follow, but someone grips my arm. I pull away. "You'll only make it worse," Angie whispers in my ear. She pulls me back gently and puts her arm around me.

"Wait, Allie." Clair pushes through the crowd toward me, her eyes full of false sympathy. "They put a new lock on your locker. Here's the combination." She hands me a blue piece of paper. "Your teachers will be issuing you new textbooks. There wasn't much that was salvageable from your locker."

I look at the paper in my hand, but I can't move. I want to scream at her for doing something so normal when everything is so wrong.

Angie tugs at my shoulder. I let her guide me toward my locker. A low buzz fills the school. It fades when I get close, grows louder as I pass by, and then fades again. It sounds like waves rushing onto the shore and then pulling back.

My locker smells like fresh paint mingled with seawater. My fingers are numb as I spin the new combination. It sticks, and then sticks again. Angie is hovering, waiting for me to open it. "Do you want me to find someone to help you get it open?"

The only one who can help just got arrested, because of me. I shake my head. The bell rings. I should forget putting away my backpack, I should forget school, I should forget everything, but I work the lock desperately, like Blake is inside and I can get him out.

I twist the lock again, and this time the door springs open. "Um, I need to head to class." Angie leans toward me. "So you're okay?"

I think I nod; whatever gesture I make sends her away. I'm too busy looking at what's inside my locker.

It's the little white purse I used for cotillion, with a note attached in Blake's handwriting.

> I needed to return this to you. I can't explain everything here. We need to talk. Come find me as soon as you get this. Please don't hate me. I love you more than anything. I'm sorry.
>
> —Blake

I blink back tears as I press the purse between my fingers and feel the shape of the ring box inside.

I turn around and come face to chest with Randall. He's mad, punching his hand into his fist. I step back, suddenly remembering that he was Trip's friend, too. Suddenly remembering that he saw Trip hit me. But he doesn't come any closer. "This is so stupid. We were all there. When would he have had time to . . . why would he torch his own paintings anyway?"

"Wait." I look up at his face and what he's saying registers. "What did you say? Why did they arrest Blake?"

"For torching the gym. I heard my dad said they found his knife in the gym. Somebody used it to strip some wires in the ceiling. That's what caused the fire."

Arson, not murder. I almost slide to the floor with relief. If James started the fire . . . if Blake is being blamed . . . I can help. I saw James at the school that night. My heart squeezes tight. If I tell on James, what will he do to me?

I leave school and head for Hoquiam. I don't know what Blake's bail will be, but I hope the ring will cover it. It's the only hope I have left. Get Blake out of jail and then we can get away together.

. . . – – – – . . .

Paul has his back to me when I come into the pawnshop. I work on making my voice casual and confident, but it sounds strained as I say, "Hey."

He turns around and smiles. "Hey, Allie. You here to shatter another guy's heart by pawning off his gifts."

I lick my lips. His teasing strikes too close to the truth.

"Some girls are just heartless." He turns back toward the other side of the counter and shuffles through some papers.

I grip the ring in my pocket and start to pull it out, but I stop when Paul turns and I see what he has in his hand.

"Can you believe some girl would be so cold as to try to pawn her engagement ring?" He slides the paper across the counter so I can see it. It has a picture of the ring in my pocket with the words "PAWNSHOP ALERT" written across the top. He looks up at me with an intense gaze. "But you wouldn't do anything like that, would you?"

I push the ring back in my pocket and pull out the tigereye. "Is this worth anything?"

He leans forward and studies it. "It's a nice piece, but tiger-eye isn't very valuable, and this one is split." He shakes his head. "Sorry, I'm afraid it's worthless."

I slide it back in my pocket. "That's what I thought."

Chapter 46

The wind is howling and ominous black clouds are blowing in off the ocean. I get into Mom's car, and for a second I think about going the other direction and running away, but I can't leave Blake to take the blame. I have to do what I can to save him. It's like I'm outside my body as I head toward the police station. My fingers are so numb that I can't even reach for the tigereye that's digging into my thigh through my jeans' pocket.

It's pouring rain when I get into town. I'm drenched by the time I get inside the police station. The lady at the desk smiles when I walk in, like I'm here for a tour.

I grip the tigereye. "I need to talk to Detective Weeks."

She pushes a button on her phone. "Allie Davis to see you, Detective Weeks." I'm positive that wherever Detective Weeks is, he's not more than forty steps from where she's sitting.

"I'll be right out," his voice answers.

He's through the door in less than ten seconds. No stewing in the waiting area, no trying to get the story straight in my head. He's just here with that stupid triumphant grin on his face. "Glad to see you, Allie," he says. "Saves me the trouble of going back to the high school to talk to you there. Come with me."

I follow him back to the now-familiar office. Detective Weeks sits at the desk, motions for me to sit in a chair across from him, and waits.

The more he just sits there, the more time that ticks by, the more nervous I get. Finally I burst out, "Blake didn't start the fire."

"Oh?" Detective Weeks sits back and laces his fingers over his knee. "How do you know that?"

"He was with me, the night before the dance. We were together the whole time," I stammer.

"The whole night?" he says calmly.

I feel myself blush. "No, he took me home when we were done decorating for the dance, but it was late."

"According to the janitor, the two of you were the last ones to leave that night, and he locked up behind you. Are you sure Blake didn't go back later, after he took you home?"

I rush forward. "I saw another guy there, just before we left. He was standing by the Dumpster. I couldn't see his face."

His eyebrows shoot up. "Do you know who it was?"

"Yes." I press the tigereye through my pocket. "I think I do."

He leans forward and writes on a pad of paper. "And?"

"James Mathey."

"Really." Detective Weeks doesn't believe me, I can tell he doesn't. "The boy who threatened you at the dance?"

"Yes." I focus on the blank wall behind him.

"What makes you think he was the one who started the fire?"

"He was following me. He told me he was following me, waiting for me to—"

"To?"

I breathe in. "To mess up. He thinks I—"

He cuts me off. "That's all very interesting," He picks up the pen and starts tapping it on the desk. "But what I find more interesting is that I arrested Blake for bringing a weapon to school, and you're talking about arson."

My heart drops so fast I feel like I'm going to faint.

"As far as I know, the fire in the school gym is still being called an accident. But if you have any more information you would like to share about that—"

I look down at my hands. How could I be so stupid?

"Since you're already here . . ." He takes a box off a shelf in the corner. "I have a couple of things I'd like you to identify for me." He pulls out a pocketknife, stuck in a plastic bag with a label attached. "I got a tip-off that your friend Blake had this at school. Have you ever seen it before?"

"No," I answer so fast that I'm sure he knows I'm lying.

"The fact that he brought a knife to school would be bad enough. What makes it worse is what's on the blade." He reaches into the drawer in front of him and pulls out a magnifying glass. He pushes the glass and the bag toward me and taps the blade through the plastic bag. "Do you see what I'm looking at?"

I lean forward. The blade is nicked in a couple of places. Caught in the edge is the same puke-brown paint that covers all of the lockers at Pacific Cliffs' combined school. I want to believe the paint came from the one time Blake helped me get into my locker, but I'm not sure. "We think this is the knife that was used to break into your locker. That he was the one who left the notes." He sits back with a smug smile. "How long did you say you've known Blake?"

"Since we were kids."

"You know him better than I do, so maybe you could help me figure out why Blake would bring a knife to school. Or why he put those notes in your locker. Or what he might have to gain by threatening you."

I don't answer. It feels like the point of the knife in front of me is being twisted into my chest. I don't dare move. I don't dare close my eyes.

"No? Maybe you should think about it." For a second I think he's going to let me leave, let me go home to think about it. But he has more.

"A couple more things and then I'll let you go." He pulls out the plastic bag with the bloody white T-shirt in it. "Do you remember this?"

"Yes."

"We got the lab results back. Do you want to know whose blood is on this shirt?" I don't say anything, but he pauses like he's waiting for me to answer. "It's your blood. No trace of Trip's blood, or anyone else's blood. But unless you wore this T-shirt to the dance, we can be pretty sure there was someone else at the accident scene. Any idea who that might be?"

I stare back at him, blank, emotionless, a look I perfected last year. The only look that kept me safe. The only look that didn't make things worse.

"No?" He goes back to the box. This time he picks out a big yellow envelope. He takes out a piece of paper and slides it across the desk in front of me. It's the same piece of paper that Paul had at the pawnshop. He points to the picture of the ring. "Ever seen that before?"

I take a breath and try to sound calm. "No."

"Insurance companies send these out when a claim is made. Mrs. Phillips filed a claim after the accident for this ring. A ring her son spent a lot of money on. A ring he was going to give his girlfriend. Are you positive you've never seen it?" He keeps his eyes locked on mine. I shake my head and work on keeping my face blank. He puts the paper back into the envelope. "I guess he never got the chance to give it to you. It's a shame. It was worth a lot of money."

I grit my teeth and don't dare answer.

"Just a couple more things, and I'll let you head back to school." He replaces the envelope in the box and pulls out another bag. "Do you know what this is?" He slides another package across the desk. Inside is the shoe I found in the bushes, the one I wore to cotillion. "Your friend James brought this to my attention. He said he found it in a little clearing where Trip used to take you off-roading. He was nice enough to take me there. It looked like a beautiful place for a proposal."

How could I be so stupid? I led James right to it.

He pokes at the oily spots on the shoes. "You want to tell me what those spots are?"

"Blood," I say as dully as possible. "My blood."

"Not this time." He leans across the table and his eyes glint with anticipation. "Your dad's a mechanic. He ever explain to you how brakes work?" My stomach clenches.

"Brakes are hydraulic; that means they have a series of pistons filled with a liquid—brake fluid—you've probably heard that before. When the brake fluid levels get too low, like if there's a leak, then the brakes don't work as well. Lose all of that fluid and the brakes don't work at all." He taps the plastic bag with my shoe in it. "Those brown spots are brake fluid."

"What the hell did you step in, Al? It looks like oil. Watch it. You're getting it all over my truck."

"In a modern vehicle, and by modern I mean post-1970s, any loss of pressure in the brake lines would set off all sorts of warning lights. But Trip's truck wasn't a modern vehicle, was it? What was it, a 1967 Chevy?" He raises his eyebrows, but I don't think I need to answer. "I checked into it. Trip's truck was never retrofitted with modern brakes. Did you know that?"

"No," I answer. "I didn't know anything about Trip's truck, or the brakes, or anything like that."

"Angie Simmons told me you guys rode from the dance to your house in the limo. You got out at your house and then left in his truck together. How long was Trip's truck parked at your house before he took you to the forest? Long enough for someone to cut the brakes?"

"I said I don't know!" I want to crawl out of my skin. I want to be anywhere but here right now. I grip the tigereye to keep from bolting from the room.

"Still nothing, huh?" He puts the bag back in the box. Then he sets the box deliberately back on the shelf, turns around, and sits back down. "I'm not your enemy, Allie. I'm just trying to find out the truth." He leans closer and lowers his voice. "I read the notes from your locker. And I talked to Ms. Holt. I know Trip was hitting you, maybe for the whole time you were dating. I think there were probably a lot of people who knew about it, but they all looked the other way. Ms. Holt told me she filed a suspected abuse report a year ago but never heard anything more about it. I bet he was responsible for the scar on the back of your head and the one over your eye. If you killed him, in the heat of an attack, then that would be self-defense." He lets the words hang in the air.

I struggle to keep the emotion out of my face. The words are on the tip of my tongue where they have been a thousand times before. Trip hit me. Trip hurt me. This is all Trip's fault. But like a thousand times before, I can't make myself say it. I let the proof that was all over my body fade away. No one will believe me now.

"But if somebody cut his brake lines, then that's premeditated murder."

A chill runs down my back. "You don't have any real proof." It comes out before I can stop it. "None of this means anything."

He smiles and leans toward me. "You're smarter than he gave you credit for, aren't you? You're right. Without a truck or a body, we don't have enough evidence to turn this into a homicide investigation."

"After all your work." I know I'm baiting him, but it seems only fair.

"Not yet." Triumph creeps back on his face. "But maybe tomorrow."

I shouldn't ask, but I do. "What happens tomorrow?"

"Tonight the tide will be higher than usual, and with the storm, we'll probably have some flooding. Things are likely to wash up that have been buried deep in the ocean. Then tomorrow morning we'll have an extremely low tide. Roger Phillips is anxious to figure out what happened to his son. So anxious that he hired a couple of divers to go down below the cliff and look for the truck. They're going to wait until the tide is at its lowest early tomorrow morning. That way they'll have more chance of finding something and it won't be as dangerous."

Divers looking for Trip's truck? Is that what Mr. Phillips meant by the ocean returning things you thought were lost?

"You have less than twenty-four hours to decide what you're going to do. Your friend Blake isn't going anywhere." He nods toward the back of the building. "It's time to tell the truth. The truth about everything. If they find that truck tomorrow and there's any evidence that the brakes were tampered with, Roger Phillips will be out for blood. You've already seen what he can do without any proof. What do you think he would do if he was sure Trip was murdered?"

I sit in stunned silence, my body numb. So numb that I don't think I could touch the tigereye if I tried.

Behind him, the boxes of evidence haunt me. Blake's shirt—and the ring, still in my pocket. Evidence that Blake was there the night Trip died. Why didn't he tell me?

Blake's voice fills my brain. "I have to tell you something about the night Trip died." His note: "We need to talk." And what he said to me the night of cotillion: "You don't have to go anywhere with him. He doesn't own you."

Blake didn't want me to leave the dance with Trip.

My shoes, covered with brake fluid. The fluid leaking from Trip's truck when we got to my house. He had already sabotaged Trip's brakes.

Blake killed Trip.

"Believe it or not, I'm sorry for all of this." Detective Weeks indicates the box behind him. I focus on draining the emotion from my face. "You've already been through a lot. You don't have to take the fall for what someone else did. Think it over, Allie. You're the only one who knows what really happened that night. What do you owe Blake, anyway?"

Detective Weeks knows.

"The threats, the message on your locker, maybe even the fire in the gym. He was trying to put the blame on you. He's scared that you'll remember and tell what happened that night. My guess is that he already knows about the ring. Maybe he even has it. He's doing this for the money and to save his own skin. He doesn't care about you." He leans across the desk, his eyes locked on mine. "You don't have to take the fall for something someone else did. Think about what you owe yourself, Allie."

Chapter 47

The wind drives the rain in my face as I stumble across the parking lot to Mom's car. I barely feel it. I barely hear the wind screaming in my ears. I barely know the storm is coming, because the storm inside me is much fiercer. I drive like I'm on autopilot past the high school, the line of condos, and Blake's house toward home.

My house is dark when I pull up. It's only about four in the afternoon, but the press of clouds makes it feel more like late evening. There's a note on the counter.

Andrew is sick. Mom and I took him to the clinic.
—Dad

I try to turn on the lights, but the power is out. I walk back to the bedroom, sit on my bed, and wrap myself in my quilt.

Sasha yowls and paces and wraps her body around my feet. She's always hated storms. I try to pick her up for some comfort, but she scratches at me until I let her go.

I'm waiting for the tears to come, but they don't. With every breath I feel more numb, like I'm retreating to a place in the center of my body where no one can reach me, where I can't feel anything.

Detective Weeks's words fill my head and swirl around my brain like the eddies that fill the little pools in the cave when the tide comes in.

Blake was there that night. He didn't save me. He stood and watched me fall and watched Trip grab me.

What do I owe him?

My fault. All my fault. The only two guys I ever loved. One is dead, one is in jail. Because of me.

"*You don't have to take the fall because of something someone else did.*"

Blake killed Trip.

I'm so numb that the thought barely penetrates my brain. But another thought stays clear. He did it for me. He did it because he loves me. Because he's always loved me. Because he wanted to protect me. Because I was too stupid to tell the truth about what Trip was doing to me.

My fault.

I can't let him take the blame.

Thanks to Detective Weeks, I don't have to. He gave me all the pieces I needed. Everything that was missing from my memory.

I know what I have to do.

I go to the kitchen and dig through the drawers to find a

match. Sasha is standing at the door yowling. The sound splits through my numbness and goes down my spine like fingernails on the chalkboard. I yank the door open and watch her streak across the yard and disappear behind the trash cans. The cold wind blows through the door and rain stings my face. The smell of the ocean permeates everything outside. It brings me back to myself.

I return to my hunt with a new purpose. I find a lighter in the back of Mom's neatly organized junk drawer and take it back to my bedroom. Inside my hutch I dig out a candle that I brought home from Grandma Joyce's house—one of my screw-ups that I chose to keep instead of melting it down and starting over. I light the candle.

The musky smell of sandalwood and dust mixes with the ocean. I breathe in the memories of rainy afternoons with Blake in Grandma Joyce's attic. My place to hide. My refuge from the truth, but only for a little while. The light reflected in the mirror above my dresser lights up my freaky eye and makes my face look haunted. The flame plays across the picture of me and Blake from the dance. It's too bad it's our only picture together. I look stiff and stressed out. I hate for him to remember me that way.

Through the mirror I can see the painting Blake gave me for Christmas—the three of us playing together as kids—innocent. Maybe he can remember me that way.

I pick up the first set of papers I find on my desk, an application for South Puget Sound Community College, a little college in Olympia. Close enough that I could have driven home on the weekends to see Blake.

I won't need it anymore.

I search my desk drawers for a pen, but I can't find one. I almost laugh at the irony of my own disorganization coming back to bite me now. I go back into the kitchen and find one lined up neatly next to Mom's "phone notes" pad. She'll miss it in a day or two, but I'm sure she has a new package ready to replace the one I take.

I feel so calm that I'm surprised when I start to write and my hands are shaking. I force myself to be slow and deliberate, focus on the words in front of me. This is important.

I write my confession. Talk about how I felt trapped dating Trip, how controlling he was. I write about being jealous the night of cotillion. How I knew he still loved Hannah. That will make her happy. I confess to looking on the Internet and figuring out how to disable his brakes. I say I punctured the brake lines on Trip's truck so they would be completely bled out by the time the limo brought us back from the dance.

I write that Trip was going around the cliff road when the brakes failed. That I knew he couldn't stop and so I jumped out before he went over. That that's how I ended up on the side of the road. How I got hurt.

I say I'm sorry to everyone for everything—Mom and Dad and Andrew and Blake, even Trip's mom, but not Roger Phillips.

At the end I write why I did it, what Trip had done to me.

It's the one secret I'm not going to take to my grave.

I lick my fingers and extinguish the candle the way Caitlyn did. The smoke curls in the fading light of my room. I watch it and think about what she said about death and souls. I wonder what it will be like on the other side—nothingness or kind of the same. I pray I don't have to be at my funeral and see what my death will do to Andrew and Blake and Mom and Dad.

Hannah will probably come, dressed in black, crying and talking about how we were such good friends.

Or maybe no one will come after they find out I was a murderer.

I leave the note on my dresser and walk out to the front door. For a minute I pause on the porch and watch the wind tearing at the empty trees in front of my house. I call for Sasha, worried about her in the storm and feeling guilty that I let her out. But she's weathered worse than this storm. I don't know how long she waited in the trap Trip put her in before Blake and I found her. Regret crushes my heart like waves against a castle of sand. If I had listened to Blake back then, none of this would have happened.

But it did and I'm running out of time.

I check to make sure I have my tigereye and the ring before I climb in the car.

As I pass the forest, the trees bend low against the wind like they're trying to grab me, but this time they don't even slow me down. I go to the cliff, thinking that it would be poetic justice to end everything here. The rain drives against my face and the wind blows what's left of my hair. I stand on the cliff and watch the last rays of the sun sink into the ocean. Like the woman in Blake's picture, only without hope. I linger too long, imagining Trip's body mangled in his truck below the cliffs. I can't stand to be there with him, even in death.

I head back into town. Pacific Cliffs never has much traffic, but tonight it's completely deserted. I park my car next to the condo that stands where Grandma's house used to be. Nobody is staying in it now. I get out and look up at Blake's house. The windows are dark and neither of the cars are there. I hope Grandma Joyce is at the police station and they'll release Blake to her.

One good-bye glance toward the window of the attic before I plunge forward, down the familiar trail, toward our cave. The wind howls through the cliffs, no longer mournful—only angry and accusing. It pushes against my back, driving me forward toward the water. The waves roar and toss. The ocean shows all of its awesome power, but I'm not afraid.

Chapter 48

Everything is muted when I step inside the cave. The water is already coming in. Inky-black and gray-green swirls wrap around the edges, flowing in and out of the entrance, gently, rhythmically. The motion stands in sharp contrast to the rage of the storm outside. I pause for a second and touch the tigereye before I start climbing toward the back of the cave.

Fear doesn't hit me until I scramble onto the ledge in the back, tuck my legs up under me, and wait. I rub the pieces of stone between my fingers, searching for the courage that the woman had promised, but none comes. Someone with courage wouldn't die like this, huddled on a slimy, rocky ledge, listening to the roar of the ocean and waiting for death to come. Someone with courage would run out to meet it, embrace it, welcome it. Not that I've ever done anything that could be considered courageous.

Maybe this—my final act—taking the blame to protect someone I love. Maybe this could be considered courageous.

But no one will ever know.

Lies.

Even my last words, scrawled on the back of my college application, are lies.

Once I could have stopped all of this from happening by telling the truth. But I didn't. And now it's too late.

Going off the cliff might have been better. I even messed up my own suicide. I didn't think about how long it would take for the cave to fill up with water or how long it would take for me to drown—too long. Long enough for me to wallow in my own guilt and self-pity. Long enough for this to not seem so noble anymore. Long enough for me to worry about Andrew at the clinic and reach for my cell phone to see if anyone has called. I left it at home. Not even on purpose. Not so no one would call and try to stop me. Just because I forgot.

Nice, Allie. Can't even get your own death right.

I hope after I'm dead I can do a better job of shutting his voice out of my head. With my luck it won't be just be his voice, but the actual Trip. His soul will be bound to mine, tormenting me for eternity.

I'm definitely losing it.

The water is coming closer. I can hear it spilling over the rocks I climbed to get here. It's only a matter of time. I lean my head against the wall to the cave. Maybe if I sleep.

My body starts to shake; the damp on the bottom of my pants and the damp all around me seeps into my blood. My teeth chatter. I wrap my arms around my chest to hold myself together.

I wonder if I'll freeze or drown first. Freezing would probably be better. I think when you freeze to death you fall asleep.

I close my eyes again. Squeeze the tigereye tight in my hand. I know it's cutting me. I can feel the edges against my palm. I might even be bleeding, but I'm so numb that I feel no pain.

"Allie."

I'm hallucinating. Hearing voices. Maybe I will freeze to death first.

"Allie!"

It isn't really him.

"Allie!"

His hands are on my shoulders, shaking me gently, bringing me back. He holds me against him, kisses me.

"Blake?" My brain is so muddled that I'm not sure where I am.

"Allie! Thank God." He leans back. It's so dark I can barely make out his face. "What the hell are you doing? The tide's coming in. It's too high. You're going to drown."

I touch him like he's not real. "How did you escape from jail? Why are you here? How did you know where to find me?"

He laughs. "I didn't escape. Chief Milton released me to Grandma's custody. With the storm coming, he has worse things to worry about than a kid who brought a knife to school." He cups my face. "I went looking for you. I was on my way to the clinic when I saw your mom's car. I knew you'd be here." His face goes dark in the fading light from the crack. He looks away from me. "Did you get my note?"

I nod and pull the ring out of my pocket so he can see it. "You have to let me take the blame. You have to leave me here."

"No!" He grips my arms, hard. "We can talk about that after we get out of this cave. The tide is supposed to be really high tonight. The cave is going to fill up with water and we'll both drown."

"Go away!" I push against him. He doesn't understand. "You have to leave me."

"I'm not leaving without you!" he yells back. "Either we both make it out or we both die."

I'm trapped again. My death means nothing if Blake dies, too. And he won't go without me. I'll have to come up with another way. Maybe once we're out of here and his back is turned, maybe then I can—

He pulls on my hand, hard, ready to carry me out of the cave. For his sake, I stop resisting. When I slide off the ledge, I land in thigh-deep water and realize how much trouble I've gotten him in. If the water is this high in the back of the cave, it's probably already filled the mouth. And the tide is still coming in.

He takes his keys out of his pocket and loops them over his thumb. Then he starts to undo his belt.

"What are you doing?" I scream at him over the sound of the water coming in.

"We're going to have to swim. We need to take off our jeans and our shoes so they don't weight us down." I take off my shoes. Then I grip the tigereye through my pocket, and the ring. I can't just leave them here. "I can't . . . I'm fine."

Blake is already in his boxers and T-shirt. We don't have time to argue. He reaches for my hand. "Hold on to me. Whatever you do, don't let go."

I nod, even though I know he can't see me. It's already dark, but we plunge forward into a blackness that's so thick I can feel it press around me. He squeezes between the rocks first and drags me after him. I stumble on my last step and slip down underneath the water, like in my dream, except there's no red satin seaweed covering my face.

Blake pulls me to my feet. "You have to stay up! You have to keep your head above water!"

But in the next few feet that's hopeless. The floor of the cave slopes sharply and I slide, staying on my feet, but my head is still underwater. I kick against the rocks, but my jeans are too heavy. I let myself sink back down. Blake will see that it's hopeless. He'll give up on me and leave me here. He'll be safe.

I barely feel it when he unfastens my belt and slides my jeans over my hips. As they slip away into the darkness, I reach for the tigerseye, but instead I touch Blake's hand.

He pulls me up so my head breaks through the water. "Breathe, Allie," he yells in my face. "You have to breathe, you have to try." His voice is pleading. "I'll help you. Whatever it is, we'll get through it together. You have to trust me." His voice, his hands holding me up, and his breath on my face bring me back.

I take in a breath and choke. Then I breathe with him. "Okay."

Ahead the ceiling is lower and completely submerged. "Do you have your phone?" Blake yells.

"No."

"We need light. Hold on." He lets go of my hand and pulls a tiny flashlight from the key ring he looped over his thumb. It doesn't give much light, but enough to see where we're going. I grab the sleeve of his shirt. A wave crashes into my face.

"Breathe," he commands again. "Now go down."

I take one deep breath and dive under the low ceiling. The saltwater stings, but I force my eyes to stay open and on the light he's holding. I feel Blake's grip on my shirt, sometimes holding on, sometimes pulling. The light fades as the water ruins the flashlight. My lungs are about to burst, and my brain is screaming for me to take a breath. I ignore it and kick harder. Inky blackness fills my mind. The flashlight goes out. I feel myself sinking with it to the bottom. But I can't let Blake die. I kick hard, one more time, and bump my head on the roof of the cave.

I lift my chin and breathe in putrid, sea-stink air. It fills my lungs and makes me choke. I realize Blake isn't holding on to my shirt anymore. I take another deep breath and dive back down again. Frantically, I paw the water, no longer sure which way is up and which is down.

My hand brushes against something soft. I grab a handful of Blake's shirt and pull with everything I have left. Miraculously, I find the pocket of air again. I force Blake's head up. He gasps in a breath. His arms move.

"This is crazy," he chokes out. "We're going to die in here."

"No!" I yell at him. "We are not going to die. We're almost out. I know where we are." My lie almost makes me feel better.

He gasps again. "I have to tell you. One thing. I didn't kill him."

Suddenly, I know he's telling the truth. "I believe you." Relief floods through my body.

He holds my face out close to his. "Whatever happens, we face it together, okay? No more secrets."

I nod, but I'm not sure he can see it through the dark.

"One more big breath, and then we swim for it." He presses his lips against mine in a long, salty-wet kiss. "I love you." He doesn't give me time to answer before he ducks back under the water.

He's dragging me—I'm dragging him. The water pushes against us until I don't know if I'm swimming forward or back. But I keep going. Finally, impossibly, my fingers brush the edge of the cave. The tide is so high that it's almost completely submerged. I try to scream to Blake that I found it, but a wave washes over my head and tries to suck me back inside. I pull myself up and rest my arms on top of the cave so my head is out of the water. Blake bobs beside me, gasping for air. He doesn't see the next wave.

"Look out!" My voice is hoarse from swallowed saltwater. He pushes me up, so the wave lifts me and carries me to the top of the cave. He gets the full brunt of it. It slams him against the rocky ledge. His arm twists and his face disappears under the water.

"Blake!" My scream rips my throat like sandpaper. I search the inky-black water, ready to jump in after him. When the wave rolls out, his fingers are still gripping the edge of the rocks. I lie on my stomach and grab his arms in both of mine. "Fight! Climb. Kick against the rocks!" With the next wave, I heave him onto the ledge.

He lies there still and silent.

I crawl over to him and lean my head against his chest. His throat gurgles. He rolls over and vomits ocean water again and again.

"Are you okay?" My body trembles and my mind feels numb.

Blake stays on his side, facing away from me. His voice is hoarse when he whispers, "I'm alive."

"We have to get out of here. We have to get warm." I force myself to my feet and turn around to help Blake. When he twists to get up, he gasps and falls back against the rocks. I lean over him. His chest is caved in just below his shoulder. I swallow my horror. "You broke something. Your collarbone or—" My brain isn't working enough to finish that sentence. "We have to get to the clinic."

His face pinches in pain as he struggles to his feet. I want to help, but I'm afraid I'll hurt him worse. "I'm sorry, so sorry." I gulp back tears.

"It's okay." He touches my face. "I'd do it again. Even if I died. I'd go in after you again. As long as you're okay." I bite my lip and nod, overwhelmed by what he feels for me and what I feel for him.

We stumble, crawl, and drag ourselves to the top of the hill where I left Mom's car. I remember my jeans, the keys in the pocket, sunk at the bottom of the cave. Despair crashes into me. Then I see them dangling from the ignition and remember—I hadn't planned on coming back.

Blake tugs at my arm. "We have to get warm." I nod and for the first time I realize how numb I am and how tense and tired my muscles are from shaking. I want to curl up and fall asleep. Sleep seems so warm and safe. I open the door and Blake slumps in the corner of the car. I know he's thinking the same thing.

I turn on the engine and crank up the heater. The first blast of cold air goes completely through me like an icy knife. Blake's teeth are chattering so hard I can hear them. My hands feel like cold rubber bricks, but I force them to put the car into gear and watch Blake as I back out. His head lolls to the side. He's going into shock. I can see him slipping away.

"Talk to me, Blake. Don't go to sleep!" I yell.

"Hmmm?" he mumbles.

"You said we needed to talk. Tell me about the night of the accident. I know you were there. Tell me why." I'm trying to sound like I'm mad at him, hoping it will get him to answer.

"Andrew." He shakes his head like he was clearing out a fog. "Andrew called me, hysterical, hard to understand, but I knew I had to find you. That something bad was going to happen if I didn't. I followed you and Trip up the road in my car. It was muddy and slick, and he was in a truck. I couldn't keep up.

"I should have gotten there sooner. I should have gotten there before he hurt you." Blake leans forward and grimaces. He starts talking fast, like this is something that he has to get out now, as quickly as possible. "I wanted to tell you what happened. A thousand times. I was afraid. I was ashamed." He shakes his head and his face crumples in pain. "I couldn't stop him. I saw you run. I saw you fall. I saw him grab you. He hit you, hard. When you fought back, he slammed your head against one of those boulders in the woods. I couldn't get there in time. I thought he'd killed you. I though you were dead." He chokes on the last words and a groan escapes his chest. He leans his head forward and stops talking.

"Wake up, Allie! Wake up! You're not going to leave me. I'm not going to take the blame for this."

The heater finally starts pouring out warm air. The windows

fog up and I brush my hand across the glass. I want to comfort him, but with all he's told me, the barrier is on my side now. I can't cross it to touch him. "What happened after he knocked me out?"

His voice comes in a hoarse whisper. "He thought you were dead, too. He was kneeling over your body and crying. He didn't touch you after that, but I did, so I knew you were still alive."

"I didn't mean to do it. She shouldn't have said no. This is her fault."

"Trip kept saying that it wasn't his fault. That you made him do it."

"I'm not going to jail!"

I can still hear him, his sobs coming out through clenched teeth. Trip was full of contrasts, sorrow and anger, repentance and justification, always in the same breath.

I grip the steering wheel. "I know," I say softly. "I remember." Blake looks up at me, shock registering on his face. "I could hear him. I was pretending to be dead so he wouldn't kill me." It all comes back to me—lying breathless, my blood warm and seeping around me. Reason told me that I was hurt, but there was no pain. I stayed still, waiting for the final blow, and then I heard Blake's voice. Hope.

"I heard what he asked you to do," I say.

"We can dump her off the cliff. We'll tell everybody she killed herself because I was going to break up with her. I'll pay you if you help me. Whatever you want."

Blake picks me up. I feel his arms around me, carrying me through the woods. He's going to help Trip kill me. I struggle to get away, but I'm too weak. So much blood. He pulls me tight against his chest so I can't get away.

I look at Blake, trying to read his reaction, but he keeps his face down. "He offered you money to help him," I say. "You picked me up and carried me to his truck. My blood was all over your shirt."

I open my mouth to scream, but he covers my mouth gently and leans into my ear. "Shh, stay still. I won't let him hurt you. I promise I'll keep you safe. Trust me."

Blake looks up. His face is so pale that it glows in the dim light of Mom's car. "He was freaked," Blake says. "Wouldn't touch you. He told me he would pay me if I came with him. If I carried you, helped him get rid of—" He turns his face to me, but it's too dark to see his eyes. "I wouldn't have—I didn't know what to do. Only that I couldn't let him touch you again. Only that I had to stay with you."

I turn away from him. The windshield wipers slap back and forth—loud in his silence. Finally he speaks again. "I held you while he drove to the cliff. He was driving crazy fast like he wanted to kill us all. I yelled at him to slow down. The guardrail was coming up fast. He slammed on the brakes, but nothing happened. I knew he wouldn't make the corner. I opened the door. I held on to you and jumped."

I remember the fear in Trip's eyes, just before Blake opened the door. Trip thought I was dead until I opened my eyes.

When the brakes didn't work, he knew he was.

My foot reaches for the brake, like if I slam on it now I could stop everything that happened before. Only I'm not sure I want to.

Blake's voice quivers. "I saw his truck go over the cliff. I stayed there with you in my arms—hurt, in shock." His back heaves. "You raised your head and handed me a little purse that you hadn't let go. You told me to keep it for you."

I search my mind but come up with nothing. "I don't remember giving you the purse." I guess it doesn't matter.

"When I heard the sirens, I ran away. I was still scared that everyone would think I'd killed Trip and tried to kill you. I ran back up the road and through the forest where I had left my car. My shirt was covered in your blood so I shoved it under a log. I hid in my car until morning." He looks up at me, his hair plastered against his face, the streetlights glinting on saltwater tears in his ocean eyes. "I'm sorry I left. I was so afraid. When I gave you back the tigereye, I was hoping you'd remember. And hoping you wouldn't. I didn't want you to know I was such a coward."

I pull into the clinic parking lot, put the car in park, and turn off the engine. I don't move. A thousand emotions churn inside me, fighting each other for dominance—anger, fear, guilt, pain.

His voice is ragged when he speaks again. "I couldn't keep that night a secret from you anymore. That's why I gave you back the ring today. I never meant to keep it. I didn't know what to do with it." His body shakes. "Please don't hate me."

He looks like a little boy again, vulnerable, the way he did on New Year's Eve. The barrier melts. I slide across the seat and touch his arm. "You saved my life, that night and again tonight. I can't—" but I don't know what else to say—too much to express. I bury my head in his neck.

He tucks a piece of my hair behind my ear. "I have one more confession to make." I pull away and face him, dreading whatever else he has to tell me. He traces the scar over my eye.

"He didn't do that to you. I did." He slides his boxers up until I can see jagged white scars on his thigh and the chunk of flesh that's missing from his hip. "When I jumped out of the car, I tried to protect you, but you hit the side of your face on the road." He touches his own scar. "I told Grandma that I wrecked my mountain bike. I don't think she believed me, but she didn't make me go to the hospital. She took care of it herself."

I trace the indented white flesh on his leg. Another scar Trip left behind.

He leans over and whispers, "When I saw Trip lose it, I realized it couldn't have been the first time." He looks at the floor. "When did it start?"

The weight of my shame hangs heavy in the air. How can I tell him the truth?

I think of James and Randall, turning their faces away and never looking me in the eye again, and Hannah pretending I don't exist. Like I was damaged. Like it was my fault. I don't ever want Blake to look at me, or not look at me, the way that they do.

Detective Weeks's voice fills my head. "You have to start trusting somebody, sometime. I just hope it's the right person."

Blake risked his life to save mine, twice. He stood by me when no one else did, even when I told him I didn't want him around. Even when I was horrible to him.

He loves me.

How can I keep my secret from him? The words start slowly. "You're right." I keep my eyes on the floor and lick the salt off my lips.

"What?" Blake looks up again, but I can't meet his eyes.

"That night. Cotillion. It wasn't the first time he'd hit me." Now that I've started I can't stop the flood. "He hit me a lot." I reach for the missing tigereye, but find Blake's hand instead. I slide my fingers into his. "Where people couldn't see. Where I could hide it—on my arms, or my legs, or on my back."

I grip his hand for strength, but I can't look at him. Now that he knows how damaged I am, how could he possibly want me? How can he ever look at me again with anything but pity?

His voice is barely a whisper. "Why didn't you tell me? Why didn't you tell your parents? Someone? Anyone?"

My mind swirls like the waters we just left—muddled, dark, too much to process. How can I explain it to him? "I was afraid." I trace the calluses on his hand. "I thought Trip loved me. I thought I had to protect him." My excuses sound so empty now that my voice is little more than a whisper. "I was embarrassed. I felt like it was my fault." I rub my thumb across the smooth inside of his palm. "I was trapped." I turn to face Blake with my teeth clenched together. "I was stupid."

He pulls his hand away and shakes his head. "No, I was stupid! I should have seen it. I knew he treated you bad, but . . . Dammit!" He slams his hand against the glove compartment. It springs open and my mom's insurance and registration envelope falls out, followed by a thick owner's manual. Blake goes ghostly pale and slumps forward, gritting his teeth in pain and clutching at his shoulder. "Ouch. Now that was stupid."

I laugh. Completely off from the mood, but it's a relief. Like letting go of a huge rock that's been wedged in my chest. Freer than I have felt for a long time. I touch his arm gently. "We need to get you inside."

I open my car door and then walk around to his side. We hold on to each other and stumble into the clinic. The bright lights and the stark white interior are harsh and blinding. The waiting room is full—a crying baby, an old woman with a walker, a little boy playing a video game. It all feels unreal after everything that's happened.

"He's hurt," I tell the nurse at the desk.

She looks at Blake's caved-in shoulder and immediately takes him back. I stand there alone, wearing nothing but a T-shirt and my underwear, wet and shivering. The other people in the waiting room stare, but I'm too numb to care.

"Allie, thank God you finally made it." Mom's embrace nearly knocks me over. I blink at her, trying to remember why she's here. "You're soaking wet and freezing. And where are your pants?" Her eyes are shocked, but she doesn't make me explain. She flags down the nurse who's taking the old woman's blood pressure. "Do you have something dry she can wear?"

A nurse brings me a blanket and a pair of blue scrubs that feel like they just came out of the dryer. I wrap up in them gratefully. "How is he?"

The nurse shakes her head. "Not good. He's having a hard time breathing. But we can't get an ambulance through. There are too many trees down. Your dad and a couple of other guys went out in his truck to see if they could clear the road."

It takes me a second to realize she means Andrew and not Blake. When it hits me, I run for the curtained room where Andrew lies. He's pale, his breathing sounds forced, and he's still. Andrew's body is always in motion, even when he sleeps, so the stillness scares me more than anything.

I ignore everyone else in the room, climb around the wires and tubes hooked to his body, and lie down next to my brother. I lay my head against his chest and focus on his raspy breaths and the beating of his heart.

I stay that way. The nurses come in and out. Mom tries to reach Dad on his cell phone. When Blake comes in, his arm in a sling, I don't move. I barely register Grandma Joyce's hand on my arm before they leave. The only thing that matters is the beating of Andrew's heart next to mine, the way it did for nearly seven months, the way it has for the last eighteen years.

Chapter 49

The clock on the wall says 3:45.

Andrew's chest heaves and his eyelids flutter. "Allie." He says my name quietly enough that Mom can't hear but more clearly than I've ever heard him say it. "I'm sorry. Never meant for you to get hurt."

"Shh, it's okay. I'm not hurt now." I squeeze his hand, trying to soothe him, thinking he's delirious with fever.

His voice drifts. "You were grounded, weren't supposed to be in the truck."

"Straight home after the dance. No exceptions."

Andrew strokes his finger across the scar on the back of my head. "Didn't mean for you to get hurt. Couldn't let him keep hurting you."

"Don't go. Stay home with me. For our birthday."

The pleading in his eyes cuts into my heart. "You don't understand.

I want to. I just can't, okay. Trip would be furious. He's been planning tonight forever."

His fists clench and his whole body shakes. "I understand, more than you think I understand. I know what he—" His fingers tangle in the lace on my sweater. It slides off and exposes my back and a swollen mass of purple and red—a testament to my lie.

I wrap it back around me fast, but he's already seen. "I fell and—"

"No." He breathes in slow and deliberate. The softness in his eyes is gone.

Trip barrels through the door, huge and intimidating. "Allie, get out here! The limo is waiting! Everyone is waiting."

"I'm coming!" I grab the purse off my doorknob and whisper to Andrew, "Don't tell, please. I have everything figured out. It's not that bad. I'm okay."

Andrew grips my arm with more strength than I thought he had. "Let me help you."

I jerk my arm away. "What can you do?"

His face falls.

"Now, Allie!" Trip crosses the floor in three quick steps.

Andrew levels a hard gaze at Trip, but Trip doesn't even acknowledge him. He doesn't hear Andrew whisper, "I won't let him keep hurting you."

Realization pours into my chest like icy seawater and flows through my body until I'm colder than I ever was in the cave. Andrew was home alone while Mom and I were at the inn. Andrew knows cars. He would know how to mess up Trip's brakes.

Andrew cut Trip's brakes.

Andrew killed Trip.

I forced my brother to be a murderer to protect me. The single damning piece of evidence, my shoe, and I led James right to it. I bury my head against Andrew's chest. "I'm sorry. It was my fault, always my fault."

"No." He pushes against my face and his eyes catch mine. "Not always your fault." He takes in a ragged breath. "I didn't mean for him to die. Didn't know he was going by the cliff. Just wanted him to know what it felt like to be helpless. Wanted to give you a chance to get away."

"I'm sorry I didn't listen to you," I whisper.

He strokes my cheek and I feel his strength flowing into me. His voice gets quieter. "Time to let it go. The tide comes in and takes everything away. Like it never happened." His voice fades.

"Andrew?" I panic. "Andrew?" I lay my head against his chest. His heartbeat is slow, but steady.

"Shhh. Time to rest." He wraps his arm around me. I close my eyes and let the exhaustion overtake me.

. . . — — — . . .

Sometime just before dawn Caitlyn comes in the room. She's wearing a long plaid coat over shorts, a T-shirt, and purple boots. Her hair is tucked under a matching purple hat. Her eyes are red and she looks like she's ready to shed another gallon of tears, but she puts her hand on her hip and says angrily, "Andrew."

His eyelids flutter open when he hears her, and his face settles into a guilty grin.

She takes a step toward the bed. "If you ever do that to me again . . ."

I get out of the bed and give up the place that rightfully belongs to her. I know she'll take care of him.

Mom stirs when I stand up. "Andrew seems better," she says. "Why don't you go home and get some rest? Dad will be back soon." I nod and squeeze her hand on the way out.

Blake is sleeping on a couch in the waiting room. I thought he had left. I lean over and kiss him good-bye on the cheek. He doesn't even stir.

Mom's car is still outside where I left it. The keys are still in the ignition. Pacific Cliffs is small-town like that—a place where people still leave their keys in their cars. A place where they leave their doors unlocked at night. A place where people feel safe.

Without knowing where I'm going, I drive past town, where people have gathered to talk about the storm and clean stray branches out of the street, past the mix of old houses and vacation condos, past the high school and the police station. I finally stop at the top of the cliff road and pull into the parking lot.

I get out and sit on the bench beside the plaque overlooking the ocean. The flowers and notes that were left behind by kids from the school are gone, blown away by the storm. Only Hannah's sad, soggy teddy bear remains behind.

The waves are gentle. The wind has blown itself out. The high tide has receded back into an extremely low tide. The water is out so far that I can see kids walking along the beach looking for treasures. I wonder if any of them will find the tigereye or the ring. A van with a commercial diver's logo on the side is parked in the sand to the right of the cliff. I wonder how long it will take them to find Trip's truck.

I sit watching the ocean, without moving, even when the black Charger parks behind me. I know Detective Weeks is coming to arrest me, but I'm through being afraid. I'm through running away.

Detective Weeks sits down beside me. "This is a great view."

"It's the most beautiful spot in Pacific Cliffs," I answer. I wonder if he'll handcuff me and read me my rights like on TV. I wonder what the gossip will be in the cafeteria and in the halls at school. I wonder what it will be like to stand trial or be in prison.

"That it is."

I take a deep breath and prepare to confess to everything so Andrew doesn't have to take the blame for my mistake. "Detective Weeks, I wanted to—"

He holds his hand up to stop me. "Before you say anything, you should know, Trip Phillips's death is going to be ruled an accident." He sounds so sure that a spot of hope cuts through the gray in my chest.

"But after everything you said last night—" My head hurts too much to try to figure anything else out.

He shakes his head. "We need to continue this discussion at the police station." He stands up and gestures to the police car. "I could give you a ride, if that's okay with you?"

I nod and follow him. The second time around, the front seat of the Charger seems less ominous. For a second, I wonder who saw me get into it this time and what the new rumors are going to be, but I have so many other things going through my head that the thought slips through without sticking.

At the door of the police station I meet Mr. and Mrs. Phillips.

She's wearing a fur coat. He's wearing an expression of triumph. The divers must have already found the truck. Detective Weeks must have lied to me, to get me to come with him. Why didn't he just let me confess? Maybe he wants me to do it in front of Trip's parents so they'll see that he did his job.

Chief Milton and Detective Weeks usher us back to Chief Milton's office. It's bigger than the office that Detective Weeks was using. The walls are covered with commendations, certificates, and pictures. The bookshelf is full of books. On the desk is a picture of Chief Milton with his wife and three bucktoothed kids.

Mr. and Mrs. Phillips and I sit on chairs around the desk. Chief Milton sits behind the desk; Detective Weeks takes a chair to his right.

Chief Milton looks around the room, takes a deep breath, and begins. "We called you here to let you know that we're officially closing the investigation into the accident that killed Trip Phillips. We're ruling his death accidental and closing the case."

Mr. Phillips jumps to his feet. "You can't do that!" he roars. "My son was murdered." He steps toward me and sticks his finger in my face. His face is purple with rage. I shrink back into my chair. "She killed him. I demand that you take her into custody!"

Detective Weeks stands between me and Mr. Phillips. "Sit down, Mr. Phillips. The divers didn't find anything. There isn't enough evidence to—"

Mr. Phillips gets into his face. "Don't tell me what to do! She killed my son!"

"No." Mrs. Phillips's voice from the chair in the corner starts out small but gets stronger. "You killed him. You taught him that whatever he did was okay. You gave him everything he wanted. You showed him it was okay to step on people to get what he wanted. You showed him—"

"How dare you!" Mr. Phillips lunges for his wife, but Detective Weeks catches his arm and holds him back. "How dare you!" he sputters again, fighting to get to her, but Detective Weeks holds him fast.

Mrs. Phillips stands up. Her voice trembles, but she speaks clearly. "Enough people have been hurt. It's over."

Mr. Phillips looks at her with an expression that's somewhere between shock and anger. She walks to the doorway and then pauses. His expression changes to horror as she lets the edge of her fur coat slip, just a little. Enough so I can see the bruise on the back of her neck. Enough so that I understand.

After they leave, I turn to Detective Weeks and Chief Milton. "You saw"—I swallow hard—"you both saw what was on her neck."

Chief Milton shakes his head sadly. "We can't do anything about it until she's ready to step forward and press charges."

I swallow again, my heart hurting for Mrs. Phillips.

"But you might have grounds for a harassment charge against Mr. Phillips," Detective Weeks says. "James confessed to everything last night when we arrested him for starting the fire in the gym. He said Mr. Phillips paid him to follow you and to put the notes in your locker." He stands up. "We'll give you some time to think about it."

"Allie." Blake comes to the door of the office, breathless, his arm in a sling. "I saw your mom's car out by the cliff and

I—" He looks at Detective Weeks and Chief Milton. "Is everything okay?"

"I think so." I look up at Detective Weeks.

He nods, then says, "I have a few more questions, Allie, for clarification on my report. If you'll follow me."

I hang back. "I don't understand."

He smiles patiently. "Without a truck or a body, none of the evidence I gathered means anything. I have no choice but to close the investigation. But I would like to know what happened to you that night and before. He looks into my eyes. "I mean, whatever you remember."

Blake hugs me with one arm. He stiffens like it hurts him, but he won't let go. "It's time to tell the truth," he whispers into my hair. "I'll be waiting outside."

I squeeze Blake's hand. Then I follow Detective Weeks into his office. I sit down, take a deep breath, and let my memories flow out with a tide of tears.

Chapter 50

"I got you something. For your birthday. And to wear to the dance." Andrew's new voice sounds deeper, more mature, less electronic. It fits him.

"Don't you mean *our* birthday?" I blot my lipstick and turn away from the mirror to face him.

"I decided you could have this one. I think you earned it." He pushes a little box across his tray toward me.

"And you didn't?" I pick up the box, lift the lid, and pull out a heart-shaped pendant, pale green, on a silver chain.

"Periodot, it's our birthstone. It's supposed to be a gem of healing." He looks up at me and his eyes soften.

Since the night at the clinic, we haven't talked about it—what really happened to Trip. It's a secret that only we share. I'll never tell anyone else and he'll never tell anyone else. Being in the womb with someone for nearly seven months creates an unbreakable bond.

"I love it." I turn toward the mirror and fasten it around my neck. "It's perfect." I turn my head and watch it catch the light in the mirror. It almost matches the dress I chose for cotillion this year: short, simple, and blue green, my favorite color. "But you should be saving your money for school."

"Full-ride scholarship, remember?" He smoothes his tux with his good hand.

I look at how handsome he is, how grown-up, and I have to swallow a lump of tears. "Are you nervous?" He's leaving for Stanford next week. My heart aches every time I think about Andrew going away to college—the two of us, who have never been apart, separated by so many miles.

"No. Yes. Maybe a little." His electronic voice is emotionless, but his hand trembles.

"I'm glad Caitlyn will be there to keep you out of trouble." She's going with him on a full-ride scholarship, too. They applied together and they've been planning this for months. Who knew a girl with absolutely no fashion sense could be as smart as Andrew? Then again, she saw something in him that no other girl did.

"Allie, Andrew, you're going to be late." Dad's voice floats down the hall.

Andrew reaches for my hand. "Are you sure you're up to this?"

I nod my head and try to look brave. "If you can leave home and go almost a thousand miles away to college, I think I can make it through one more cotillion."

His eyes meet mine and he squeezes my hand. "I'll miss you, sis."

I swallow hard. "I'll miss you, too."

"Hey, babe." Caitlyn breezes into the room. "Are you about ready?"

I release Andrew's hand and move out of the way so she can kiss him.

"You look amazing," he says as she pulls away.

"Thanks." She beams at him. She's wearing a gold sequined dress with swirls of brown and orange all over it. It looks like a mix between a tiger pelt and a retro '70s disco dress. When she smiles at my brother, I wonder why it took me so long to realize Caitlyn is beautiful. She sits down on his lap. "Shall we go?" He nods and backs up his wheelchair.

I follow them into the living room and stand by Mom while Dad takes pictures. "You look very pretty," she says, and wraps her arm around my waist. I lean into her shoulder. Five months of counseling and a lot of long talks with both her and Dad have gone a long way toward fixing things between us. It's going be hard for me to leave for college in a couple of weeks, but at least I'll be close enough to come home on the weekends. I had to rewrite my college application. No one ever saw my suicide note. The day Andrew came home from the hospital. I took it to the mouth of the cave and burned it. I decided the ocean already held too many of my secrets.

When we're done taking pictures, I follow Andrew and Caitlyn to the limo and climb in after them by myself.

. . . . — — — . . . .

Mrs. Phillips greets us as we walk in the door to the inn. She's wearing a silvery blue dress that matches her eyes. Her arms are bare and tan from her recent trip to Florida. Someone behind us whispers, "Divorce looks good on her." I have to agree with them.

Andrew and Caitlyn head for the dance floor, but I stop and take in the effect. Blue and green lights dance across the dark wood floor. The wind machine makes Blake's sail paintings billow like they were at sea. The ballroom at the inn looks almost as magical as the high school gym did the night Blake told me he loved me for the first time.

The city council wanted to use Blake's paintings for cotillion, as a sort of pre-exhibit exhibit, with them all displayed in one place before they're spread out all over town. It took him a long time to clean off the soot and restore them. I can still see some fire damage on some of the edges, but I think it gives them character. They look more weathered and authentic.

Between the paintings, guys in black tuxes and girls in colorful flowing formals float across the dance floor, like waves on the ocean. In the middle of it all is Kasey, surrounded by her court, wearing her sash and crown, the new Beachcomber's Queen. Blake is beside her.

I turn toward the redone painting, *Hope*, and my own face smiles back at me. I press the pendant at my neck while the wind machine ruffles through my hair. It would take a long time for it to grow back to the length it was before, the length that the girl in the picture has, but I've decided I like it short.

"Hey." Blake walks up behind me. "Why didn't you tell me you were here?"

"We just got here." I nod toward the makeshift stage where Marshall and his band are setting up. "Did you get the problem taken care of?"

He rolls his eyes. "We had to drive all the way to Olympia to get a replacement part for Marshall's amp, but he wasn't about to miss out on playing at the Pacific Cliffs Inn. I only hope his band doesn't shake the plaster off the walls. I promised Mrs. Phillips no damage."

He wraps his arms around my waist and kisses me on the back of the neck. "I'm sorry I didn't get to do the picture thing, or ride with you to the dance."

"Don't worry." I lean back against him, "You can make up for it later."

He rests his chin on my shoulder. "So, what do you think?"

I take in the whole room: his paintings blowing in the artificial breeze, the lights playing across everyone's faces, the music—slow and sappy, Kasey giggling with the other girls from the pageant, Angie sulking in the corner while Randall tries to apologize, Marshall tuning his guitar onstage, Caitlyn and Andrew making slow circles in the middle of the dance floor, Mom and Dad chatting with people from town by the refreshment table, even Hannah and her unknown trophy date flipping through a scrapbook of Beachcomber's pageants past.

It feels like I belong here. It feels like home.

I turn around, wrap my arms around his neck, and whisper in his ear, "I think everything is absolutely beautiful."

Blake brushes back my hair and slides his fingers down my scar and along my cheekbone. He cups my face in his hand. "Yes. You are."

I touch the stone at my throat and think about what I am now—not perfect, still scarred, not completely whole, but not broken either. For the first time in forever I feel good about myself, like I'm okay.

Maybe even beautiful.

Acknowledgments

Way back when I started this process, I remember reading the acknowledgment sections for the books I read. One author said something like, "It takes an army to write a book." At that point, working alone on my laptop, I couldn't comprehend how that could be true. Now I know. I'm grateful for the opportunity to say a huge (if grossly inadequate) thank-you to my personal army—the people who have made this dream a reality:

First, to my biggest supporter, cheerleader, and beloved husband, David. I love you! I would be nowhere without you. Next, to my four kids, David, Sabrina, Zach, and Daniel, who have supported me through this journey even when they had to eat cold cereal for dinner and do their own laundry. Thank you to my amazing extended family: my parents, Dale and Linda Shaw, who taught me to work hard, do what's right, and live my dreams; Kristy, my only blood sister, who has walked every step of this journey with me; my mentor, sister-in-law, and shoulder to cry on, Angela Morrison, for teaching me pretty much everything I needed to know to get me to this point; and my brothers and my "extended" sisters (sisters-in-law) for their support and willingness to read.

Thank you to my lovely agent, Sara Megibow, for being adviser, cheerleader, counselor, friend, and sometimes even mom, and for believing in me from the beginning. Thank you to Anita, Kristin, and Lindsay at Nelson Literary Agency.

Thank you to my editor, Mary Kate Castellani, for pushing me when I needed to be pushed and pulling me back when I needed that, too. You're a master of your craft! Thank you to the rest of the unseen army at Walker.

Thank you to the members of the most incredible critique group I could have stumbled upon: Val Serdy, Joan Wittler, Blessy Mathew, Sarah Showell, Michele Gawenka, and Monica White, for reading and reading and reading and telling me the truth even when I hated you for it. Thanks to my first teen readers: my daughter, Sabrina, and her best friend Ashlyn; Abby for giving it to me straight; and my niece Ashley for her simple, encouraging question, "Is there any more?" Thanks to my adult beta readers: my sister, Kristy; my almost sister, Christie; Mom; Stacy; Lucy; Lynn; and Miranda. Thanks to my literary agency mates, my Apocalypsies group, SCBWI Western Washington, SCBWI South Sound, the Class of 2K12, and my ANWA sisters. Thanks to Ann Gonzalez for helping me hone my craft and for giving me the writing prompt that sparked this story.

Thanks to Jason and his family—Marianne, Kevin, and Julie—for teaching me about inner strength and compassion.

Thank you to the many survivors of abuse for your strength; you are in my prayers.

Thank you most of all to the Divine Creator and Author of the universe; I know I am nothing without you. I know I have been truly blessed.